DONNY MUMFORD

OLIVER'S
ADVENTURES
A SEQUEL OF OLIVER'S WILDWOOD VACATION

WARNING

This book contains sexually explicit scenes and adult language. It may be considered offensive to some readers. This book is for sale to adults ONLY.

* * * * * * * * * * * * * * * * * * *

Please store your files wisely where they cannot be accessed by underage readers.

Please feel free to send me an email. Just know that these emails are filtered by my publisher. Good news is always welcome.

Donny Mumford - **donny_mumford@awesomeauthors.org**

About the Publisher

4Fun Publishing, a member of **BLVNP Incorporated**, 340 S. Lemon #6200, Walnut CA 91789, info@blvnp.com / legal@blvnp.com
NOTE: Due to the highly emotional reaction of some people to works of erotic fiction, any email sent to the above address that contains foul language or religious references is automatically deleted by our anti-spam software and will not be seen. All other communications are welcome.

DISCLAIMER

Please don't be stupid and kill yourself. This book is a work of FICTION. Do not try any new sexual practice that you find in this book. It is fiction and not to be confused with reality. Neither the author nor the publisher or its associates assume any responsibility for any loss, injury, death or legal consequences resulting from acting on the contents in this book. Every character in this book is over 18 years of age. The author's opinions are not to be construed as the opinions of the publisher. The material in this book is for entertainment purposes ONLY. Enjoy.

Oliver's Adventures

A Sequel of Oliver's Wildwood Vacation

By: Donny Mumford

© Donny Mumford 2015
ISBN: 978-1-68030-368-1

Chapter 1
The Roommate I

This summer I worked, fell in and out of love, and had the time of my life vacationing at Wildwood New Jersey. Playtime is over now, though; tomorrow, I'm off to college. It's my freshman year at the University of Pennsylvania. All the preparations have been done and I'm nervously ready to go first thing in the morning. After a good night's sleep, we start out very early in the morning, like five o'clock, to be accurate. It's a five-hour drive for me in my Mini Cooper convertible. The car was a graduation present from my rich, albeit, mixed-up brother, Christian. I get to drive my car, and my parents insist on going with me, but in their SUV. Actually, me driving to college is a major deal and initially, I didn't think I'd be allowed. Freshmen living in dorms aren't normally permitted to have a car on campus. I side-stepped that technicality by applying for an "Assistance-Group" exception. I was accepted and got a sticker to park my car on campus. The Assistance Group is a very old campus organization with the mission of providing free assistance to incoming freshman. I'm now a member of this do-gooder group and it seems an easy way to get two credits each year, but mainly, I just wanted a parking pass for my car.

The Assistance Group members are asked to help another freshman in any number of ways. Maybe I'll be an aide to someone who needs help getting around, a student on crutches perhaps or a blind student, God forbid. Or maybe I'll have to chauffeur someone to a doctor's appointment or, hell, I don't know. If a student needs assistance, I'm their boy. I don't know that much about it because I didn't read all the materials they sent me. I also have no idea why I was admitted to the group, not that I really care. I've never been much of a joiner, but I really needed to have my car with me. How else would I get to see friends back home? So, no problem, dude, sign my ass up for whatever. The University of Pennsylvania is inside the city limits of Philadelphia so there aren't any rolling hills or expansive lawns on campus. There's a lot of cement and black-top and a lot of brick and ivy-covered old buildings. It's all new to me: the energy and excitement of big city life, plus the atmosphere of a major Ivy League university all wrapped together, wow! I liked everything about it when exploring the campus during my high school's senior class trip last May.

After arriving on campus, I need to wait forty-five minutes for my dad and mom to arrive. Dad drives agonizingly slow. Pretending I recently arrived myself, I tell dad, "I haven't had time to scope out the reception and admissions area, but I believe it's down this street." Mom smiles proudly, but my Dad makes a face like he know I'm full of it, and of course I am. I had plenty of time to drive around and find out where we should go. Registering turns out to be an extremely tedious experience, that's the best thing I can say about it. We won't be starting classes for two days, but there are orientation meetings that freshman should attend. That still leaves a lot of free time for me to get reacquainted with the campus. As part of registration, I'm assigned my dormitory building and my room, so off we go to have a look at my room and unpack the cars. When we get there, I'm pleased with both the dorm I'm in and the room. I immediately think about Cristobal, who I met during my class trip and with whom I had my very first sexual experience with. A very pleasant and exciting one it was too. I was in his dorm and right off it's apparent how much better my dormitory is than his. Better because my dormitory is centrally located near all the main classroom areas, dining rooms, recreation facilities, etc. But, by far, the number one reason my dorm is better is because there's a private bathroom for each of the rooms on the first floor. And, my room's on the first floor. No waiting for elevators, but much more importantly, no community bathing and shitting and such. On the wall next to the front door, a three-by-five card has been taped. On it, written in big block letters, "NICKERSON/GALLO". I now know the name of my roommate, but that's all I know about him. I'm Oliver Nickerson, by the way. I have a full boat academic scholarship to this prestigious university and I'm proud of it, but humbled by it too.

My folks and I check out the actual room and like all dorm rooms, mine has twin beds, two desks and a bookcase. The bathroom is unusual because it has all those fat chrome bars for a handicapped person, so maybe my roommate is handicapped. I hope not, for his sake, and for my sake too. Dad and mom look at the room and say, "Small, isn't it?" I give them an annoyed look because they just don't get it. We move my stuff in from the cars without much sweat. Jeez, I wonder if getting this dorm with the private bathroom is just another part of the lucky streak I've been on lately. It's awesome! Finished unloading my stuff, there's still no sign of my roommate, so off we go for lunch. I'm starved. We have lunch off campus and then tour the University grounds, endlessly it seem, but finally my parents are ready to head back home, and by then, I'm quite anxious for them to be on their way. I tell them it's best to get back home before dark because dad doesn't like driving at night. The goodbye was quick, just some awkward hugs and kisses. My brother Christian left home, and now me, so I do feel kinda bad for my folks as they're leaving. The bottom line is that they're wonderful, caring parents, but I want desperately to be on my own. Plus, I have the Assistance Group meeting,that most of my fellow freshman students refer to as the, "Ass-Kissing Group" because it's so difficult to get into. Most of them would like having their car on campus, but too bad for them. Anyway, the meeting's at three o'clock in the library. I'm anxious to get this meeting over with and I'm dying for a cigarette. The folks don't know about my recently acquired nasty habit, but a college student should smoke, don't ya think? Fortunately, my on again, off again boyfriend, Frankie, taught me how to smoke, more or less.

Puffing away while walking toward the library, I can't help but hope my luck holds up as far as any kind of group assignment goes. I'd much rather just be on-call, assuming they have something like that. And, of course, I've got the same concern most freshmen have about who my roommate will be, who this 'Gallo' guy is. The dread of getting an asshole for a roommate is huge. I have no choice in the matter of course. Freshman year, we have a roommate assigned, period. I filled out a questionnaire about my likes and dislikes so hopefully they do try to match kids up with similar interest. That questionnaire is okay as far as it goes, but it doesn't address the asshole factor, so I still need to get lucky. First, the great dorm room and now, please, a great roommate. There are only twenty Freshmen in the Ass-Kissing Group each year, so it's kind of an exclusive group. This year, all but three of the members are girls. The falculty member in charge says everyone is going to get some kind of assignment, so obviously I'm going to have to do more than be on call like I was hoping for. In the meeting, an older, no-nonsense woman with a hairy mole on her chin, passes out the assignments for all twenty of us and gives instructions with each one. As each kid gets their assignment, he or she goes on their way. Finally, it's just me and the old lady. She says, "Okay, well you must be Oliver Nickerson. Right?" I nod my head and she goes on to explain that my assignment entails the biggest commitment of this semester, a big responsibility. I smile, nod my head again, thinking, "Oh shit!"

My roommate is my assignment. He's in a wheelchair, temporarily. A car accident of some kind and I'm to be his care-giver. The lady said I'd received this assignment because I'm the only one out of all the kids who applied for admission to the group that checked off the 'yes' space on the application for, 'able to provide extensive care-giving'. Well hell, I'd checked every block because I was desperate to bring my Mini Cooper to college, and as I've said, getting in this Ass-Kissing Group was my only hope. I mean, what are the odds some Freshman's going to need nursing care? God damnit! I have no luck. Calming myself, I realize that if I want to stay in the program, this wheelchair kid is my baby. Plus, thinking about it, how much assistance could he need? Well, quite a bit, I find out as the lady, with me staring at the mole, goes on to explain. For one thing, he needs to be fed because both his elbows were broken in the accident. They're in hard casts. He also has a broken kneecap, which is the reason for the wheelchair. Hmmmm, now that I re-think this, it does sound like a lot of trouble. On the other hand, I rationalize that how long does it take for bones to heal, six weeks or so? I get to keep my car the entire year no matter if my duties are completed in six days or six months. The mole lady confirms this will be my only commitment for the year. What the hell, it could have been worse I guess, but still I want to kick myself in the ass for checking off every freaking block on the application. I hadn't even read the damn thing, just put a check in each one. Well, anyway, now I know why I was accepted in the group so quickly.

Walking over to my dorm, it dawns on me that the fabulous dorm and room location are because of wheelchair boy too. It had nothing to do with my luck. I'm feeling sorry for myself again. Please, dear God, don't let this wheelchair kid be a fatso or a ball buster or an asshole. Six weeks of being a primary care giver is starting to seem like a bigger deal with each step I take toward my dorm. I light up another cigarette nervously, worrying about the mess I'd gotten myself into this time. My needy wheelchair roommate should be in the room by now, for sure. I'll soon know what kind of kid I have to deal with. It doesn't take me long to walk to the dorm and I'm kinda nervous when I get there so I stand outside and have yet another cigarette, wishing my brother was around to pump up my confidence and give me some advice. Finally, I go in the front door of the dorm and take two steps to my left and, ta da, I'm in my room. Very good and convenient room. The card with our two names printed in block letters is still there. Popping a couple of breath mints, I stare at his name, GALLO. Italian? My hand on the door knob, ready to turn it with trepidation, I'm thinking, 'Good guy, or asshole?' I open the door slightly and hear the unmistakable sound of a long rumbling fart. What the hell? Sticking my head tentatively around the edge of the door and there sits this bean pole of a kid in a wheelchair, leaning to one side with one buttocks lifted off the seat straining out this five or six-second fart. He doesn't see or hear me because his concentration is totally fixated on that fart. His eyes and mouth squeeze tightly shut as the motorboat sounding fart rumbles out of his asshole. As the first fart runs down, he takes in a big breath and forces out a short blast of follow-up flatulence and then relaxes against the back of his chair, a look of relief on his face. I continue to stare with my mouth hanging open as the fart cloud envelopes me and that horrid sulfur/fart smell overwhelms my senses. I go, "Holy shit, gross!"

The bean pole whips his head around with a face as red as an apple, and says, "I'm so sorry, but it's a condition I have. Are you Oliver? Where ya been, man? I need to go to the bathroom bad!" I stutter, "We wel well then, ga go ahead and go." I say that as my brain is trying to make sense of the situation. He has a cast on both arms that cover the lower part of his bicep, his elbow, and the upper half of his forearms. There's a short metal rod connecting between the cast on each forearm to a contraption on his chest that hangs over his shoulders. The cast are set so that his arms bend in toward each other. I find out later this is to allow him to use his laptop computer, but that's all it allows his hands to do. The rods prevent any other movement of his arms. He has no way to touch his head, or his crotch, or his back side. My brain goes, "Oh, noooo...." The kid has a humiliated look on his face when I'd stuttered, "Go ahead" and he mumbles, "I can't go by myself. You need to help me." I think, 'Well obviously you're fucked over good this time, Oliver. Poo poo boy looks so pathetic though, I take pity on him and say, "Oh yeah, sorry. I wasn't thinking." I roll his wheelchair into the bathroom which, as I said, is all set up for a handicapped individual, but not for the way my roommate's handicapped. He can hobble up off the chair on his one good leg and collapse on the toilet seat, but he can't pull down his pants, aim his dick, or wipe himself when he does a poop. Can't pull his pants up when he's done either. I feel sorry for the kid, but this whole deal seems like it's way more than just assisting someone who needs a little help. This seems like a fucking full-time job that should be undertaken by someone who's trained for it. I'm mumbling to myself various things along those lines, when he says, "Please, I'm going to pee my pants. Help me get on the toilet." I'm like, "Oh, um, ah, sure," and I awkwardly try to help him over to the toilet, him, hopping on one leg. I pull down his pants with one hand and with the other, hold him around his waist so he can balance himself on that one good leg. Then, with his pants down, I lower him to the toilet seat.

He immediately starts to pee but it's firing off to the side and some of the piss spray is coming out between the rim of the toilet and the toilet seat. "Oh, you need to adjust my penis, please...." I go "Huh?" and then "Oh, yeah," and reaching down, I straightened it out so the piss stream hits the inside of the toilet bowl. What the fuck, I decide to hold onto his dick till he's done with his pee. Nice dick, uncut, about six and a half inches long. Then another hissing sounding fart from bean poll's ass, followed by a long poop. "Fuck!" I grunt, as I walk out of the bathroom. I hear a pathetic, "I'm really sorry" behind me. Well, this sucks! I put my head out the front door for some fresh air. Jesus, how am I ever going to do this? In less than a minute I hear, "I'm done, Oliver." Reluctantly, I go back in the bathroom and see him trying his best to twist around and bend down at the same time, hoping to flush the toilet by hitting the lever with the bottom part of his elbow cast. I say, "What the fuck?' and push the lever to flush. "I'm sorry," he says again. All I can do is shake my head while helping him lean into me, balanced on his one leg again and, using a lot of toilet paper, I wipe his ass three times with him grimacing and grunting, undoubtedly because of the rash in his butt crack. Flushing the toilet a second time and pulling up his pants, I guide him back in the wheelchair. As I'm washing my hands, I hear, "Thank you so much, Oliver. I really had to go." I say, "No problem. Chill, dude." Pushing him back to our room, I'm thinking, 'Okay, what the hell, at least let me take the time to look him over and maybe get some fun out of this. I've been a boy-watcher since I was about eleven years old. Love to look for cute aspects in a guy's face. Hey, wouldn't it be a pisser if he's gay?'

Back in our room now, he sits there in his wheelchair staring at me as I sit in a desk chair evaluating his looks. Skinny as a bean poll, like I said, and he isn't as tall as I initially thought, probably not much taller than me. Olive complexion with dark blue eyes and dark brown shaggy hair. A few minor, random pimples on his chin. His nose is definitely going to be too big if it continues growing, but for now, it strikes me as kind of cute. He's very young and innocent-looking. Hard to believe he's even old enough to go to college. I guess, overall, he's handsome, but his face is unremarkable in any one particular area. Everything goes together good though. Actually, on second thought, his eyes do qualify as remarkable. They're not only big and a very dark blue, but they shine with a lot of warmth. Narrow, dark eyebrows over fairly long black eyelashes. I like his 'looks' and he has a humble manner about him too, sitting there patiently with an agreeable expression on his face, his lips slightly parted, and huh, brilliantly white teeth too. What the hell, he seems very likable. I decide I'll stick it out and help him as best I can, and it might be fun giving him a bath, for example. See, sometimes I can be an optimist.

"What's your name, dude?" He says, "Joey Gallo. Um, weren't you expecting me?" I explain I'd seen his last name on the card outside our door, but that I'd just now come directly from the Ass. Group meeting where I'd been informed I'd be taking care of him. Pointing at the file on the desk that I'd carried in with me, I say, "I haven't had a chance to read about you yet. I've known about you, in a general sense, for the last ten minutes, that's all." He tells me he's read some about me from the paperwork he received earlier. He wants to know if I've run into his mother, who went off looking for me some time ago. Apparently, she'd been under the impression I was to be here at one o'clock, taking over Joey's care. Taking over for her, I suppose. Looking puzzled, I say, "I can't imagine where she'd got that idea I was to be here at one o'clock. I wasn't even assigned to care for you until about three-thirty. Hell, the meeting wasn't until three o'clock." He shakes his head and sort of sighs, saying, "My mother can be problematic at times, very stern too, and pushy even. She scares some people, to tell ya the truth." Then he does a small, nervous, pretend laugh and averts his eyes. I do my pretend cough. He goes on to tell me she'd been to see her plastic surgeon earlier in the day and gotten her regular treatment of Botox injections so her face is stiff and sore which just adds to the frustration she always seems to feel. He says, "Life is a challenge for mother, or maybe life in general just pisses her off. Me being in this condition just about put her over the top. I know she's thrilled I'll be out of her hair now, and into yours." Joey looks up at me with a worried look. He wants to see if I'd be upset, I guess. I give him a half-hearted smile.

He speaks in a quiet voice, not so much shy as humble, like I mentioned earlier. The way he acts and speaks, and his sincere expression, make me realize how vulnerable he must feel, and how very dependent on me, a total stranger, he is. For some reason, a strange nurturing feeling comes over me and now I actually want to protect him and take care of him. I feel even worse for him when he tells me about his accident, which happened almost a month ago. He'd been driving his Mustang convertible with his best friend riding shotgun. They were goofing around, not paying attention, and their car rear-ended a UPS truck that pulled out in front of them. It caused Joey's car to swerve out of control, crashing into a fire hydrant. Neither of the boys was wearing a seatbelt. Joey flew out of the car, hitting his head on the top of the windshield and landing unconscious on his elbows and one knee, all three joints were cracked. He also has internal injuries when his gut connected with the steering wheel on his way over the windshield. This is causing him some bloating and blockage, hence a lot of farting.

When his best friend flew out of the car, he landed on the pavement breaking his neck... he died instantly. Joey begins crying while telling me about it and I think about Tyler, who was my best friend. He killed himself diving into an empty swimming pool that I should have pulled the tarp on, but didn't. I was a long time getting over that. I'll probably never get over it even though the consensus of is that Tyler committed suicide and it wasn't my fault. Anyway, I feel compassion for Joey and do my best to console him. Joey doesn't want to be comforted though. Blubbering now, "No, please, it's alright. I'm dealing with it myself, internally. I'd rather have it that way. Mostly, it was the worst fucking bad luck. A fucking fraction of a second difference in the speed of my car or the speed of the UPS truck and we don't collide. Eric, my friend, was doing some grab-ass with me and I took my eyes off the road for a second and the shit hit the fan, so to speak. I can't put into words how sorry I am about it all. I wish to God I could tell Eric that." Joey gives me more details as his crying dies down. It's horrifically sad. Youthful deaths are the hardest to get over, I think. Not only my personal failure to deal with Tyler's death, but all the other heartbreaking stories every day on the news about some young kid getting kidnapped or raped or murdered or killed in some kind of accident; our's is a scary and dangerous world! The heartbreak and heartache can be beyond words, Joey's right about that. I light up another cigarette because it's stressful listening to this. Joey says, "Oh my God, can I have a drag?" We share the cigarette, with me taking a drag and then holding it up to Joey's lips for him to take one too. He lips the filter with each drag and I taste his saliva, while thinking about Frankie's spit, and my dick starts to get hard.

Then, all of a sudden, I'm thinking, did he say, 'Joey and Eric were grab-ass buddies? Hmmm, gay?' Oh man, I know it's just wrong thinking about a possible sex situation. Sometimes, I hate how insensitive I can be. I hit my forehead to try and get my brain working on something besides gay sex. Concentrate on this poor kid and his sorrow and his sad situation. And the situation you're in too, ya knucklehead! That's my advice to myself. Joey's so polite, apparently without an ego, and it gives me a guilty conscience to let my mind wander to sex all the time. Moving past the morbid topic of teenage deaths, we talk in general about each other and I get the sense that Joey's the kind of kid that was popular in High School. Not a leader, but they'd be very few classmates who would have anything negative to say about Joey Gallo. That's my guess because he seems to be an unassuming go-along kid. A positive thinking kind of kid, but very introspective too. Joey handled his sadness and loss much better than I'd handled mine with Tyler, but he was a lot older when his accident occurred and therefore more mature. He has a pleasant sounding, youthful voice too, and he wants to talk although I can tell he's nervous. He tells me he'd been in a gymnastic club with his friend Eric for the past five years and this past summer, he was recruited to be on the University's gymnastic team. The gymnastics coach and some of his teammates let Joey know he's still on the team and they're rooting for his full recovery and stuff. A teammate will be picking him up each day for practice even though all he can do right now is observe. He gets excited talking about the gymnastic stuff and I see his cute little grin for the first time, sweet.

Within a half hour, Joey Gallo and I are getting along good and it's one of those deals where you feel you've know someone for a while even though you just met the person. I'd begun to notice more about the body on this kid too. He's a bean poll, but a very fit bean poll. Well, fuck, a gymnast with a fit body! Duh! The subtle muscle definition, I can see in his otherwise thin arms and legs, the parts not hidden inside the plaster casts, is eye candy to me and it's intriguing to think of the rest of his body. I start thinking more and more about that bath I'll need to give him when the door bangs open behind me and in comes Mrs. Gallo. She's not happy. Joey cheerfully says, "Hello, Mother." Ignoring Joey, she points at me and with a snarl in her voice, asks, "Are you the Nickerson boy?" I nod and stand up as I'm saying, "Yes, Ma'am. Oliver Nickerson. Nice to meet you." Mrs Gallo is a tallish woman with a reddish, sharp-featured face. Because of her reddish hair and rather pointed face, my first impression is that she looks like a woodpecker. Joey obviously takes after his father's side of the family, or else, he's adopted. Mrs. Gallo stand stiffly as she lectures me, "I've wasted half the afternoon looking for you and I can't tell you how frustrated I am at this moment. You were very late getting here and that's a big problem because I have no intention of leaving the care of my invalid son to someone who isn't dependable and ...." At that point, Joey cut her off with, "Mother, it isn't Oliver's fault. He didn't even know about me till an hour ago." Mrs. Gallo transfers her stare from me to Joey. She didn't move her body, but her eyes go flat and gray like stones. With that same snarl in her voice, she says, "Joseph, don't ever interrupt me when I'm speaking." Joey looks away, mumbling, "Sorry, Mother." She quickly walks over and sits on Joey's bed, muttering something under her breath. Something about Joey's father that I couldn't quite make out. It looks as though she's trying to frown too, but the Botox injections prevent her face from moving much.

Giving up on the frown, she turns her attention back to me and demands, "Is that right? You just found out about Joseph an hour ago." I tell her exactly what happened at the meeting. It appears for a moment she doesn't believe me, but then she says, "Okay." She tells me she'd give me another chance, but she clearly isn't happy about things in general. "Now, about what you need to do for Joseph", she says, and then, counting off the items by hitting the palm of her hand with the index finger of her other hand, and her woodpecker head nodding up and down with each point, she gives me a detailed list of instructions for the care of Joseph, er, Joey. She informs me that Joey and I have the same courses and I'd be responsible for getting him to class, "On time each and every day, mister." Also, that he has medication that needs to be taken precisely at six hour intervals and his skin under the shoulder braces must be massaged morning and night to prevent the skin from...... and on and on she goes, but I've stopped listening. When she runs out of breath, she rummages through her briefcase and comes up with computer print-out of the instructions she'd just given me verbally. Joey looks as if he's in pain all through her recitation. I'm kind of fascinated at the gall of this bitch. I'm doing them all a great favor, for free, and she still insists on giving me a bunch of shit about it. Go figure. Mrs. Gallo abruptly gets off Joey's bed, and says, "I'm very late due to this screw-up that you two are partially responsible for." Joey and I look at each other with expressions on our face like, "Say what?" She picks up her briefcase and her oversized purse, saying, "I was going to take you both out for lunch, but that's not possible now. Running all over the campus looking for you, Arthur, put me way behind schedule." Joey and I give each other that look again. Arthur?

Mrs. Gallo makes a 'face' she probably thinks is a smile, and goes, "Don't look so frightened, Arthur, my bark is worse than my bite." Joey says, "Excuse me, Mother, but his name is, Oliver." She tries for a confused look, and says, " Oliver who, Joseph?" Then she gives Joey a kiss on the top of his head that causes her pointed nose to twitch. Looking at the nose I wonder, 'More plastic surgery?' She says goodbye and warns us she'll be checking up on us, we could count on that. The last thing from Mrs. Gallo is directed at me, "Joseph needs his hair shampooed, and I mean today, Arthur. I suggest you get to work on that right now. Don't fuck up, boys! I'll be watching." The door slams behind her. Joey looks over at me shrugging his shoulders, "I'm really sorry 'bout that, Oliver. We can pick our nose, but we can't pick our family." I'm glad to see Joey can make a joke out of his mother's bizarre behavior. Keeping it light, I mumble, "Well, actually, Joseph, at the moment you can't pick your nose either. You're double fucked, dude" He has a nice laugh and it makes me smile at him. "Do you want your hair shampooed?" I asks. Joey says he'd like that very much. His mother, he tells me, can't abide doing anything that involves touching a dirty part of the human body, unless the human body is hers. "Mother hired a nursing aide to come in twice a day for three hours each morning and evening to take care of my hygiene concerns," Joey explains. "But the poor old woman she hired didn't have her heart in the job at all. She sucked at it, actually." I go, "Extremely awkward situation," and Joey sums it up, "My humiliation was humongous the first week or so, but what could I do? Bodily functions don't care if I'm humiliated or not." I ask how much longer for the hard casts and he tells me the bad news, ten more weeks. I mutter, "Fuck. Let's not think about it though. We'll go in the bathroom for a shampoo and then dinner at the University's dining hall #3. Okay?" "Thanks, Oliver. Someday I'll pay you back, man, I promise you!" I mumble, "Sure you will."

As I'm pushing his wheelchair into the bathroom, he tells me how the old nurse did the shampoo routine with him. She put a chair up against the sink, leaning it back with the front legs off the floor, Joey sits in the chair facing away from the sink, his head over the sink. So, using his desk chair, that's what we do except I fold a hand towel to put under his neck for comfort. "Hey, that's nice, Oliver. Wonder why the old nurse never thought of that." I mumble, "No fucking idea, sport." This being a handicapped-appointed bath, there are a number of extra items available and one of them is rubber tubing with a shower nozzle on one end; the other end gets attached to the spigot. I use that to wet and rinse Joey's hair, which works fine except his shirt collar is soaked before we're done. This is my first time though, and it'll get better as I learn from experience. Funny, but I don't mind shampooing his dirty hair; I like boys quite a lot, even straight boys. There's only about a ten-percent chance Joey's gay if I can believe the estimates of gay/straight ratio statistics. Straight or gay, he's still a boy and I'm fond of boys, so shampooing his hair is kind of fun for me. It makes me think of my friend, Alexander, who works with guys' hair every day in his profession as a barber, cutting and shampooing guys' hair, and getting paid for it too. Shampooing

Joey's hair also makes me feel good because I'm helping him. Wetting his hair and running my fingers through it, then massaging in the shampoo and working the thick suds through his hair gets to be a little sexy and I discover it's a bit of a turn on. This primary care thing might work out much better than I thought. When I've shampooed and rinsed his hair, I use the hairdryer that's provided, combing through his full head of hair as I dry it. Yep, this is really sexy. Joey can't thank me enough too, which is an added bonus. He says this is the first time his hair has been this clean since the accident. Makes me feel real good.

Getting him a dry shirt, I discover that he's got a supply of specially made shirts that zipper up both sides and under both short sleeves. The front half and the back half of the shirt are connected at the mock turtle neck and across the top of the shoulders and sleeves. When I unzip both sides of his shirt, I merely slip it over his head. With his arms in a cast like they are, I couldn't get a regular shirt on him. Never realized how complicated things can get. Anyway, I pull his wet shirt over his head and whoa! Joey's got himself a hot torso. It's tight, smooth and hairless with awesome definition, but I shouldn't be surprise, him being a gymnast and all. Still, I can't help staring at his sexy body. Then, realizing he's looking at me staring at him, I do a fake cough and look away. Oh man, I don't believe I've ever seen a body this toned! I don't mean it's the body builder type, they can look freaky, but Joey's body's not gaudy with muscles, just excellent definition. He's no bean poll like I initially thought. Even just sitting in the chair, his stomach has those small ripples of muscles under the skin, nice pecs and great biceps, but like I said, not overdone at all. His olive-toned skin is so smooth I make sure to touch his bare shoulder as I'm taking the wet shirt off. Damn, he's hot. Frankie's hot too, but Frankie and I are the bean poles now that I've seen Joey's body. What ain't so hot though are his armpits; they reek. Not sexy BO like this kid, Myers, from back home. Joey's pits stink in a bad way, needing to be washed and deodorized. I mutter, "Dude, ya ever hear of deodorant? It's this new invention ya might want to consider." Joey looks down and says his favorite two words, "I'm sorry." Then he nods his head toward a small satchel and says, "My toiletries are in the bag over there, but I can't put deodorant on myself and that nurse didn't do it either. Oliver, I can't do anything for myself!"

He sounds frustrated and embarrassed and now I feel like an insensitive prick. I could have used a little tact.

Giving Joey a pat on the shoulder, and a smile, I go, "Joey, you're going get better care from me, dude, I promise. Don't hesitate to ask me for anything you need, we're gonna bond 'cause I'm gonna take care of you the right way." He grins, mumbling, "You're awesome, Oliver, thanks." I dig his deodorant out from a number of toiletry items. It's Old Spice Original and has a crisp, clean scent. Camouflages the BO, but Joey's gonna need a bath soon. He says, "Thanks. You can't imagine how awkward this is for me, but I already feel more comfortable with you, Oliver, than I did with anybody else who's took care of me. Trying to cover-up my earlier inconsiderate remark, I tell him, "I was just breaking your balls about the BO, just kidding with you." He mutter, "No problem," as I rub his head telling myself, 'This kid is very likable.' Putting one of his specialty shirts over his head and zipping up both sides, then asking, "How we doing, Joey?" and he says, "You're my hero, man. I mean it. I was so nervous about who'd be my care giver at college and now you're the best thing that's happened to me since the accident." I ruffled his hair again.

It's a beautiful early evening in Philly as I push Joey's wheelchair toward dining hall #3. I'm feeling pretty good about myself and lucky too. I mean I've got a hot, helpless boy in my care and touching is a requirement, but I need to be sure I don't take advantage of the situation. Also, it would be totally awkward for him if he knows I'm gay so I gotta watch myself with that too, at least for the time being. I'll need a low gay profile, which might be dicey where Chis is concerned. Chis being the boy I met and had sex with when I was here for my class trip. Well, the trip was to Philadelphia, but I spent most of it here. Anyway, when we get to the dining hall, I swipe both of our dining hall cards at the desk and in we go. Mostly only freshman are on campus at the moment so it isn't very crowded. Great looking buffet style food set-up and it's smelling real good too. Joey says, "Yum." He asks me to get him whatever I get for myself, so I settle him at a table and pile some food on a tray: boneless fried chicken, mashed potatoes and gravy, sweet cut corn, sweet potato souffle, and a mixed salad with Russian dressing. Two of everything plus two glasses of iced tea and a straw for Joey's glass.

Setting everything on the table, it occurs to me I'll need to feed him, duh! I ask if he minds me using the same fork for both of us. He's no germs freak and tells me he doesn't mind if I don't, it'll made it simpler feeding both of us. A mouthful for me, and while I'm chewing, I feed Joey a mouthful. Thank God he chews with his mouth closed, that's one of my pet peeves. Guys that chew with their mouth open making all those revolting mouth sounds and drives me batty. We're just two highly cultured boys, using the same fork, eating our dinner. I feel the stares from other kids, but Joey's used to it by now and I'm sure I'll get used to it pretty soon as well. Everything's tasty and we eat everything on our plates with almost no talking, just smiles and a few quite burps and one embarrassingly noisy fart from Joey. He goes, "Goddamn, I'm sorry, Oliver, but I can't control that." I mutter, "Don't worry about it. Fuck the rest of the diners if they can't take a joke." Then I point at Joey while exaggerating pinching my nose so nobody will think it was me who farted in dining hall #3. Joey laughs, although I don't notice anyone else laughing which makes me laugh, shaking my head. Hell, we don't know any of these people. We enjoy our dinner which bodes well for future meals. I've heard stories about bad food in college dining halls, but this seems like the exception. We're both too full to try the desserts, so I push Joey's wheelchair back to the room. Outside our dorm, Joey asks, "Can I bum a cigarette off you, Oliver? I'll buy some tomorrow and pay you back. We both smoke a cigarette as I on a bench outside the dorm sneaking peeks at Joey as I'm holding his cigarette to his lips. I'm already kind of attached to him and being responsible for him probably has something to do with that. I've always been kind of a responsible teenager, but it's also Joey, he's very likable as I said earlier. He's hot too, so that doesn't hurt either. Leaning over, I rub his hair again, nice hair, and he grins at me. Damn!

Almost done with our cigarettes, I ask about a bath and Joey says he'd been trying to work-up the nerve to ask me to help him with one. He hasn't had a bath in three days. "Well, Joey, tonight's your lucky night; one bath coming up." In a serious manner, he tells me this already has been his lucky day because I'm his roommate. Sweet! I smile, and as were getting ready to go inside, I see a familiar Mini Cooper convertible coming down the street. I know who the height-challenged driver is too. I really want to talk to him so I wave and whistled and the driver looks over once, then does a double take and pulls over to the curb. I yell, "Davis, how ya doing, dude? I'll be right over." He waves back and then gives me the finger. Laughing, I push Joey into our room telling him I'd only be a minute. He wants to go on line and check his emails so I get him situated and then run out to talk with Davis Moore, who was Cristobal's roommate last year. I'd emailed Cristobal a number of times, but they all came back as 'Undeliverable'. Davis and I do the handshake and a one-arm hug, as Davis goes, "Oliver, great to see ya again, How's the ankle?" I go, "Well, I sprained the ankle six months ago and it's been fine for the last five months and three weeks. How many new tattoos did ya get over the summer?" Davis has more tattoos on his five-foot-three-inch body body than makes any sense, but there it is. We do some small talk, and then I ask, "You rooming with Cristobal again?" Davis has a concerned expression on his face, asking, "Didn't Cristobal get in touch with you the entire summer?" I shrug, shaking my head. Davis explains that Cristobal is taking a year off to attend an art institute in France. He adds, "Yeah, he fell love with, with um, Paris." He'd hesitated before saying, 'Paris'. Obviously, he was going to say, 'A boy in France', or something like that, but he didn't want to hurt my feelings.

I mutter, "Oh..., um, jeez. I'm kinda disappointed. Ya know, because, ah, you know, the last thing Cristobal said to me was, 'Don't forget me, Oliver'. I sure didn't forget him, but I guess he forgot me." Davis squeezes my arm, saying, "I can't lie to you, Oliver, there's someone he fell in love with while touring Europe. Cris has too many boyfriends for his own good. Don't take it personally and, hell, you probably have to beat the cute guys off with a stick anyway. If I were gay, I'd be on your doorstep right now." Davis couldn't have been nicer, but damn, I feel my eyes stinging. I hate that I do the wet eye thing so easily. I do my fake cough, wiping my eyes with my forearm and sort of turn my head doing another fake cough. Davis saw my tears though, and mutters, "Damn that Cristobal. He emailed me in July that he'd fallen for this art student in Paris and he'd dropped out of the tour to be with the guy. He promised me he'd send you an email explaining he wouldn't be here this semester. You know, Oliver, Chris is a great friend, but he falls in and out of love every month. You deserve someone more dependable. Hell, he messed me up too because I had to scramble around for another roommate." I've heard enough, I don't need anymore explanation, I just want to drop it. Even so, I find myself babbling to Davis, "Cristobal and I sang together on Mall Street, do you remember, Davis? Cris said he got more money in his hat when we sang together than he'd ever gotten alone. I was hoping we'd do the singing again. Hell, I memorized the words to a couple of the songs Cris sang last spring. The last thing he said to me, that last morning we had together, was he hoped I wouldn't forget him, but I already told you that, didn't I?" Davis looks uncomfortable, but he's very nice and just mumbles, "I think ya did, yeah. Cristobal is the original free-spirit, Oliver. He doesn't realize he hurts people as he goes through his privileged life, but he actually doesn't have a mean bone in his body. He just doesn't think things through all the time. Don't think too badly of him. He means the things he says when he says them, and then someone new comes along. I know he thought you guys had a very special time together. He told me that. He was very taken with you, he really was."

Davis is so nice, but I'm doing a little pouting, surprised I'm so beat up about this. I finally shrug, muttering, "The key word is 'was,' he was very taken with me. Great to see ya, Davis. I gotta go 'cause I'm taking care of that kid in the wheelchair you saw me with back there." He pats my back and we tell each other we'll get together soon and have a beer. Maybe we actually will get together, but I doubt it. Davis is totally straight and whenever I see him, I'll be reminded of Cristobal and my first real love, or at least what I thought was real love at the time. Davis drives his Mini Cooper away with a wave. His Mini's the reason I got my Mini, and I should have told him that. Walking slowly back to the dorm I'm thinking, 'Okay, obviously no Cristobal in my life now, my first sexual lover has officially dumped me.' Then I remember all over again how sure I'd been that I was in love with him, and maybe I was too. Then, fuck it! Goddamn him, this was something I've been dreaming about for almost six months now, recreating Cristobal and my night together in the bathtub with the wine that I couldn't stand, but pretended to like, and all the sex that followed, and him saying, don't forget me and the whole two wonderful days.

Shedding a few tears, I think of Frankie and my eyes clear up a little. I go in to start Joey's bath. My last thoughts of Cris are childish, but just the same I think, 'Fuck you Cristobal and fuck that slut French fairy boyfriend of yours. I got a boyfriend too you know!' At least I think Frankie's still my boyfriend. Heading into my dorm, my hands in my pocket playing with myself a little, I'm thinking about what might have been. Walking in our room with my head down, Joey turns his head to look at me with a big smile on his face, and says, "Wait till I tell you this joke my friend just emailed me, Oliver," and then it's deja vu all over again because he tells me the same joke my swim team captain whispered in my ear trying to loosen me up for my valedictorian speech. That seems like a long time ago now. The joke is the one where the little boy's playing with himself in his bath holding his nuts. He asks his mother if these are his brains. She says, 'Not yet, they're not.' Joey laughs and I try to laugh, but it doesn't come out right. Kind of a bizarre coincidence that joke reappearing in my life. I wonder about coincidences. "What's wrong, Oliver? Your friend in the Mini gave you bad news? He's wicked short, isn't he?" I shrug and mumble, "Yeah, but he's strong as an ox." Then, pretending it's no big thing, I add, "He told me that someone I thought would be here this year isn't going to be. A little disappointing, that's all, Joey. Let me tell you about that joke." And I tell him the story behind the first time I heard it. Joey asks, "You were valedictorian of your high school?" I lighten up and go, "Of course, weren't you?" He laughs again, and I ask, "You want that bath, dude?" He does and I let myself get totally involved in bathing him. It's turns out to be fun, but more complicated than I anticipated.

After I take off his zippered shirt and pull down his cutoffs, Joey tells me how to disengage the rods connecting his forearm casts to the chest apparatus, and then that apparatus comes totally off his shoulders. He take this opportunity to exercise his shoulder joints by moving both arms slowly in circles for about thirty seconds, and then he loosely clasped his hands together on his stomach so he'd move his elbow joints as little as possible during the bath. All he has on are his boxer shorts. After his arms exercise, I put a covering of water proof plastic material on each cast, including the one on his leg. All three waterproof covers have tight elastic on both ends to prevent any water from getting inside. Joey's very conscientious about doing whatever the doctors tell him so his elbow joints heal properly. He's determined to be a gymnast again and I have a feeling Joey's conscientious about everything. I'd had the water running in the tub for ten minutes and it's more than half full now, nice and hot. With little trepidation, I pull down his boxers while steadying him with an arm around his waist. He's got a great set of nuts to go with his pretty penis, everything swinging slightly when he straightens up. Joey's apparently not self-conscious about being naked in front of strangers. For over a month, his body had been under other people's control and that's just the reality of it, so I guess he's just going with the flow. What choice does he have? In my head I take note of his very dark pubic patch and fantasize of buzzing them like Pete did. Other than that, it's just a continuation of an extraordinary body. I can't help wondering how that olive-toned skin of his penis would taste. Then I sort of wake up and notice how his boxers have been partially masking a strongish body odor from the crotch area, but considering it's been three days since his last bath, he doesn't smell all that bad. His body's a smooth tightwire as I hold him, helping him get in the tub. I purposely put the side of my face against his hard chest with his chin hitting the top of my head as I hold onto him while the leg with the cast goes over the side of the tub. Ha ha, I can't touch enough of him to suit me and he doesn't seem to mind at all. Again, he's probably used to it by now.

As he starts to slip, I grab for his hip but get his right buttocks instead. Jesus, it's like a big, hard, tight muscle with no flab at all. I think to myself, 'He could crack walnuts between those ass cheeks of his.' Gulping and feeling a bit dizzy, I imagine my hard boner in between his smooth, hard, muscular buttocks. My cock actually becomes a boner as I help him get the other leg over the side of the tub. He gets both feet in the water, but I need to step inside with my damn sneaker to keep him from slipping. With water up to my knee, I assist him sitting down, and he says, "Oh my God, this feels awesome, Oliver." I'm hoping he hasn't noticed my pants bulging out in the front as I awkwardly try to keep my crotch away from him, and almost fall over doing that maneuver. Joey laughs his soft, good-natured laugh, saying, "We'll probably get better at this with practice. Don't ya think?" I mutter, "I sure as hell hope so, and maybe next time I'll take my sneakers off first." Everything I say seems to make Joey either smile or laugh. This kid grows on you fast, let me tell ya. I have to smile back at him, he has the cutest, most innocent smile. It's remarkable that someone in his helpless condition, with the losses he's experienced, can still have a positive outlook. He hasn't said one thing about feeling sorry for himself and I know if it was me I'd be wicked pissed-off and mad at the world. When his bath sponge is loaded with gel, I start by washing his neck and back, all the way down to those muscular buttocks of his. Scrub, scrub, scrub. I'm determined that he feel super clean with his skin tingling when I'm done. Scrubbing his chest, stomach, shoulders, then the parts of his arms not encased in a cast. Joey makes quiet contented sounds as I do wash him. Then he lifts one arm at a time so I can scrub his armpits extra hard. His head lulls against mine at times and I let my lips slide across his forehead whenever I dare. His clean hair is soft as I rest my cheek on the top of his head and it becomes very sexy for me. None of this bodily contact appears to bother Joey.

It's such a hot experience for me, ya know, having this much personal bodily contact with a straight boy, and particularly a straight boy with a body like Joey Gallo. My boner's about to break off my body, it's so hard. My arms are around his neck to reach over and give his other side a good scrubbing. It's impossible not to touch his shoulders and his slippery upper body while washing all parts of his torso. Very sexy, to say the least. Man am I happy I checked off that space on my application. Nowhere on his body is he soft or flabby, skinny muscles everywhere my bare hand touches. Flawless, satiny skin except for those few acne bumps on his chin which I give special attention to. Just the feel of his breath on the side of my face is a turn-on. His breath's so fresh and clean-smelling. It's dreamy after awhile and I begin more gentle swipes with the thickly lathered sponge as I let my mind wander to fantasize about Joey fucking me. I can just imagine those strong, thin, wiry arms and legs of his wrapped around me so tightly I can't move as he drives his long cock inside me. I envision his cock being somehow extra strong, like the rest of him, humping up my hole as he squeezes those absurdly tight ass cheeks with each deep penetration. Then, as I scrub the parts of his legs not in a cast, my boner dripping in my jockey shorts, I switch it around and fantasize my boner up inside his wiry body with those hard buttocks of his squeezing my cock and me squealing in ecstasy as I shoot the load of my life up inside that tight, tight hole of Joey's. In my fantasy, I hear someone moan quietly. When Joey asks, "What's wrong, Oliver?" I realized I was the one doing the low moaning and I'd stopped bathing him, staring out in space. "Huh? What...oh, ha ha ha...sorry, Joey, I almost fell asleep there. I'm a little bit wiped-out right now because I got up at four o'clock this morning and drove for over five hours to get here. It's been a long day for me, that's all."

Joey's apologetic, but I say, "It's not your fault, Joey. I'm good, dude," and go back to scrubbing his legs and what legs they are too. Perfect boy's legs just the way I love to look at and dream of touching. I always think how I'd like to put the side of my face against legs like Joey's. Feel his leg against my cheek. I rub my bare hand over the small amount of hair on his calves, the rest of his legs are smooth. No surprise to me that his feet are like everything else on this kid, perfectly formed, like a drawing in a high school health book. They're kind of small, but other than that, just about perfect, no weirdly shaped toes or veins bulging, or corns or anything. Holding his foot up out of the water, I'm thinking how I wouldn't mind sucking his toes and lapping the nice arch and then sucking on the heel. That made me think of Frankie again, the only other boy I've ever had that foot fantasy about. Frankie's feet are pinkish and Joey's feet are an olive/tan, both of them with flawless skin and not a single hair. Oh, fuck! I'm tired now and getting punchy and even goofier than I usually am. Bathing him is sexy as hell and I'm enjoying this deepened awareness and appreciation of Joey's body.

Finally, only his private parts are left to do. Going right at them with a ton of thick gel lathered on that sponge, I scrub his groin, balls, and cock. Then wrapping the sponge around his penis, I pull up the length of it four times and it get firmer each time I do it. Joey's grunting quietly so I do it again. Using my fingers covered in bath gel, I clean under the foreskin and all around the head of his hardening cock. No protest from Joey as I'm rubbing down around the bottom of the head, and then all over it with the ball of my finger pulling open the pee slit slightly. Joey gulps audibly. Then, turning my finger around, I rub all around the inside of the skin. Glancing up at him, I see he has his eyes closed, puffing out his cheeks, continuing the quiet grunting, going "Umm, umm, ooh, ah, ah oooh." Then I pulled the fore skin back off the head and rinse it real well. Putting my arm around his neck to keep him from sliding down in the tub, Joey leans his head against mine, real cosy-like, and I force that sponge under him and in between his ass crack and scrub down there. Joey goes, "Ahh ahh, oh my god that feels awesome, Oliver. I have a rash there and the scrubbing is incredibly excellent. It's like scratching the biggest itch I've ever had." I mutter, "Okay, Joey, I'll get it real clean and then put on the ointment your mother told me about." He nods his head next to mine against the side of my face, and I want to lick his forehead, but I don't. He can't even speak; it feels so good having that rash finally taken care of. After scrubbing his asshole and in between his buttocks, I throw the sponge in the hamper and pulled the tub's stopper to let the dirty water out. Attaching the hose with the shower nozzle head to the spigot, I rinse Joey's body thoroughly.

He's quiet as I get one of my big fluffy towels from home that my folks insisted I bring with me to college. It's just right for this job. He's sitting in the tub, and without looking at me, he says, "If you weren't so nice, I wouldn't mention this 'cause I know it's weird. It's like, don't think I'm gay, but, um, if you would just jerk my dick a few times it'd give me some peace and I'll be forever in your debt. It's been so long since I had a climax, I won't bore you describing my agony." I act shocked, jokingly saying, "Are you fucking out of your mind? Nineteen-year-olds do not wank each other's puds unless, of course, it's some kind of an emergency. Is this an emergency?" Joey does his light laugh again and said, "Why, yes it is. My pud needs emergency wanking, this is a fucking 911 wanking." I go, "Oh, that's a little different then. I'm not experienced in this at all as I've only jerked-off myself fifty thousand times, but I'll do the best I can for you."

Smiling, but blushing at the same time, Joey, mutters, "You're awesome." I suppose I should be blushing too. Taking hold of his cock in my fist, I start a steady stroking, dragging the foreskin over and off the head of his cock and right away Joey is moaning and sliding down in the slippery tub. I put my arm around the back of his neck and hold his head against the side of my face to hold him up as I continue jerking him off. He maintains the same position, clasping his hands together on his stomach not resisting having his head against mine at all; in fact, he nestled his head into the crook of my neck in a comfortable position doing little puffs of warm air against me. Could he be gay? And why am I assuming every boy I meet is gay? His boner quickly gets ridiculously hard, and I'm talking metal pipe hard! The fore skin is still coming off the head of his cock as I stroked down, and then up on the wet glistening head, but his boner has stretched so the foreskin can no longer cover the head. Over and over I stroke his excellent cock with Joey quietly going, "Ah Ah Ah." I really enjoy looking at that dark pink swollen cock head with the gaping pee slit, precum drooling out with each stroke. Wetting my lips with my tongue, I swallow noisily. Squeezing his hard boner tightly now as my own boner inside my boxers bumps against the outside of the tub. He doesn't last long and it's a good thing too, I'm gonna cum in my pants any second now. He starts humping his hips and grunting and moaning and thrashing about, leaving a big saliva wet spot on my neck as he moans. I'm careful that his bouncing around doesn't result in him cracking one of his cast against the porcelain tub. Watching with fascination, I see the head of his now seven-inch poker expand right before my eyes and then a magical foot long spurt of cum weakly slipped out his pee hole with Joey going, "Eeeee" and with the next stroke of his steel boner, a long hard stream of creamy cum shoots out spattering against the spigot at the other end of the tub. Joey screams "Eeeeeeeee Ohhhh Ahhhhhhhh" as he fires four more shorter spurts. This was his first real climax for over a month. Just thinking about that causes more pre-cum soaking into my underpants. I continue to stroke his cock until all the cum in his balls drools out of his big cock.

Joey can't talk. He's gulping and breathing hard. Finally he gasps, "Jesus, Oliver, how will I ever pay you back?" I go, "Hmmmm? We'll see, dude. We'll see." He goes on and on enthusiastically about how awesome I am and how I managed to do this in a way that he didn't really feel too embarrassed or terribly awkward. I enjoy hearing the praise, and why not, I'm proud of myself for not wimping out about it in the first place. Struggling to get him out of the tub, I him sit on the lid of the toilet while I dry him off and then help him hop over to his bed, still naked. Now I need to put ointment on that chafed ass of his. After that, I'll get clean boxers on him, but first I take a peek at my crotch to see if there are any tell-tale wet spots. No pre-cum has leaked through my cargo shorts yet, so I look through his toiletries kit and find a rash ointment. I get Joey laying on his back with his legs up while I put a lot of that white ointment on the inside of his hard butt cheeks and all along his reddened crack. It's a nasty looking rash that must be painful at times, especially doing a dump. Ouch! I push some cream inside his asshole, my finger slips in up to the first joint. Joey makes a long hissing sound. Pushing the cream up further, he lifts his buttocks up and moans. It must have been raw up there and the cool creamy ointment is feeling so good. Fingered him as long as I dare without any complaints from Joey, gives me the passing thought again, 'Wouldn't it be awesome if Joey's gay?' Naturally, with Joey in this position, his legs up and his hole pulsating, my cock's so hard again I need to look away and get a grip on myself. The thought of sliding my boner up between those muscular, hairless buttocks of Joey's comes over me again and I swear I feel faint. Blinking my eyes, I concentrate more on helping Joey and less on my horniness.

When I can't stretch out the ointment treatment any longer, I put clean boxers on Joey and he lays in his bed contentedly. He tells me he hasn't felt this good since the accident; not even close to this good and he sounds so sincere I believe him. Needing to wash my finger three times before the Desitin smell is history, but it's worth a stinky finger to put cream in and on Joey's ass. Feeling good, he says he wants to mess around online so I get him set-up at his computer and go in to take a shower myself. In the bathroom, I start the shower so the sound of the running water covers up my jerking off and any squeals I might make. I've been very turned on for a while and now I'm supernova hot. Sitting naked on the closed toilet lid with my legs straight out, I fist my cock for ninety seconds before shooting off almost as much spunk as Joey shot off fifteen minutes ago. Holy shit! Tantalizing ripples spread out from my cock and balls and the relief is there, but the sexual part of climaxing with a partner is not. This jerk was a necessity after taking care of Joey got to be sizzling hot and I got uber aroused. Damn, this nursing deal ain't all that bad. Of course, Joey's a real turn-on which makes it all the more special. If he was some fatso goofy-looking nerd, it probably wouldn't be fun at all. I sit on the toilet seat for a minute after climaxing before I have the strength to get in the shower. Long day and plenty of excitement, I am beat.

As the shower water pours down on me, I realized just how tired I am; exhausted, actually. The shower's fantastic and afterwards, as I brush my teeth, I remind myself to brush Joey's for him, which I do right after I finished with mine. Then we get in our separate beds for some much needed sleep. Joey doesn't need to wear the shoulder contraption with the rods while sleeping on his back. I make sure he's comfortable before getting in my own bed. Even though it's fairly early, we say good night and the next thing I know, the sun's shining through our window. Joey's lying in bed, looking over at me. I'm surprised to see it's almost nine o'clock. WOW, what a fabulous night's sleep and I feel much better. Joey looks just as good to me this morning as he did last night. We mutter 'good morning' and then I go in to do my bathroom stuff first, actually looking forward to taking care of Joey again too. I could have awakened and thought, 'This is simply too much trouble,' but I don't feel that way at all. Probably the novelty will wear off in time, but for now, this is a blast. As soon as I'm done with the bathroom, I take Joey in there for his morning activities. Brush his teeth for him again, then help him get on the toilet and hold his dick for him while he pees. He also does a poop so I wiped his ass afterwards without thinking too much about it. He mutters, "Thanks, Oliver," as I use a washcloth to wash his hands and face, and then take him back to his bed, lying on his stomach this time. According to Mrs. Gallo's computer print-out sheet, bed sores on his back and the back of his thighs need ointment. This ointment is a prescription drug with steroids to promote healing. Also in the instructions, I'm to massage the shoulders where the apparatus chafes all day long. There's a moisturizer for that too. These last few nursing chores are the last ones on the nursing list. These, along with the evening ones I did with Joey last night, and feeding him constitute my total care-giving responsibilities and would normally all be done in the evening, but I was too tired to finish them last night. Looking at the list, I think to myself, 'I can handle this.' The rest is just making sure he gets to where he needs to be on time.

Joey's forced to surrender his body to whichever caregiver is working on him. It's cool though that he rolls this way or that whatever I want, with his arms and legs limp. He didn't give a thought to me moving his nuts from one side to the other in cleaning and so forth. The instructions hadn't said anything about massaging his ass with the cream, but I assumed that's just an oversight. I massaged his ass for three or four minutes. Neither of us says anything, but every minute or so, Joey makes a quiet moaning sound of pleasure. Needless to say, my boner pokes my boxer shorts straight out again, but fortunately, Joey's on his stomach with his eyes closed and misses my bobbing pole. The last thing I needed to apply is the Desitin creme. That stuff needs to be applied inside his crack and up his hole again. I can see right away that last night's treatment has already noticeably reduced the redness of the rash, so this nursing chore might not be necessary a few days from now. My index finger, covered with the white creme, pressed against his anus and then slides in his hole, this time up to the second joint. Joey's so relaxed and loose he offered no resistance and I, more or less, finger-fucked him for a minute or more. I notice him lifting his crotch off the bed somewhat, probably boner-related. When I don't dare finger his hole any longer, I run my finger from the top of his crack to the bottom near his nuts, three or four times with my fingers slippery with more of the Desitin. He does a long quiet moan wiggling his crotch against the bed sheets.

"Oh, fuck, Oliver. You're the best, dude. I haven't felt so, um, so free of discomfort since the accident. All my itches and scratches and burns are all fixed by you." He chuckles and adds, "Come to think of it, I never felt this good before the accident either." Then a soft laugh. I say, "Hey, Joey, glad to hear it, man. Now we'll get you turned over and I'll put some of this lotion on your chest and the front of your shoulders." He said, "Oh no! No way! I won't be turning over for a while, Oliver. Go have a cigarette or something." I chuckle, "Oh, I get it, Joey. Yeah, sorry 'bout that," and I just have to laugh out loud because we both have wicked boners. He's willing to admit his, but I'm hiding mine. I pat his bare ass a few times, just because I feel like it, and say, "Well, would you like your friend squeezed again?" He gives a half-hearted protest saying he couldn't keep asking me to do that, but soon enough, he gives in. Getting jerked-off simply feels too good to pass up, especially if your snake has been stroked a total of once in the past month, are you kidding me? I tell him I need to take a pee and then I'd spank that naughty boner of his. He goes, "Thanks, Oliver," but the words catch in his throat as he nervously does what I now recognize as his phony laugh whenever he feels embarrassed. What I need to do is put on a big T-shirt and then secure the head of my boner under my boxer's waistband. I want to hide my boner because I'm far from ready to have Joey realize how much all this turns me on. He'd probably realize I was gay fairly soon anyway, hell, I haven't exactly kept it a secret on campus. But I don't want him to know just yet. Soon, but not right now. Guess I'm just working up the courage to tell him. I want us to be more comfortable with each other before I tell him, you know, so he has a chance to realize that there's more to me than me just being gay.

When I have my own boner under wraps, I get Joey turned over. As usual, he keeps his hands clasped as low on his stomach as the casts on his elbows will allow, which is almost as far down as his belly button. His seven-inch boner is sticking straight up. "This is pretty embarrassing, Oliver. I'm used to being man-handled, but this is a brand new kind of man-handling, if ya know what I mean." Then he laughs nervously again, and adds a mumbled, "But nice, um, very nice of you. I'm not complaining!" He's having a little trouble talking. I go, "Shhhhh, just relax," as I massaged the oily cream into the front of his shoulders, then some on his chest and stomach. Avoiding his crotch for the moment, I start massaging his feet and then up his legs slowly, all the way up his skinny, but powerful legs till they connect at his groin. His boner swells and pre-cum drools down the shaft, as Joey moans, "Ohhh my god, that massage feels good." I'm quietly grunting with each quick intakes of oxygen myself by now, wiping a lot of the slippery gel on his nuts and then down near his hole, which I'd covered with Desitin earlier. Finally, my slippery hand grabs around his boned-up penis and my fist goes up and down his long shaft with the head of his cock showing itself when I stroked down and then retreats back into its skin shell when I stroke up. Over and over with both our cocks, mine against my stomach and his encased by, and drooling pre-cum on my hand... our cocks drip, drip, drip pre-cum. I like watching the head of his swollen cock as the pee slit expands with pre-cum bubbles coming out of it. Joey generates more pre-cum than any boy I've ever encountered. His cock head glistens with it. He's openly moaning now and making the hissing sound from sucking air in between his lips as he rolls his head from side to side on the pillow, and then, "Ah ah ah ah" with each tight, relentless long stroke I do on his hard, hard boner.

He holds out longer than last night, but not much. Arching his back, grunting twice and then gasping as he sends another long string of white creamy boy cum over his feet to splat on the hard wood floor at the foot of his bed. The second and third shots land on his leg down by the calf and some on his thigh. Joey, breathing hard, mutters, "Will you marry me, Oliver?" and we both laugh harder than that remark deserved. My stomach is wet with my own pre-cum and I'm right on the edge of spontaneously climaxing. Shortly, he's breathing normally again so I say, "Be right back" and I go quickly into the bathroom for a fast couple of strokes on my boner using the same hand that has Joey's pre-cum and creamy spunk on it and I fire off another hot shot of cum so hard it made me see stars. Sitting down on the edge of the tub, I take short breaths until my heartbeat's almost back to normal. Holy shit! Is this ever hot!

After getting us both cleaned up and dressed, we go for breakfast. Neither of us mentions my rush to the bathroom or Joey's jerk-off, instead, we're quiet with our own thoughts as I push his wheelchair to the dining hall. Later, while I'm wiping some grape jelly off Joey's chin, a thought explodes in my head: 'Hey, this is Darleen and Frankie all over again. I'm playing the Darleen part and Joey's playing Frankie's part. The care I'm providing Joey has to be very similar to the way it was when Darleen nursed Frankie that year following his accident. Another bizarre coincidence in my life and I wonder what it all means? Of course Frankie was very capable of jerking himself off so that's different. I bet the rest is pretty much the way it went with those two. Frankie and I have never discussed the specifics of the nursing Darleen provided, it's just that it was humiliating to Frankie in the beginning, but he eventually felt comfortable only with Darleen. Weird stuff. Joey already seems real comfortable with me, but he's been doing this for a month already with one caregiver or another. As I'm feeding Joey a fork-full of scrambled egg, I glance at his face and discover he's staring at me intently with those big dark blue eyes of his, staring at me like maybe I really am his hero. When he sees me look at him, he smiles at me sweetly. It's a very nice feeling having someone think you're their hero. At the same time, it also occurs to me that being someone's hero is a hell of a big responsibility too.

After breakfast, we attend a couple of morning orientation meetings. In between them, we chat casually about sports and music and try to make a few friends along the way too. Then, for laughs, we whisper insulting comments to each other about other freshman who aren't as cool as we think we are. We do manage to meet a couple of other guys and girls that we both feel meet our standard for acquaintances... haha. They're all real interested in Joey's accident and the fact that I'm his caregiver. Everyone acts amazed at that, but I'm not sure if they're amazed I can do it or amazed that I'm willing to do it. The extent of hygienic care Joey requires should be apparent to all. I don't mind, I want to make friends for sure, but I'm very much aware that I didn't have a good history of success in that department during my high school years, and I'm still not sure why. In any case, I've decided to concentrate on what's most important at the moment, and that's taking care of Joey. I'll let friendships develop naturally without me making a conscious effort to force the process. I may have tried too hard in high school. Just let it happen, that's my new philosophy. During the first orientation meeting, I paid attention, but soon realize Joey's conscientiously typing notes from the meeting into his laptop. After that, instead of paying attention, I daydream throughout the remainder of both meetings. I'll read Joey's notes later.

I'm daydreaming about the way unexpected situations seem to happen in my life, like Cristobal's absence, and realize how much I'd been looking forward to continuing our relationship. I'd built up my first sexual experience to a significant degree and Cristobal had become a huge turn-on for me. All summer I thought about Cris, like the time he danced with me that first night, and how he kissed me a little later. Both were first time experiences for me. And of course, I had my first real gay sex with him. Cris was so experienced it hardly hurt at all, even the first time. That sexy feeling of another boy's penis inside me was awesome, especially after I'd fantasized about it for all those years. It's a memory I'll never forget. I expected him to do me again all my freshman year, but he's not going to and I'm realizing the full extent of how disappointed I am. Actually, I guess I'm pissed off at Cristobal for leading me on in my innocence. He took advantage of me. Then, daydreaming about the weekend I had with Christian, I'm wondering if he took advantage of me too. If he did, I'm positive it wasn't planned, it just developed on its own with the help of alcohol. I realize another thing, too, that sort of surprises me; I've no desire for another sexy time with Christian. It was special at the time, but mostly I think it was something I did for him because of all the wonderful things he's done for me in my life. And then there's Alexander, who I do have the urge to have sex with again. Fucking him earlier this summer was another first time experience and quite a hot one too. Well, except when he acted feminine, which was only rarely. I get a hard boner thinking about his beautiful light brown skin, the sexy smell of him, and that handsome face and that great, dense hair of his. It's hot grabbing fistfuls of his hair when pile-driving his tight hole.

During the second orientation meeting, I think about Frankie and the summer we had together, and his beautifully cute face, and our spit-swapping makeouts, and the couple of times I sucked his perfect cock, and him fucking me in his garage full of junk. Smiling to myself, I think of his wise-cracking personality, but mostly I go back to daydreaming about the two times he fucked me. Oh my god, I really long for more Frankie. We'd laugh so hard we couldn't catch our breath and then there were the serious talks we had too. I can almost smell Frankie's scent, his sexy natural scent. I love running my fingers through his bright red burr haircut, his silky hair on his perfectly shaped head. I could eat him with a spoon, he's so delicious; and it's fun thinking about licking his pinkish smooth body from his feet all the way up to his red hair. Loved sucking on his nuts and rubbing his closely cut pubic hairs and watching his big cock get hard, then lapping and sucking it. And then there's Myers and the shy, super-hot mailroom boy, Pete too. These memories suddenly make me feel lonely because I don't actually know anyone here. I mean, I know Davis' name, but I don't know him. I was depending on Cristobal to show me around and introduce me to his friends. It's obvious that I'd been depending too much on him. And, now that I know he's not going to be here, I'm starting to wonder why I ever thought college was going to be any different than high school. I'll just be an outcast from a larger number of smarter kids here at the university.

Yeah, except there's Joey, and what a stroke of good luck he's turning out to be. So I do have a friend here and I'll make others too. And I'll be hooking up with Alexander once in a while, Frankie too, so what's my problem? I can't allow all this daydreaming to get me depressed, that's the old Oliver who searches out depression, not the new adventurous Oliver. Hell, none of the other freshman in these orientation meeting know anyone here either, it's not just me. I do too much daydreaming. Instead of that, I glance at Joey and damn he's hot. I'll concentrate on that thought. After the second orientation meeting Joey and I go to lunch. While pushing his wheelchair, he's describing the hot chick who sat across from him, something about her body. I just nod my head like I know what he's talking about. Two blocks away from the dining hall, I see two guys jogging towards us. One of the guys points at Joey and me, saying something to his friend. They're amazingly light on their feet and it's fun watching them run. I roll the wheelchair to one side of the brick sidewalk to let them pass by, but they pull up on front of us, not even breathing hard from the run. One of the boys asks Joey, "Are you Joey Gallo?" Joey nods his head and the jogger introduces himself and his friend as members of the gymnastic team. They're supposed to hook up with Joey for lunch. The orientation meeting finished earlier than they expected so they got there late. Both guys are juniors and they're here on campus early representing the team and greeting freshman gymnast. Joey introduces me and the gymnasts invite me to join them for lunch at a place called Smokey Joe's. After lunch they'd take Joey off my hands so he can meet other members of the gymnastics team. I feel like a fifth wheel, but can't think of a way to decline their invitation without offending them.

Both gymnasts are short, about five feet five inches at most, but obviously fit. Fantastic bodies on these two and they don't walk so much as they sorta glide along. One of the two is very cute, but the other is not. The cute one's name is Randy Rider and the goofy-looking one is Bob Crane. They're both kinda funny and likable. They're being nice to Joey because he's a new teammate, but they're nice to me too. The cute Randy puts his arm loosely on my shoulder as we walk side by side to this bar/restaurant. Goofy pushes Joey's wheelchair ahead of us. They're both quite confident and why shouldn't they be since they've been at college for two years already. Everything they say seems to be tongue in cheek, silly, or just plain outrageous. Joey and I laugh easily because the juniors put us at ease and treat us like equals. Being a part of this foursome made me feel like I'm part of a clique and that I'm a University of Pennsylvania college student, and most everybody else in the world isn't.

The not-cute one, Bob Crane, has the fabulous body alright, but an unfortunate face and bad hair to go along with the hot bod. He's cursed with early male baldness with a receding hairline and a small bald circle at the crown of his head. His temporary remaining hair is wimpy, straw-colored, and cut short. His eyes are small and too close together as they peer out under a straight line of thick eyebrows above a too long nose. It's fortunate for him that he's smart and good at gymnastics or he might be headed to the 'loser' bin. Also he's very quick with funny asides and a seemingly good guy. The other gymnast, Randy, is quite a different story. He's funny and very bright also, but oh so very cute as well. Randy's hair is cut too short for my taste, but it's that type of luxurious two-tone blond hair that's thick and even though it's short, it has a slight curl and I wouldn't mind running my fingers through it. Not only does Randy have perfect hair and a perfect body, he's also model beautiful as well as cute. To be honest, Joey and I are cute, but Randy is up a few notches on us. He's up there with Frankie on a much higher plateau of cuteness. He has the kind of face I like to stare at because the more you look at it, the more you realize how special it is, and all-boy as well. This will not surprise you, but my dick's moving around in my boxers and I need to concentrate to keep from wetting my lips, and my pants. I consider Randy a little unexpected temporary gift for me to ogle. Everything wrong about Bob's face is just right with Randy's. He's another one of those boys with that special peaches & cream complexion that always looks clean and lickable. Fine light eyebrows over very bright brown eyes that appear to change shades. Nice perky nose with a dozen small, light colored freckles across the bridge and very cute cheekbone structure that give him the appearance like he's grinning all the time. His chin's just right, too, with no cleft. Natural pink, bowed lips and awesome dimples when he smile. His smile shows off his very white teeth and a slight separation between the front ones. The perfect imperfection, if you know what I mean. Like I said, he's eatable.

Wow, Randy takes my breath away walking next to me with his arm casually on my shoulder, looking me in the eyes when he talks. At one point, he asks me if I'm alright because my breath's coming out in short snorts. He has a smirk on that wonderful face of his when he asks me that; I think it was a smirk. I mumble, "I'm fine, thank you," and he continues telling me how I'm going to need a really good fake ID to have any prayer of getting served in bars around the campus. He goes, "In case you're not aware of it, Oliver, fake IDs are exactly like real IDs except they're fake." I mutter, "Huh?" and he adds, "Yep, they're usually produced by a frat dude entrepreneur, one who has mastered the mysterious art of laminating. The safest bet is an ID without a hologram, which means choosing IDs from states that don't know what holograms are: like Alabama, Arkansas, and Mississippi." I finally blurt out a laugh, but he pretends to be serious, telling me I can find out about all kinds of shit like that in the College Humor Guide. I don't know if there's such a thing or not. With Randy, it's hard to tell.

The side of his tight body rubbing against mine every step we take is definitely getting to be boner-time for me, but we arrive at the bar just before I spring one. I slide into the inside seat of the first empty booth we come to, adjusting my semi-hard pecker as I slide. Randy slides in tight beside me as I take a deep breath wondering if he's gay. He looks over at me, then inexplicably pinches my ear lobe and holds it, proclaiming, "No piercings?" I'm like, "Huh? Oh, that is, um, no. None." But, by then he's calling out to another kid he knows who's sitting at the bar. I don't understand their exchange, but they both laugh; college lingo probably. Smokey Joe's is a cool bar full of college students and other young kids pretending to be college students. For lunch, Bob feeds Joey clam chowder that came in a hollowed out round loaf of bread. I have a Philly cheese steak, which I fed to myself while bumping elbows with Randy. Both Randy and Bob have big cheeseburgers with French fries and fried onion rings. Big lunch for guys that size. They said that soon they'd have to watch their diets, but they liked to binge when they can. The food's okay, not great. We have a pitcher of beer with our meal although actually I'd rather have a coke. I drink the beer listening to Randy giving us freshman advice about college life. He tells us that as freshman, the first weeks of college present us with our only shot at hooking up with people who are ridiculously out of our league, status-wise. He claims it's because the social strata has yet to be established, and once it's established, losers like Joey and I won't have a chance with the in-crowd. Where have I heard that before? Randy gives us an example, "Let's say early in the first week, Oliver here is chatting up this hot chick and by some miracle, he manages not to say anything blatantly racist or incredibly stupid. She's a freshman too and will probably think to herself, "No way would I consider talking to this loser ordinarily, but this ain't high school so maybe stuttering is cool at college, I really don't know. I better go out with him just in case it is."

The things Randy says are mildly amusing in themselves, but he presents them in a very funny way and Joey and I laugh pretty good. I love that Randy used my name in his example and that he sort of included Joey and me in on the joke. Plus, he squeezed the back of my neck to show me he's only teasing about us being losers. He follows up the squeeze by rubbing up the back of my head and then ruffling the hair on the top of my head, as he says to Bob, "Freshmen are so cute, ya just gotta love em." I'm all jittery and then I think to myself, 'Was I stuttering again?' I hadn't realized it. I do my fake cough glancing at hot Randy who looks back at me with a killer grin, and with a mysterious expression doing something with his eyes. Another fake cough from me and for some reason, I'm blushing. Bob's telling us about his first roommate, who informed him, "FYI, dude, but I'll be occasionally smoking pot in our room." Bob said to his roommate, "That's so weird, dude, because I occasionally tell on people who smoke pot." Bob and Randy think that's a riot. Then Randy says he was worried about his first roommate when the kid suggested, "How about we push these dorm beds together and make a big king size bed?" This made all of us laugh. By now Joey and I laugh at anything these two say. They just seem very cool to us. At one point Randy's giving Joey and me tips on how we too can be cool at college. He goes, "No truly cool person speaks loudly. You need to speak real low in conversations, and always act bored. Say a few, small words, but every once in a while, drop in a really big one just to prove you can, but you're too cool to bother. See?" For example, someone says to you, "Hey," and you mutter, "Sup?" and they say, "I like your T-shirt." You say, "Sup?" again, and it goes like that for a bit and then somewhere along the way you drop in one of the big words you've memorize." By now, I'm playing with myself under the table because Randy's pressing the side of his thigh against the side of mine. As we're finishing the pitcher of beer, Joey asks me, "Ya want to come with us to meet some of the other gymnast, Oliver?" I say, "Sup?" making Randy laugh and do the back of my neck squeeze and hair rub again. My boner is full and hard by now. I squeak out, "Can we get something for dessert?"

We all get chocolate ice cream sundaes because Bob informs us it goes best with draft beer, which is puzzling. I take my time eating my sundae hoping my boner will go down. Not wanting to leech on to the gymnast, I mention to Joey I need to email my folks and do some other stuff, and I'd catch up with him later. After lunch, all of us go back in the same direction we came and on the way, Randy explains to me about the difficult training program necessary for gymnastics at their level. He claims it creates full body muscle development and he pats my ass emphasizing that this part of the body needs exercising too. I'm wearing flimsy nylon-like basketball shorts and Randy, after patting my almost bare ass, grabs my left buttocks and pushes some of the material of my shorts up my hole using his middle finger, telling me, "Yeah, even this muscle gets worked on for gymnastics and both buttocks get very muscular and hard," making me think of Joey's buttocks. He adds, "Now, Oliver, your ass is firm, but not hard like a gymnast's ass," as he's pushing the material of my shorts further up my asshole until I'm walking up on my toes going, "Ugh...oh oh...Ah ah." I hold onto his arm to keep my balance as he chuckles and massages my ass cheek, saying in his normal speaking voice, "Here, feel the difference," and he lets go of my ass, taking my hand and presses it against his ass. His ass feels just like Joey's. We're walking behind Bob who's again pushing Joey in the wheelchair, so all this ass-grabbing goes undetected by them. I'm still on my toes, clutching Randy with one hand and pulling at the back of my nylon shorts with the other. My efforts to pull the material out of my hole were not immediately successful, but I do spring another boner. After a few steps, Randy points at the bulge in the front of my shorts and lightly touches the head of my cock through the thin material, muttering, "Get a grip, dude. Jeez, I won't be able to show you insightful things about gymnastics if ya keep popping boners." Than he hugs me around my waist, saying with a grin, "I'm just breaking your balls, Oliver, 'cause I like ya. Don't get all flustered." I managed to smile back and gulp while trying to say, "Sup?' I'm betting that Randy's gay.

He calls up to Bob, "You'll never guess what happened to Oliver?" Bob doesn't even look back when he says, "Let me guess. He's the victim of the infamous 'Randy Rider Wedgie' and he can't get his underwear out of his asshole." Randy said, "You're not as much fun as you use to be, Bob." Maybe he's not gay after all. And then we're at the point where they go left and I go right. We all say goodbye and two minutes later, Randy jogs back to me and asks, "You're okay, right, Oliver?" I say, "Um, yeah, I'm fine," and looking me right in the eyes, Randy says, "We've got to hook up soon, dude!" Then he's gone and I stand here watching him glide away, again thinking he's gay. When he's out of view, I slowly walk away not really sure what was going on, but my boner's back. Randy's one of the confident ones and I'm attracted to his type, but what attracted him to me? And, is he gay or, like he said, just busting my balls? What I don't need is another conundrum confusing my life, like with Frankie most of the time. It's not unheard of for a gymnast to be gay of course and the thought Randy's gay and interested in me has me hustling back to the room for an emergency afternoon jerk off. In the bathroom, I do it thinking about Randy and a little about Joey too. And, whoa, do I ever explode with cum. A burning climax as spunk streaks from my pee slit. Then I worry that Randy was making fun of me and I'm just too stupid to realize it. Later, after emailing my parents, Alexander, and Frankie, I pick up Joey at the gymnasium and while pushing his wheelchair back to our room, ask what he thinks of Randy. He thinks he's cool, but doesn't mention anything about Randy maybe being gay. Well, there's no way I can bring it up, so it's unclear. I lay on my bed and fantasized about Randy and Joey being gay and what a threesome we would make once Joey's bones have healed. The two tight and toned gymnast do the skinny and very willing Oliver Nickerson. God damnit, I popped another boner already.

I get my iPod out and listen to The Killers' CD. I absolutely love "Can you read my mind?" and I memorized every word hoping to sing it with Cristobal on Mall Road. Fuck that! Checking my emails, I see one from Mom & Dad, one from Alexander, two from the twins and one from Frankie. Now I'll finally find out something, maybe.

Chapter 2
Joey

Listening to my iPod, I'm checking my email. Joey, my roommate, is being well taken care of by his gymnast teammates so I'm enjoying some free time. First, my parent's email. No surprises there. They got home fine and are hoping I had a good first day. They're probably thinking back to my first day in high school, which was a nightmare, and they've got their fingers crossed that things are going well for me here. I reply, 'Things are going great for me so far, thanks!' then give an outline of my responsibility as my roommate's caregiver. I make it seem simpler than it actually is so they won't worry. Next is Alexander's email, which unfortunately, continues to reflect the same tone of his recent ones. Friendly, but not like, I can't wait to see you, Oliver. Not like that. It appears Alexander, like Cris, is less excited about seeing me than I am about seeing him. It's not like he says he doesn't want to see me, he actually says just the opposite, but it doesn't seem like he's excited about it. Alexander makes it all sound like we're arranging an appointment for a job interview or something. Very business-like. He doesn't have a free weekend in September, but says, 'October is looking good.' Hopefully he can fit me in some time in October.

Ya know, maybe I need to rethink my feelings for Alexander. Right now my feelings about him are this: I really, really want to see him. I can't help thinking about all the hugging and kissing that we did together. His body feels good, and he smells good too, and I love how he tastes. All that hugging and kissing started right after he sucked me off that first time. And that was right after he'd given me my hot haircut. I haven't had a haircut since. For me, haircuts are a low priority item normally, but Alexander makes getting a haircut more like an event. It's hot because he's hot! I want to lay on his bare back and fuck him for at least an hour and then we'll hug and cuddle some, and later I'll do him doggy style and then we can hug and kiss some more and after that...haha. In other words, reenact what we did last summer. This isn't rocket science, I want to have sex with him, that's all. He turns me on. I know I don't love him, but I like him a lot. We had fun with the sex for sure, but a lot of other kinds of fun too just hanging out together.

Getting up from my desk, I wander downstairs and buy a coke from the dorm's vending machine. There are all sorts of snacks and soft drinks available from machines down in the finished basement of this huge old home that long ago was converted into a college dormitory. The room next to the vending machine room is the laundromat, which is convenient, but pricey. By the time I get back to the room with my peanut butter crackers and my Coke, I'm in a funk. How come I get so over the top attached to boys and they don't get the same way with me? I can't pretend to myself I'm not hurt that Cristobal could so easily blow me off, and now Alexander is acting a lot less than thrilled about me visiting him. Those kinds of things hurt my feelings. Alexander tells me his barbershop is doing great business, but he doesn't mention anything about having a boyfriend, so why isn't he excited about seeing me. He was hot for me last summer. Fuck! This is putting me in a depressed frame of mind. Back at my laptop, I decide I'll keep my reply to Alexander upbeat. I type, "Okay, Alexander; whenever, dude. Just so ya know though, I can't wait to see you and I need a haircut bad so the sooner the better. Just mention a date that works for you and I'll make it work for me. Oliver.' Hitting 'send' I sit back in my desk chair trying to figure out my weird feelings. Rejection sucks of course, but I think my weird feeling is partially caused by that email that's sitting there blinking at me; the one from Frankie that I'm purposely leaving for last because I never know what to expect from him. I'm afraid it will be bad news of some sort. I need good news where Frankie's concerned because I have unbelievably strong feelings for him. Feelings of need or infatuation or something that's strongly emotional when it comes to Frankie. Those feelings I've decided to call love.

Maybe I still don't know what love is, but the way I feel about Frankie is what I think love is. So, I'll check Frankie's email a little later, but right now I'll see what the North twins have to say. They always boost my self-esteem with their undying love and admiration for me. Haha, that may be overstating it a bit, but they do call me their other big brother and they never have anything but positive things to say about me. They say they love me and that sort of thing which makes me feel good. They also claim that I'm the big brother who pays attention to them. Not like Alexander who just wants to play golf with his buds and then, every so often, give the twins haircuts and then it's, 'run along boys.' I most certainly would never tell those two to 'run along.' Carbon copy examples of all boys with perfect tight matching bodies and identical faces so cute you'll walk into a telephone poll staring at them on the street. I know what I'm talking about too because I've been looking at every boy that passes my way for the last ten or twelve years now. Nathan and Noah, in many ways, are immature for eighteen, but that's because their parents have sheltered them and babied them all their lives. They go to exclusive private schools so they can be together all day at school, like they're together all the other times of their lives. Those two are inseparable which is fairly normal for identical twins, but the North twins definitely take it a couple of steps further.

They've sent me quite a few emails since we went our separate ways last summer after Wildwood. I'm still marveling at that fabulous happenstance of renting our summer place next door to Alexander and his twin brothers. Well, right now I need someone to pump me up and these two are perfect for that so I open their first email which starts-out, "Hi Oliver. We miss you terribly and can't wait to see you. The earliest time we can get away from school will be during Thanksgiving break, but we want you to drive up to St. John's Prep to see us sooner than that!! PLEASE!!." It's nice to be missed, but then they hit me over the head with this bit of news. 'Noah wants me to tell you that we know you're gay, Oliver. We've known almost from the first day on the beach, but we don't care. Last summer, Noah and I went back up to the house to find you when you were late coming down to the beach. I didn't want to spy on you at first, but Noah said to me, 'What if Oliver is in some kind of trouble and needs our help?' So, anyway, we snuck up and looked in your bedroom window and saw you fucking Alexander. We didn't have any problem with that and so we didn't bother to bring it up to you until now." I can't imagine where this is leading, but I need to stop and get away from this email. It's really embarrassing they saw me fucking their brother. I go for a walk smoking my Marlboro lights while trying not to think about anything. Thinking about nothing isn't possible for me though, and it seems to me that every single plan I had for my first freshman year is going up in smoke already. I don't know about Frankie yet, but my premonition is that it's not going to be good news. Cristobal is history and Alexander has other things besides me on his mind. And, the knowledge that the twins had seen Alexander and me fucking is very disturbing. My face gets hot and red just from thinking about that.

The things I expected to be awesome are turning out to be big disappointments. On the other hand, what's up with that Randy guy? Possibly something hot might develop there before the semester is over. Feeling a little more optimistic thinking about Joey and Randy, I open the front door of the dorm and run right into a kid coming out. He knocks me up against the door jam, then grunts, "Watch where you're going, asshole!" My automatic response is to say "I'm sorry," which I do but it doesn't help. The other kid is pissed off, and says, "You dumb shit, look at this." He's pointing at his polo shirt where a coffee stain is shining wetly. I guess his coffee spilled on him when we collided. I go, "Oh man, I'm really sorry. I didn't see you coming out. Ah, can I wash your shirt for you, or something?" This kid's big, in a squat kind of way. Maybe an inch shorter than me, with an extra eighty pounds on him. Not some fat slob though, it's hard fat with muscles. A lot of real white skin showing with big freckles on his face and on his bare arms too. Dark red hair cut in a military flat top with shaved sides. Big face with pinkish eyes, and he's breathing nosily through his nose making a wheezing sound with each exhale. Huh, he never quite closes his mouth either. I get the feeling he's always looking for trouble and that's a familiar type from my high school days. We had tough farm-boy types like this and they were always bullies. This kid might have been a farm boy, but he's a smart farm boy because you don't get into the University of Pennsylvania unless you're smart.

When I offer to wash his shirt, he grabs a fistful of my T-shirt twisting it as he pulls me roughly over to him, and snarls, "Are you trying to be a wise ass, ya skinny punk?" breathing his bad breath in my face along with an offensive spray of spittle. "Na, no ,na I..that is.." My stuttering is the last straw for him, I guess, because he whacks me across the top of my head with his fat, open hand. "Keep out of my way girlie-boy. I do not like fags!" and then he shakes me, which rips my t-shirt at the neck. One more smack across my forehead and he rips my tee almost off me, saying, "We're even now, ya little cunt." Then a push up against the door jam again and he walks away, saying over his shoulder, "Ya got me on a bad day kid, but anyway now ya know, don't fuck around with me. You need to stay out of my way!" The door slams behind him. I get tears of rage in my eyes and a thumping heart. It was so fucking unfair! He didn't see me coming in the door any more than I saw him coming out. Plus, I said I was sorry even thought we were both equally to blame. He didn't care, instead he beats me up because, well, because he can. This is turning out to be a horrible start to my college career. And, that fat bastard is in this dormitory too so I'm going to have to be on the lookout for him all the time now. I feel like shit that I didn't stick up for myself. At the least I could have verbally stood up to him except after my terrible high school experiences, I'm not used to being confrontational myself. I'm in the habit of being passive because that served me well in high school.

I go in my room and lay down on my bed, but I won't let myself cry, which is what I feel like doing. All my energy goes into not crying and I don't. A small victory, but I feel so lonely and lost all of a sudden. I want to go home, back to my old room and work on the loading dock with Frankie during the days. Frankie and I would eat each other's lunch every day and swap spit when we kiss and get our wet boners bumping against one another. Then when Frankie is out sick or something, little Pete can suck on my fingers and then give me a rough fuck with his huge cock in the lavatory, or I'd give him a good fucking when his hole isn't too sore. That's what I want to do. What I do instead is fall asleep. My cellphone wakes me. It's Joey wondering where I am. He sounds like he's in an echo chamber. Oh, it's the speaker phone mode he's forced to use because both his arms are in a plaster casts, "No, hurry though, Oliver. Whenever you get here is fine. It's so much fun watching these gymnasts go through basic routines." I ask, "How did Randy look?" Joey's like, "Randy? Oh, the kid from lunch? I don't think I saw him after we left you. I'm with the freshman. How you doing?" I tell him I feel a little sick, nothing serious. Turning off my laptop, I head over to pick him up feeling better because Joey's a bright spot for me. I leave the rest of those depressing emails for later. Joey's the best thing that's happened to me in college so far. I'll bet that boy needs another bath before bed too. That perks me up as I play with myself on the way over thinking there's a chance I'm too obsessed with boys. By the time I arrive at the gym, I'm feeling okay again.

What a cute, warm smile I get from Joey when he sees me. It's only a five-minute walk back to our dorm, which is a good thing because Joey has to pee badly. I jogged him back and almost spill him out of the wheelchair coming off a curb too fast. We get to laughing at that as Joey says, "Fuck, Oliver, I'm going to pee my pants as it is. Don't make me laugh." It's odd how comfortable we are with each other already. In our bathroom, I get Joey on the toilet and hold his dick for him as he pees. I need to bend over to do that and I let my forehead rest on his shoulder. He leans the side of his head against mine. Neither of us says anything, and it's sweet. After his pee he says, "Run for the hills, Oliver. I've been holding this fart in for two hours and I've got to do a dump too." He doesn't have to tell me twice. At my desk, I hear his long, loud motorboat fart followed by, "Ahhh, ohhh yeah" as his doody plops into the toilet water. Shortly, I hear, "Get in here now and wipe my ass, Oliver." I do it, but his pretend way of ordering me to do it gets us laughing again. We're in silly moods, like Frankie and I used to do all the time. I'm happy to be in this silly mood rather than the gloomy mood I'd been in earlier.

Later, when we're in the dining hall, I tell Joey about my encounter with the dormitory bully. Joey's appalled that something like that would take place here at the University of Pennsylvania and I guess I am too. It's just that I was kind of use to it in high school. That kind of thing wasn't all that rare at a high school in the western part of upstate Pennsylvania, in my experience anyway. Halfway through dinner, two guys come over to join us at our table. Gymnasts of course, but neither of them is Randy. Mac somebody and I didn't get the other kid's name. These guys are really built, but too muscle-bound in their chest, shoulders, and biceps for my taste. Probably a turn-on for plenty of other gay guys though. Neither of them seems gay in the least and neither of them is particularly cute either. And to be honest, they pretty much ignore me as I feed Joey. The three of them talked exclusively about esoteric gymnastics stuff. That's fine with me.

After dinner, the four of us go to their dormitory and watch the Phillies lose another baseball game, not that I care because I'm a Pirates fan. No beer or anything, just Gatorade. Later, back in our room, I get Joey in the tub again and do a shortened version of last night's bath. No boner in the tub so I don't mention a jerk-off. As I'm getting him out of the bath, Joey reminds me I need to put the cream on his rash. I was going to do that anyway, but I'm glad he was the first one to bring it up. With Joey lying in bed on his stomach, I first do the massage routine and I can feel how relaxed and loose Joey's body is while I'm doing it. Spreading the cream between Joey's hard buttocks, being sure all the red areas are covered, and then gently pressing on his hole until my finger slides in. This time I push in all the way past both joints and up to my index finger's knuckle. Looking at the side of Joey's face to see if there's any negative reaction. His eyes are barely closed, slightly fluttering, and he's gently biting his lower lip. I slowly finger-fuck him with the entire length of my finger a half dozen times and he moves his head on the pillow the way you do when something is feeling real good. When I pull my finger all the way out, he involuntarily moans, "Ahhh ohh." Putting more lube, er, Desitin on my finger, I pushed back in and finger-fucked him until he says, "Oh, Oliver, I'm going to cum." He lifts his crotch up a bit and shoots a lot of spunk on the sheet. With each spurt of cum, his hole closes tightly on my finger and both of his strong, perfectly shaped buttocks close on the lower part of my hand. I honestly don't believe I could have pulled my finger out even if I wanted to, which I don't. Imagining my boner in there instead of my finger causes the front of my cargo shorts to bulge out. A small wet spot quickly soaks through. I quietly moan, "Ahhhh, ah." Joey said, "Oh, man. I'll never be able to repay you for taking care of me so well, Oliver."

In the bathroom, I pull out my t-shirt to cover the wet pre-cum spot on my shorts and then grab a dampened washcloth. At Joey's bed, I help turn him over, away from the cum, and clean him up being extra conscientious about cleaning his dick as he grunts quietly, sucking on his lips. Is Joey gay? I need to ask myself that question again, but I'm not asking him because so far this arrangement is very acceptable to me. When it's unreasonable to continue cleaning his cock and balls any longer, I get a pair of clean boxers for him and then help him hop over to his desk where he sits in front of his laptop to go online. Changing his messy sheets, I give him a grin to show I don't mind changing his bedding. I'm in the bathroom, in the shower, jerking off and almost pass out with the force of my ejaculation. That kid's body gets me hot. After my shower, Joey and I stay up having a long bullshit session telling each other about our lives. I tell him about the death of my best friend, Tyler, and we commiserated with each other about our loss of best friends. Of course Tyler was only fourteen so Joey and his best friends were best friends a lot longer and I've had five years to recover. He tells me, just as I'd suspected after meeting his mother, that he's adopted. He was adopted when he was one day old so he's spent his entire life in the Gallo family as an only child. His father travels all the time for his job as a business consultant. A great guy when he's home, but he's not home very often and maybe that's because of Mrs. Gallo, although Joey doesn't say that. On and on we go, taking turns telling each other stuff about ourselves. Joey never mentions a girlfriend, dating, or anything at all about his sexuality. Neither do I.

We get to sleep about four o'clock in the morning and sleep in the next day till almost two o'clock in the afternoon, which means we missed the last orientation meeting. We don't care though, we both care more about bonding during our bull session last night. Joey's on his stomach again for the diaper rash cream, which is what it actually is. The rash is almost gone already, but neither Joey nor I mention that minor detail. His boner poppin' for me just thinking about being finger-fucked again. Joey's sort of squirming on the bed waiting for it too. Obviously, it feels very good for him too, although it's not clear if it's just relieve from the itching and dryness of the rash, or the finger fucking part. Probably it's both. Squeezing a lot of the cream on my finger, I spread it slowly up and down his ass crack and then, using my longer middle finger this time, I push my slippery finger all the way up his hole and fingered it with curving long strokes over and over until Joey squeaks out, "Would you please help me turn over and then take care of my snake again, Oliver?"

Smiling to myself, I mutter, "Sure, Joey," and help him turn over. I can't tell who's breathing harder, Joey or me. His boner looks very long as it stands straight up from his dark pubic patch, and it appears to be vibrating. Taking it in my fist, I stroke it with the longest strokes possible, from deep in his pubes up to the tip of his fat cock head and I swear I've never felt a harder boner. What a turn-on seeing that swollen head of his cock drooling pre-cum as the lips of the pee slit opens and closes repeatedly. I've never seen anyone's pee slit open as wide. Joey's needs to open very wide though because of the copious amounts of pre-cum that's drooling out and running over my fist and then down the long shaft of his pretty, pale tan boner to collect messily in his pubes. Pulling the uncut skin off the head of his cock when I stroke down and pushing it back up to cover part of the wet dark red cock head when I stroke up. It's mesmerizing to me, but after only within three minutes, tops, Joey moans out a long, "Ooooooooooh," arches his back and the first creamy cum spurts out of his pee slit followed immediately by a long, hard, fast moving string of cum that shoots out about four feet until gravity takes over and pulls it down. It lands as a four foot line of creamy wetness from his thigh to his ankle. Again Joey goes, "Ahhhhhhhh, oh oh oh" as he shoots a shorter version of the long cum blast and then a few little spurt follow. Now it's just drooling cum that slowly runs over my fist to pool on his big oval, hairless, nuts joining the pre-cum that ended up there earlier.

My lips parted, I stare at his boner in my hand wanting desperately to taste that creamy, white spunk, but of course, I don't. Joey blows out a half dozen burst of air with his face red, then he mutters, "Fuck, Oliver. Damn, how do you do that? I never cum this hard jerking myself off. Oh my God that felt good. Thank you so much, man. I feel so close to you, Oliver. Like we've known each other all our lives. You're the best, dude, ever, you really are." Smiling back at him weakly, then in a strangled voice, I mumble, "Thanks, same to you, be right back," and turn to walk quickly into the bathroom, licking some of his cum off my fingers as soon as I close the door. The taste of his cum has me moaning quietly to myself, my cock's painfully hard and I barely have the bathroom door closed before pulling my pants down and stroking my boner, desperately needing to climax. Just thinking about my cock in Joey's hole is a huge turn-on. I suck on the same slippery finger that was in Joey's asshole and almost immediately fire a stream of cum up onto the medicine cabinet mirror. Breathing hard with my heart pounding like a drum, I savor the sensation of climaxing while wondering, what is it with Joey and me?

The after effects of my orgasm sizzle about my body doubling me over at the intensity of them. All these fabulous sensations spreading from my groin all around my pelvic area get my eyes blinking and it's so ridiculously awesome I grunt out a laugh looking at myself in the cum-stained mirror. Jesus! I'm doubled over with a red face, and this is just from jerking Joey and myself off. What the hell would happen if we ever have real sex together? A heart attack comes to mind. Holy shit, this is wicked hot. Sitting on the edge of the bathtub, coming down from that high, I, all of a sudden, feel self-conscious. Joey obviously knows that I just jerked myself off, so now what do I do? Picking up another damp washcloth, I clean the mirror and put myself and my clothes back together and sheepishly go back out to face the music. Joey's grinning from ear to ear when he asks, "How was it?" I smirk, muttering, "I'm sure I don't know what the fuck you're talking about." We both smile and I clean up the cum Joey shot all over himself. "I never knew college was going to be this much fun. Did you, Oliver?" I go, "Sup?" and we both laugh, but there's no other reference about our masturbation morning.

First day of classes tomorrow morning, so we've carefully double checked that we have all the books we need, and we verify when and where we need to be, and how to get there. We're ready and anxious to get going with our freshman year at this prestigious Ivy League University. Having the same schedule is a huge help and it's kinda fun being together all day too. Joey and I have become tight already. The intimate nursing care is obviously a big factor in that, but we sincerely like each other as well. I couldn't hope for a better roommate. Joey's probably the best roommate in the entire history of the University. We'd slept through most of this day so after a late lunch I need to hustle Joey to his gymnastic practice. Then I go back to the room to finish reading my emails and maybe take a peek at Frankie's email. Nathan's reads, 'Lately we've really begun getting into the whole sex topic thing and we want to try it and of course we went right to our brother for help, but he said, flat out, that he would not help us with it. We're late bloomers sex-wise, but Noah says we'll start with gay sex, that being convenient'. Oh no! They want lessons from me about how to do gay sex safely.

This is insanity! Going out for a walk around the campus again, I chain smoke trying to think how to answer the twins' email. I'll need to talk to Alexander about this. It's like those twins were raised in a bubble. They don't know shit about the real world. Alexander's barbershop closes at six o'clock so I'll call a little after six tonight. Maybe I'll be able to detect something from Alexander's voice to give me a clue about him and me too. First and foremost the twins, I know we have to resolve that, but I'm still concerned about me and Alexander? I wish he didn't get me so hot, but other than Pete, Alexander's the only boy I've ever fucked as a 'top'. I like it although not as much as the other way around, except Alexander's terrible at being a top. Of course, that could change… maybe.

I need to sit down, which I do on a conveniently placed bench and let the real world back into my brain. Joey's at the gym until five-thirty so I walk over there to get him. He's so psyched about the gymnastic team and excitedly telling me all about it as I try paying attention. He needs to use the toilet, so after that he gets set up at his desk checking emails, which he gets a lot of. That's not surprising because I'll bet he was very popular in high school, and on the gymnastic team too. Teammates form close bonds and tend to stay in touch. A little after six, I tell him I need some air and wander outside to make the cellphone call to Alexander's barbershop. I'm a little nervous for a couple of reasons. One, I don't know what kind of reception I can expect from Alexander, and two, just bringing up this matter of the twins may make me seem perverted, but what else can I do? There's no way around it, talking to Alexander is positively necessary.

He answers on the second ring by automatically giving the shop's name and saying that he's sorry but they're closed. I try being funny, "But, but this is an emergency! Don't ya understand fool, I need a haircut tonight." Alexander's chuckling, "How's my favorite white bread? I hope your skinny ass is close by for a surprise visit because I miss you and I want to taste that cock of yours sooooo badly. I want to lick your hole and have you fuck me till I squeal like a banshee. Where are you, bro?" Well, that sounds encouraging. He's excited that I might be in the area and I hear disappointment in his voice when I tell him I'm still an hour and a half away, in school. We do small talk for a minute and then I asked about us getting together. The problem with that for Alexander is the week he'd be away at a hair stylists' convention in Atlantic City. Also, his biological father wants Alexander to visit him in Texas and there's been a problem getting someone to cover for Alexander at his barbershop during his absence. Further complicating Alexander's life is the slowness of the breaking-in process for his recently hired barber, who will keep the business going when Alexander's not there. All legitimate reasons for his inability to set a date for us to get together. Oh, how tedious is a working man's life. But, the long and the short of it is that Alexander does want to see me for fun and games just as much as I want to see. Emails can't convey tone of a message like Alexander's voice can. It sure makes me feel better about myself because someone still considers me their sex buddy. I don't know about Frankie because I'm afraid to read his email, although I've got to do that soon.

Alexander and I make a firm date to get together the second Saturday in October, and just knowing a date has finally been set makes me feel so good it's a bit embarrassing. Am I that horny? And it's also nice that I didn't detect the slightest feminine sound from him. I'm pretty sure his business requires he not sound or act feminine. I want to get my hands in his dense hair and taste his mouth, and he gives me the best blow job! With that settled, I hesitate for a second trying to get the courage to bring up the reason for the call. Alexander recognizes my hesitancy, and goes, "Oh no, what is it, Oliver? Something bad?" Then I come right out with it, "We got problems with the twins." He says, "Oh, that nonsense about them trying gay sex together? Don't make a mountain out of a molehill, Oliver. They're like babies and it's all my mother's fault. Let them work it out. They're eighteen fer chrissake!

He's finished with that topic and goes on to tell me what he intends to do about my haircut next month. I'm leaning up against a brick wall outside our dorm, not paying too much attention to that, as I unconsciously grope my junk thinking what a blast it would be teaching Nathan and Noah gay sex. Ha ha, but relieved the situation is left to take care of itself. Then I hear giggling. Looking up, I see three girls staring at me from the brick sidewalk, miming me playing with myself. My face gets red and hot as sweat pops out on my forehead. I stop the groping of course, but the girls have already turned the corner. Hmmm, I think I recognized one of the girls as a gymnast. I think Joey was talking with her when I picked him up earlier. Life sucks some times. "Are you still there, Oliver?" Alexander asks. What the hell? Oh yeah, my cellphone. I tell Alexander about getting caught just now playing with myself and he laughs and I do too. Fuck it. Yeah, it is pretty funny and his laughter is contagious anyway.

Feeling good that everything's cool between Alexander and me, I say goodbye. Walking back to the dorm, adjusting my package again, I hear more giggling. What the fu...? It's two of the girls walking back the other way now, and they're pointing at their crotches. I look down and somehow I've sprung a boner. I'm a fucking walking boner. My bulging crotch makes it obvious, and I again get the red-hot face with sweat drops running down the sides of my forehead. FUCK! The girls walk on laughing and shouting something at me about a sleeping bag. For the tent...? I didn't catch it all. Hurrying inside, I wonder how I get myself into so many embarrassing situations. Ya know, I hope my boner popped up because I'm thinking about me and Alexander, and not because of the twins.

In our room, Joey's laughing as he and some bud from high school exchange dirty jokes online. He gives me his cute grin and wiggles his fingers to say, 'Hi.' Online, I email the twins wishing them good luck with their gay sex. Then, what the fuck, I open Frankie's email and the first word in the first sentence is the last word I want to read in an email from Frankie, and that word is 'Darleen'! The email starts off fine, with the salutation, 'Hi Olive, I miss you,' but then it goes downhill fast after that, "This is a surprising development, Oliver, but Darleen and I had a long talk the first night here at West Chester University. We'd signed up for this co-ed dorm last Spring. First night here we stayed up all night talking about all the experiences we've been through together. It brought back a lot of memories. She admitted to me she's been a total bitch (her word, Oliver) for some time now and she's sorry because it's a lot her fault (and some yours) that she and me broke-up. She's determined to win me back and to that end she's already lost eleven pounds and her minimum goal is to lose another twenty-five pounds.' I stop reading for a second and scream "FUCK! FUCK!" Joey asks, "What's wrong?" I tell him I bit my tongue, he goes, "Oh, sorry to hear that, dude," and he goes back to texting or whatever he's doing. So Darleen wants to lose thirty-six pounds and win back Frankie. If she thinks getting her weight under two hundred pounds is all it takes, she's in for a surprise. The two hundred pounds is an exaggeration of course. I'm just royally pissed at this turn of events. That snatch simply will not go away! Going back to Frankie's email, I read, 'Darleen feels we (her and me) need to begin an active sexual relationship immediately. She feels her lack of attention to my needs has allowed you to step in and take....well, again, these are her words, not mine...take advantage of me." I knock the laptop over screaming, "FUCK YOU, BITCH!" Joey turns around again and asks, "Your tongue again, Oliver?" He said it in such a funny way I had to blurt out a laugh. I go, "No, I bit my lip this time." He says, "Well at least ya didn't bite your dick." And I laugh again because he has this pretend serious dumb look on his face that makes me laugh. "When we going to dinner?" he wants to know. Just seeing him makes me feel better, I go, "Soon, ya hot shit ...soon."

Frankie's email went on a rant about how he didn't want me to feel hurt or angry because, after all, I know how he feels about me. Really? He says it's just that he can't say the words as easily as I can. He explains that since I'm gay, I can say stuff about love, but Frankie's straight and that stuff doesn't come as easy for straight guys. He went on again about him knowing positively he isn't gay and except for a few times with me, and the times that queer maniac Fallon had forced him into it, Frankie's never had anything remotely to do with 'queer stuff'. With me it's somehow, he says, different because he does it to help me out and because he doesn't want me to have to turn to a pervert for someone to fuck me. He's happy he's able to help, but he's really looking forward to having sex with Darleen so he can prove to everyone once and for all that he's not gay. On and on it goes... he knew he'd love hetero sex, and except for making a random exception in my case, he'd never ever do any of the gay stuff again. BUT, he and I will be the best and closest buddies ever in the world and, as he said earlier, once in a while, as a favor to me, he'll fuck me as much as I want him to. A rambling email that's hard to follow at times. He ends with, 'Please, please, please don't be mad at me, Oliver. You mean so much to me, you really do. Email me back and tell me that you L... me. You know what I mean. Your best bud ever (who feels the same way for you), Frankie.' The gist of all this is Frankie loves me and will have gay sex with me, but he really wants to do hetero sex with Darleen because he's not gay and because, even though he's never had sex with a female in his nineteen years on this particular planet, he's absolutely positive he'll love the hetero sex much, much more than that nasty queer stuff. The same queer stuff that he'll nonetheless do for me as long as I want him to, and since we're the best, closest buddies the world has ever seen, and because he knows I'm gay and in love with him, that means I'll want him to fuck me often, but he'll be doing all that fucking as a straight dude because he'll have his hefty wife, Darleen, proving he's not gay. Oh brother! What a crock of shit!

Out loud I said, "Fuck you, Frankie" and slam my laptop shut. Joey makes no comment, just turns and gives me a concerned look. It's a look indicating I have his support in whatever it is that's upsetting me. That's how I interpret his look and I feel a strong urge to kiss him on his cute, but almost too big nose. He's so innocent and cute looking and it's so beautiful when the boy smiles, as the song goes. He's eighteen and I'm a year older because I took that year off from school when Tyler died, but Joey looks younger than me. All of a sudden he averts his eyes so I guess I was making gooey eyes at him again. Damn, I gotta watch myself or I'll scare him off. I say, "I'm okay now, Joey. Let's eat." Even as I'm helping Joey get in his wheelchair, I'm already aware I didn't mean my nasty comment about Frankie. You can't turn love on and off. Once it's on, it takes a lot to turn it off. I don't want to think about it right now through. I ruffle Joey's hair, asking, "Shampoo after dinner?" Joey said, "Oh, can't we do all the things again tonight, Oliver?" Hot damn! I mutter, "Sure, Joey. Whatever ya want, dude," trying not to drool. We have an okay dinner and afterwards we do the shampoo, the bath, and the jerk-off. I jerked him off in the tub and he leaned his head next to mine very sweetly the whole four minutes. I could feel him giving my neck a tiny baby kiss that almost had me blowing a load in my shorts. I let my lips brush his cheek when he was finished firing off his four shots of cum, and then kept my arm around his neck until he'd calmed down from the climax. We don't discuss the cuddling or the little kiss, but I feel very protective of him. I hate to admit it, but I can see why Darleen got so possessive of Frankie after being his primary caregiver for a while. Naturally, I'd never hold it over Joey's head like that bitch does to Frankie, you can be damn sure of that. This kid means a lot to me already so I'm going to take good care of him. Laying on his stomach on his bed I cream his asshole and ass crack getting some finger-fucking in during the whole process and then it's time for bed.

We get to sleep quickly, waking up well rested and ready to experience our first day of college life. Each of our four professors spends a lot of time telling us we probably won't make it because the work's too hard for lazy nitwits like us freshman. There is a lot of reading and studying that need to be done out of the classroom for starters, and right from the first day too. From day one, the work load is at a heavy level. Joey is real smart though, and I am too, so we work out a way that one of us does this and one of us does that. It frees up free time and we need it because it's slow work getting him ready for class every day. Joey especially needs the extra time because he has gymnastic practice six days a week. I love working closely with him on our studies and quickly recognize that he, like Frankie, has his own personal scent which is very nice, and oh yeah, sexy hot too. Of course I detected it while bathing him, but the more familiar it becomes, the hotter it seems.

We're in a routine now with no need to ask questions about anything, everything is automatic now and I make sure Joey's the cleanest invalid ever. His ass rash was completely cured, but we continue the treatment anyway. You know, just to be sure the rash doesn't reappear. When we run out of Desitin, I began using creamy Vaseline which actually works better for the finger-fucking. We're cautiously affectionate with each other with little things like letting our heads rest together when tired as we read a passage in a study guide or from the computer screen trying to figure something out. Or, during his bath, the sides of our faces often rub against one another and sometimes our lips lightly drag across each other's cheek or forehead. I try the lightest kiss at the corner of his mouth one night as I jerk him off, but Joey turns his head away and quietly murmurs, "No, Oliver," so he must suspect now that I'm gay. I'm not sure about him yet and that's because our minor affectionate behavior might be because he feels close to me with all the intimacy involved in taking care of him. It's funny how quickly I get attached to certain boys, and I'm feeling more and more attached to Joey every day.

I'd emailed Frankie back the same night I'd read his email and told him I love him and that, "Sure, Darleen deserves another chance to win you back, so just let me know the results of the contest whenever it ends. That is if it ever does end." He emailed back ignoring my sarcasm saying that he hopes I'd be in his life forever, but for right now, he's promised Darleen two months without my name being mentioned in her presence. That's the crap he tells me. It's hard to believe I love someone so stupid, but I do. I'd like to hit that bitch Darleen in the back of her head with something heavy. Frankie says he's being completely honest with me, but I know he's not being honest with himself and I'm pissed about that. Between Darlene and me, whoever Frankie's with last is the one he claims he loves. So now it's settled that I not only won't see

Frankie for at least the next two months, I also won't be able to email him. That Darleen is afraid I'll talk some common sense into his fucked-up head. I suppose two months is how long they figure they'll need for Frankie to successfully mount that cow. There's so much wrong with Frankie's thinking, but the bitch has brainwashed him so completely for so many years he can't easily escape her clutches. I have no realistic option except to give him the time to find out for himself what he already knows but refuses to accept.

It's been two full weeks without me seeing or hearing from Frankie, and two weeks into Joey's and my college experience. I still think about Frankie every day. Not the viper though, I don't think about her, just Frankie. Sometimes I feel sorry for myself, but what the hell can I do? It hurts to be in a one-sided love affair and that's what I've been in pretty much from the first day I saw the light red hair on that incredible cute boy. The one wearing those Harry Potter eyeglasses and who quickly captured my heart. He's so full of life and bubbling over with that crystal clear saliva that I'd love to taste again. What can I say, as much as I hate this fact, Frankie's on hold in my life and that is that. I miss him terribly. Fortunately, college provides a lot of things to occupy my mind and I do have Alexander to look forward to. Plus, Joey every day, too and I enjoy every second of my time with him. Joey and I are getting the workload for our college courses under control and just beginning to feel comfortable with it. As I said earlier, it helps tremendously that Joey and I have each other to share the load with. All we hear in class from other freshman is constant bitching about how hard it is keeping up. Joey says the ridiculous workload must be a form of hazing that the professors put on freshman to toughen us up. I say, "Sup, Joey?" He goes, "Sup with you?" and we do that for awhile, just screwing around.

Chapter 3
Bully

It's a gorgeous Saturday in late September and I'd just dropped Joey at gymnastics practice. I really like being with him, but I also really like the three hours or so each day when I'm not with him. It's not like I have free time though because there are other things besides taking care of Joey I need to do. For instance, while today is a perfect day to be outside, first I need to do our laundry before I can enjoy the day. With Joey's old plastic laundry basket overflowing with our dirty clothes, I head down to the laundromat with my pocket full of one-dollar bills and lots of quarters. I'm wearing my flimsy old nylon basketball shorts, a t-shirt about four sizes too big for me, and flip flops. The perfect attire to do laundry. Thinking about Frankie, my arms occupied with the laundry basket of dirty clothes, I back into the laundry room door pushing it open with my ass and once inside, turn around too quickly, knocking a pile of clean folded clothes off a table that's too close to the door. Fuck! A fraction of a second later, someone has a fierce hold on the back of my neck, shaking me. "You did that on purpose, ya little cunt!" and then a big slap on my ass with the palm of his hand that causes me to drop my basket of clothes and yelp out, "OW!" Totally unexpected." The vise-like grip on the back of my neck and three more hard smacks on my ass. What the fuck!? Tears pop out of my eyes mostly from the embarrassment of being spanked, but it hurts too.

I yell, "Stop that! Fuck, that really hurts!" My plea is rewarded with another hard slap on my ass that has me squirming to get away, but held in place. I can't even turn around to see who's doing this. Both my hands go behind my neck grappling at that strong hand back there. The thin flimsy material of my basketball shorts make it seem like I'm getting spanked bare-ass and the smacks really sting. Hercules gives me one more hard, "SMACK!" tries to move my ass forward, then lets go of me. Turning around, infuriated, I see my attacker is that squat kid who's coffee I knocked all over him on the second day I was in the dorm. "You again!" he snarls, getting his arm around the back of my neck bending me over and he spanks my ass some more with the found of his bare hand slapping my ass ringing out in the room, "SMACK! SMACK! SMACK! SMACK!" A continuous slapping of my left butt cheek leaving it red and burning like wild fire by now. The last smack somehow caused my bladder to shoot a short spurt of pee. A dark wet spot appearing on my light blue basketball shorts. I'm stuttering now, "Yo, pa, pal, pa please, I said I was sorry." Muscle man yells, "Shut the fuck up you stuttering dink, or I'll spank you all day."

He still has me bent over, facing away from him so he can't see the pee stain and I don't want him to see it, so I stop squirming and keep quiet. He goes, "You're a total loser, we've established that. And I guess we've established that I've got an anger management problem when you're around me, so why don't you stay the fuck away from me?" I don't say anything because all I can think about is my stinging burning ass and my peed-on shorts. He lets go of me and says, "Just stay like that, don't move. Let me think." I stay bent over with my forearms on the folding table looking away from him. The world is full of bullies. I may as well be back in high school. I don't even know this animal's name, and I haven't seen him again since that second day in the dorm. He rubs my ass, mumbling, "Stay..." Then, like he's talking to himself, "Okay, I hate doing laundry and dorky you just knocked mine on the dirty floor." Then he speaks louder, saying, "So the solution is you're going to do me a favor and do my laundry for me. Right?" I don't say anything. Wild man says, "I can't hear you," and he grabs my neck again, asking my name. I tell him and he goes, "Oliver? That's the perfect name for you, you skinny pussy. You're gonna do me a favor, and I'll do you one, okay, Oliver?" I hesitantly ask, "What favor?" and he smacks my burning ass twice, "SMACK! SMACK!" Really hard smacks causing more pee to spurt out of my shriveled dick. The pee is running down my leg now as he pushes my face against the table.

He's taking a couple of deep breaths, then sounded aroused, he says, "My favor to you, Oliver, is I won't do anymore of this," and he smacks my ass again, "SMACK!" More pee flows out running down the front of my leg. "And your favor to me is once a week, you do my laundry. Do we have a deal, Oliver?" I don't want to be a wimp, but I can't think what else I can be at the moment. Still worried about stuttering, I can't make myself speak. He talks in a sing-song voice now,

"All you need to say is, yes, Richard. Then we'll do each other a favor and become buddies." With the hand gripping the back of my neck, he squishes my face on the table top while smacking my ass hard again, and it almost lifts me up on my toes as he demands, "Say it! Say yes, Richard." I yell, "Yes, Richard!" and he lets me go. He's breathing hard, worn out from smacking my ass. The pain coming from my buttocks comes in waves, stinging and burning waves. This guy's dangerous and he doesn't know his own strength. Also, he wasn't kidding about having trouble controlling his temper. Richard's now talking in a low, barely controlled manner, "You'll re-wash all those clothes you knocked on the floor. Then dry them in the dryer and fold them neatly the way I like them folded. See the way my other laundry's folded?" I'm still bent over the table, but he's not touching me now so I move my head and look at the folded shirt he's pointing at. "You'll fold everything neatly like that. Then bring it all to me on the top floor of the dormitory, room 30. If you do your favor for me real good, I will do my favor for you real good. If you don't do your favor too good, I won't do mine too good either."

I'm still leaning on that table bent over, hoping Richard's leaving soon, "And don't fuck up both our college careers by running to tell someone that the big bad Richard spanked you. You and I will settle this ourselves. Right, Oliver?" I mutter, "Right, Richard." He goes, "Room 30," and when he opens the door leading to the parking lot, the beautiful day outside shines inside the laundromat for a few seconds. I look back and see him leave shaking his head like he's still mad at me, and at himself too, probably. Some bullies actually have a conscience. Putting my head back down on my forearms, holding my breath, I'm waiting for the pain on my buttocks to subside. Can I believe this shit? My ass burns like hell, but the pain is fading to a dull ache. There's no one else in the laundromat, but that could change at any second so I gathered his clothes off the floor and got them started in a washer. I don't want to take a chance he'd come back and find his clothes still on the floor. Then I grab the first pair of shorts I see from our dirty laundry basket and go in a utility closet to change out of my peed-on shorts.

The cut-off jeans I'd grabbed were Joey's, but the important thing is they don't have a big wet pee stain on the front. They're stiff and scratch a little because I'm not wearing underpants. The basketball shorts have netting as a substitute for underwear and I guess you're supposed to wear a jockstrap. I've never been a big fan of jockstraps. Leaving the closet, my face blushing with humiliation, I get Joey's and my clothes going in a washing machine and then light up a cigarette thinking Richard's a worse bully then I ever encountered in high school. Or maybe I just had the misfortune of upsetting an unbalanced individual. Not unheard of considering my bad luck. As long as I was hurrying to get everything in the washing machines, I was okay, but now that I'm just standing here smoking; I feel like crying because I realize how powerless I am. I scrunched my face up and hold my breath till the urge to cry goes away and a smoldering anger replaces my urge to cry. Why in the name of God does this shit always happen to me? Then, knowing it's stupid and I'm not going to do it anyway, I fantasize calling Christian and asking him to have Glen get his mob guys to kick Richard's ass up and down the fucking street. I want to be there laughing at him when it happens too. After entertaining that childish thought, I wanted to sit down. That unfortunately isn't an option at the moment with my ass still stinging. I hate that prick Richard so much.

Calming down, I change the direction of my thinking and try rationalizing my situation. What's the big deal anyway? In life, sometimes you need to eat crow, swallow your pride... whatever. You know, in order to get along in the world. Richard had one thing absolutely right, I'm not going to run crying to anyone saying Richard spanked me. Fuck that! Who would I tell anyway? Ya win some and ya lose some. I'm trying to think of one I'd won one when Randy comes in with a full laundry sack over his shoulder. I haven't seen him since the first day in campus. His cute face brightened when he sees me. "Dude with the wheelchair gymnast, right?" I go, "Yeah, Randy, I'm Oliver, remember?" Putting his laundry sack near an open washing machine, he goes, "Of course I remember, how can I forget you? You're the freshman who asked me to push your shorts up your asshole for ya, right?" and then he laughs and, grabbing a fistful of my hair, he pulls my head down to bump foreheads with him. Smiling at me, he lets go of my hair, telling me, "You're in desperate need of a haircut." I shrug and he smiles again, and asks, "You're in this dorm, are ya?" I go, "Uh huh," and he adds, "Hope ya don't mind if I use one of the washing machines. All the ones in my dorm are being used. This is the third laundromat I've been to. Busy on Saturdays."

He dumps his clothes and a detergent gel into a washing machine as I watch his every move. After putting the money in, he gets the washing machine going, then asks, "How'd ya get stuck with the nursing job, Oliver? You one of those Ass Club guys?" I explain about me wanting to have my car on campus and as a freshman, this was the only way I could do it. He tells me when he was a freshman, he had his uncle, who's a doctor, write the University saying Randy needs access to a car. "Ha ha, the suckers bought it. Huh, I can't even remember the exact diagnosis or reason Uncle Mark used. Well, it was two years ago." He sits in the only chair in the room, an old beach chair someone left here. I lean against the folding table as Randy tells a few stories about the trouble he and his roommate got themselves into during their freshman year. He has a nice personality to go along with all the other great things about him: two-toned blond hair, bright shiny brown eyes that seem to change from light brown to dark brown as I look into them, his perpetual grin with that cute mouth with brilliant white teeth that have the slightest separation between the front ones. All that perfection to go with his tight body and the ease with which he moves. Everything about him makes me feel squirmy and juicy and tingly all over. Awesome sensations from just looking at him and listening to his cute voice. Yeah, there's such a thing as a cute voice.

I mostly listen and stare at him, occasionally making appropriate one or two word comments. We smoke and he talks. I nod my head and grin or laugh at the funny stuff, He gives me two dollars and sends me for Cokes from the vending machine on the floor above us. Randy never seems to run out of college stories and it's a fun way to pass the time. Both my wash and Richard's are done. I maintain eye contact with Randy listening to him talk as I put the wet clothes in a dryer and feed the machine money. His clothes finish the spin cycle and while walking past me to the washing machine, he says, "By the way, Oliver, you're the cutest freshman on campus. Did you know that? I make it my business to check, heh heh." That was totally unexpected and I can't think what to say. He goes on, "Yeah, you know you're cute, dontcha?" He's standing right in front of me, in my personal space. I'm staring at him like a fool as he casually pushes the palm of his hand against my forehead lifting my hair up, muttering, "Even cuter with your hair off your face." He needs to reach up some because I'm about three inches taller than him. This attention from Randy is so flattering, but I don't know how to respond to it so I continue staring at him with my lips parted and my face turning red.

After a long second or two, his hand deliberately and slowly slide down the front of my face, he cups my chin, and asks, "Do you have a gymnast's buttocks yet, Oliver?" His other hand reaches around me and tightly grab my right butt cheek. I flinch in pain because my ass is still sore from Richard's spanking. Randy sees my look of pain and immediately apologizes saying, "Sorry. I'm just goofing around. Why's you ass sore anyway?" I lie, telling him I'd fallen hard on my ass. He goes, "Oh, that's a shame," and he grabs my crotch playfully, asking, "Did ya fall hard on this too?" I mumble, "Randy, don't!" He massages my package through Joey's cut-off jeans and I start getting hard, so I yell, "Randy!" again. With a hand on each of his shoulders for balance, he grins at my discomfort. My right hand moves to the back of his neck for a second before quickly running it up the back of his head feeling his beautiful hair between my fingers. He lifts his head and his pink tongue licks across my lips. Laughing, he lets go of me, mumbling, "You're hot, Oliver. If I wasn't in a relationship you'd definitely be on my radar screen."

Dropping my hands, I stand in front of him, swallowing hard and breathing little bursts of air, still unable to think of anything to say. I have a semi-hard cock partially poking out the front of Joey's cut-offs. Randy brushes the bump with the palm of his hand and my dick gets harder. He goes, "Oh, sexy! You make me laugh, Oliver. A walking boner, that's what you are; a cute walking boner." I called myself that recently. Randy digs in his pockets with both hands, asking me if I'd put his clothes in a dryer for him. "I've gotta see a guy. Actually I'm late now." Finding the money, he gives it to me for the dryer and leaves saying, "See ya, Oliver. Thanks, dude, I owe ya one. Just leave the clothes in the dryer when they're done. I'll get 'em later."

He leaves and I stand here stunned, then slowly lick my lips to taste his saliva. My boner continues pushing my pants out in front. Huh, after that disturbing experience with Richard, this wonderful attention from Randy. It totally changes my outlook and makes me feel good. I don't feel like such a loser now. It's almost like I'm friends with Randy Rider, a junior no less. Maybe things will be better for me in college than they were in high school after all. So far it's been a little of this and then a little of that, some good and some bad. Everything considered, I've got a good chance of doing okay here. Mostly because of Joey. Through him I've met a few guys, plus I've always got a friend since Joey and I are always together. Well, except for three hours a day.

Taking a deep breath, feeling okay, I check on my three wash loads wondering how Randy knew I was gay. Maybe it takes one to know one. Later, when I'm done folding Richard's clothes, and halfway done folding Joey and my stuff, I remember Randy's washing machine and dump his clothes in a dryer. Picking up all of Richard's stuff, I carry it up to the third floor. On the third floor, most of the rooms have their door open so I hear various types of music coming out of the rooms. Two guys with towels around their waists are coming out of the lavatory at the end of the hall. Well yeah, a community bath does have its advantages, I guess. Ones I hadn't thought of. On the whole though, I'd still rather have our private bathroom for our private activities. There's a lot of different sounds from the different rooms, not just music. Talking, some shouting and laughter, and it all makes me think that this is closer to the way Cristobal's dorm was when I was here last spring. On our floor it's quiet for some reason.

Finding room 30, I knock on the door and a muscle-bound kid answers it. He has a nervous look to his bland brown eyes and a twitch in his long pointy nose. "Yeah, whaddaya want?" Then Richard pushes the kid aside, saying, "It's my laundry guy, Phil, nothing to do with you. You need to get back to work on that writing assignment for me." Phil nods his head at Richard and swaggers over to his desk, as Richard tells me, "Put those things over on my bed. I'll check then later and, oh yeah, be sure you find out the day next week I need my laundry done, check with me Tuesday and I'll know by then. Now, isn't this a much nicer and more civilized way for us to interact?" Nodding my head, I put the stuff down on his bed thinking about my sore ass, then leave without saying a word. Richard says something to Phil and they both snicker. Thinking, 'Fuck you, Richard!' it occurs to me that by not disagreeing with him, I'd actually agreed to do Richard's laundry next week too. Then I realize that's what he meant from the beginning. Fuck it, who cares? I don't want to think about that now. It's was more fun licking my lips again thinking about Randy and about what he'd said to me, the thing about me being the cutest freshman.

Damn, I wish he wasn't in that relationship he mentioned. Back to the laundromat, I grab my cleaned clothes and put them away in Joey's and my bureau. Now I can finally enjoy the beautiful weather. I take a long ride in my Mini with the top down trying to look bored the way Randy suggested at lunch that time was a cool look. Later, I find out that my dorm's third floor has all freshman members of the wrestling team. Swell! Phil and Richard, hopped-up on steroids and looking for trouble with me in the middle of it. Oh well, it's just my bad luck fucking with me again. September goes by fast, even though I check with Richard each Tuesday and do his laundry the day he tells me to, that's not major enough of a negative to detract from all the positives of college life with Joey. Doing the entire bath routine every day is sexy fun. We haven't made any progress towards more intimate stuff so I'm pretty sure my first evaluation is correct: Joey's straight. Still, he's an affectionate straight boy and seems truly grateful for the tender care I'm providing him. We've become good friends. I suppose he's comfortable enough with his own sexuality that he has no trouble handling our minor intimate activities, and maybe he even enjoys it. He's going with the flow and I'm enjoying the touching and especially the finger fucking and the jerking off that I do for him. I know he enjoys those two things, and why wouldn't he? I mean the rectum and penis are loaded with sensitive areas, tons of nerve endings begging to be stimulated. Joey told me a couple of times about the circle jerks he and his buds did as young teens, so me jerking him off isn't totally a new concept for him.

At times, Joey will say things that infer he's aware I'm either gay or bi, but he never actually uses those words. I'm almost positive he knows, and he knows that I know he knows, but what's the point of bringing it up, ya know? Why complicate things that are going so well already? We're tight buds; one gay, one straight. You can tell when someone likes you. It's obvious from the look on their face when you wake up and see each other, or when we meet after his gymnast stuff. It's the look that says they're real glad to see you, and the smile too. Hard to fake a sincere smile.

The first weekend in October is on my mind now because I'll soon be visiting Alexander. I'm anxious to relieve my built-up sexual tension. Jerking off okay, but can't compare with Alexander blowing me, and me fucking him with lots of making out in the process. All the stuff I like doing with cute guys. Things are fine at school except for the blip of trouble with Richard and the laundry. The first Tuesday, I go up to Richard's rooms for his laundry, only Richard's roommate, Phil, is the room. He says, "The laundry's next to the door. Oh, and Richard's says every Tuesday is going to be laundry day. If one of us isn't here, come back later." Richard's basket of dirty clothes was there alright, and so was a laundry bag with more dirty clothes. "PHIL" is written on the laundry bag with a permanent marker. I say, "I'm not doing your dirty laundry, Phil," and he goes, "Yeah, you are. Richard told me to put my shit with his. And listen, pussy, make damn sure to use separate machines and dryers. Don't get our shit mixed up."

Well of all the fucking nerve! I started to say something, but I was royally pissed-off which makes me stutter, so I stop talking. Phil paid no attention to me anyway. He goes, "Oh yeah, the money for both wash loads is in that brown envelope. Get moving, I got places I need to be." With his hand he makes that 'shoo-along' motion. It's so outrageous that to keep the peace in the dorm, I need to do both their dirty laundry. The week before last, when I went to pick it up their laundry Tuesday afternoon, Richard was in the room and I tried to complain about having to do Phil's laundry too. In a very dismissive manner he told me, "Oh for Christ sake, all you do is whine. Phil is taking over the responsibility of overseeing your laundry duties because you and I simply do not work well together. So, Phil is doing this for me, and as a favor to him I'm letting him include his laundry. What's the big deal? Ya got to come up here every week anyway. You and him can work out the favor he'll do for you. Jesus, try to get along, Oliver, we're all in this together."

So I've been doing both laundries and when I pass Richard or Phil in the dormitory or on campus they say, 'Hi.' What the hell, it takes two minutes to pick it up, two minutes to put in a washing machine, and two minutes to transfer the clothes to a dryer. Folding takes another ten minutes, and then another two minutes more to carry it upstairs, so all together maybe twenty minutes a week. I have to be in the laundromat anyway for Joey's and my wash, so ya know. Of course, there's the principal of the matter, but fuck that. I'd rather not make waves and now nobody from the third floor bothers me at all. A number of the wrestlers are real pricks and they bully some of the other kids in the dorm, but not me because of Richard. Phil's tough on me laundry day though. He was starting the second week. He gets off smacking my ass a couple of times because I mixed up a few things from his wash with Richard's. He's one tough kid so I quickly memorized what belongs to who. It seems like Phil enjoys smacking my ass because he does it frequently and, unlike Richard, I think it does turn Phil on. Once he not only spanked my ass hard, but he made me redo the folding of his clothes while he lay on the bed watching me do it. Twenty humiliating minutes a week, a few smacks on my ass, and the rest of the time things are pretty good. Overall, a big improvement over my high school experience. I'm emailing every couple of days with mom and dad, but only tell them the positive aspects of life at college. They're thrilled everything's going so wonderfully. They've always been loving and supportive so why worry them about something they can't do anything about anyway?

The week before my visit with Alexander, one of the gymnasts give Joey a haircut. The guy's the self-appointed team barber and he cuts all the gymnasts' hair. The haircut he gave Joey looks real nice on him. It's short, but not extreme in any way, and now his shorter hairs are curly as opposed to wavy like when his hair was longer. His new haircut just adds to Joey's cute looks. Or maybe it's just that the more I like a boy, the cuter I think he is. Whatever, I enjoy Joey a lot, short hair or long hair. He needs to see his doctor back home sometime in October and he's arranged the doctor's visit during the weekend I'll be in Delaware with Alexander. Hopefully Joey will have only six weeks left with the plaster casts. That's if all goes well with the doctor's X-rays. Both of us are looking forward to him getting the casts off, except that'll end our bathroom routine with the finger-fucking and jerking off. Still, for Joey's sake, I'm hoping things go well at the doctors. Studying together, I'm in the habit now of propping us up on my bed with pillows so we can read together and work on problems for our courses on my laptop, side by side. Often I've got my arm around the back of his neck keeping him from falling off the bed, both of us leaning against one another. He likes to rest his head against the side of my neck right under my jaw when he gets tired, and sometimes he falls asleep like that. We have a lot of homework so we're usually studying late at night. A few nights we even slept together in my bed fully clothed. We just conked-out.

We go to class, eat meals in the dining hall, go to gymnastics practice, do our bath routine, and then closely work together on our homework until Joey or I fall asleep. Next day, the same thing all over again. We're together all the time and we do a lot of touching. We've become totally comfortable with that and I don't even bother hiding my boners anymore. Joey gets his own from time to time too without even so much as a comment because they're so common now. I love all of it, but I'm getting blue balls from yearning for actual gay sex. My weekend with Alexander is seven days away, but before that we have a party to go to this weekend in the gymnasts' dorm. Their actual official team practice begins Monday and this is their last chance for a booze party till after the gymnastics season. As Joey's primary caregiver, I'm allowed to attend the party. It's Friday night and I've pushed Joey to the gymnasts only party. The coaches aren't even invited. Joey says none of the gymnast will be doing any drinking after this party, not until their schedule meets are over. Everyone seems to be drinking, so we both get beers and one of the seniors lectures us freshman about booze and college. He tells us that drinking in college is a paradox. On the one hand, everyone thinks it's the most important part of college, while on the other hand, it **is** the most important part of college. Then he goes, "Wait a fucking second here, that's not a paradox! Oh well, PARTY!!!" Another upper classman yells, "Children, listen up. College is the only time in your life when you can blame any, and I mean any boorish, semi-legal behavior on being, 'I was so fucking drunk, dude, just so fucking drunk,' and people will laugh and think you're way cool. Being drunk is your excuse for anything you do." Upper classmen rule us freshman, but most of them are funny and the party's a blast. Around eleven o'clock, Joey slurs to me that he's getting extra drunk from drinking his beer through a straw. One of the gymnasts at our table says there's some truth to that. You do get drunker drinking beer through a straw. Who knew. It's a guys and girl gymnastics team so there's dancing and proposals for sex. It gets very loud and unruly. Near midnight, one of the older gymnasts, whose name I've forgotten, taps me on the shoulder suggesting I take Joey back to our dorm. I'd been talking to Randy and not paying too close attention to Joey who I see drooling beer out as he sucks it in

Oh yeah, Oliver, like that." Oh my God, does his cock get long and fat. The uncut skin's still loose enough that it moves up and down that hard boner easily on and off his the head. With each stroke he sighs and moans, "MMM, ooh, ooh, mmmm," leaning back against my chest his feet jerking in the water. Maybe a minute and a half before his boner expands so his foreskin no longer covers the head and I pick up the speed of my stroking with Joey squirming against me, splashing in the water.

Glancing at the mirror above the sink, I see our reflection: Joey's tightly clenched mouth, his eyes closed as his head's moving back and forth on my shoulder with his short curls tickling under my jaw and cheek. As always, his arms lay on his stomach with his hands loosely clasped together to keep them from moving. I wiggle the middle finger of my free hand in the soap gel and reached under Joey's ass to push it up his hole with him lifting his ass slightly helping me get my finger inside him. Finger-fucking him as I stroked his cock gets Joey's thrashing around in the water between my legs, so I cross my legs over his thighs and lock my ankles. His back's pushing against my stomach and chest as he moans with pleasure, but he's effectively captured within my grasp, I get a second finger up his hole and match the stroking of his long boner with my finger thrusts in and out of his asshole. He immediately groans and calls out my name thrashing around within my tight hold on him. The very warm water is deep enough that only the tip of dark red head of his cock is out of the water. My fingers slide tightly over his prostate button each movement back and forth in his rectum. This is so hot!

Joey's gasping for air, struggling in my tight hold. In thirty seconds his body gets stiff as a steel wire, his back arches as he bucks his hips squealing out a high pitched sound and shoots cum straight up in the air. I watch fascinated as his string of cum shoot up about three feet and then falls right back down into the bath water. His creamy cum swirls in the water above our legs making pretty patterns. Then with a desperate gasp from Joey, another shorter string of cum, and then another with Joey quietly moaning now, "Oh Oliver, oh Oliver." His strong buttocks closed tightly on my fingers with each ejaculation. I've been right on the edge of organs and then it happens. Feeling that fantastic other worldly sensation of climax, my eyes close and I can only whimper as cum soars up from my nuts exiting through my boner into the bath water against Joey's buttocks, and another hard thrilling sensation in my balls and cock follows the first with more cum streaming out of my cock. I'm feeling faint with pleasure. The cum slowly rises to the top of the bath water floating around us. Then I squeeze out two more smaller drools of sperm-i.e. semen, grunting with the pleasure sensations swirling around my groin. Without thinking, I kiss the side of Joey's cheek, then lift my hands up to hold his face against mine, kissing him again.

Joey said, "Oooh, man, I feel funny, Oliver." I kiss him again as more of his cum drools out the end of that long cock of his. Then I lick the side of his cheek because I simply can't help myself. The feel and smell of him is too enticing. I know I need to get ahold of myself and with a concentrated effort I do. My orgasm sensations fade away leaving me feeling weak but fine. Pulling the plug, I stand up and rinse us off with the handheld shower, while keeping Joey upright until I get out of the tub. I'm trying to clear my head but I'm kind of drunk myself so clearing my head isn't easy to do. We clumsily get out of the tub with Joey leaning against me for support. After setting him on the closed toilet lid, I grab a towel and dry Joey's torso and every place I can reach in front. Then it's no small task to help him stand on his one good leg so I can dry the back of him. When he's dry as I can get him, I get him in his wheelchair and dry myself.

Joey's head lulls to the side as I push him to his bed, both of us still naked. Joey opens his eyes and mumbles, "Can you stay with me in my bed awhile, Oliver? I don't feel good." No problem. I get both our naked, still damp bodies under the sheet, wrap my arms around Joey's chest and hold him against me. He rustles around the little bit he can to get snug against me and, just like that, he goes to sleep. In the morning we both wake up with a boner and a hangover. We don't talk about last night, but Joey's clingy so he doesn't seem to be upset we're naked together in one twin bed. After a bit, he takes a deep breath and falls back to sleep. Staying awake for a while, I enjoy being naked in bed with him, and then I fall back to sleep too. Another hour or so of sleep we wake up about the same time, still with the hangovers but not the boners. We drink two bottles of warm orange juice each along with three Tylenol. I go through our bathroom ritual like a robot, minus the bath, taking care of Joey's toilet needs. Then just before wheeling him back to the bedroom, Joey asks, "I don't suppose you'd shave my pubic hair, would you? It's a little easier taking care of me down there." Wow, get an unexpected question! "I'm your caregiver, Joey, whatever works for you is fine with me." He's all smiles and seems strangely eager to have me do this.

Sitting his naked body on the edge of the tub with his legs inside the tub, along with me, I've got the battery operate barber clipper that I discovered the first night when I was looking for the hand-held shower nozzle. The nozzle and clippers were just two items out of about twenty various things provided in this handicap appointed room. Clicking the clippers on, I run them carefully through Joey's pubic hairs clipping off all of the dark curly hairs. The hairs fall into the tub and then I wash them down the drain. He doesn't have any hair on his ass or his balls so it's just the pubic patch. Joey stares at his shorn pubes feeling the bristles. His cock had firmed up noticeably using the clipper work, but there was a buzzing sensation from them, so ya know. Cutting his pubes, plus Joey's apparent arousal, gives me a hard throbbing boner I need to fight down the urge to stroke it.

The boner's no big deal because we've come to take boner as a given considering the intimate nature of the care he requires. As I'm putting the clippers back in the drawer, Joey says, "Um, this looks cool, dude, but they're scratching my nuts now." He's still rubbing his fingers around the sandpaper feel of his clipped pubes. I go, "I'm not done, Joey. Just a minute." Back in the tub, I wet his bristly pubes, lather them with lots of the shaving cream that was also among the supplies for this room, then use the supplied disposable razor to shave his pubic area while my left hands moves his cock out of harm's way. It's clean and smooth as a baby's bottom when I'm rinsing the shaving cream remnants. It looks cool and his cock looks longer too. Joey chuckles, muttering, "This is giving me another hard-on, Oliver." I grin at him, but not wanting to be too obvious I ignore his 'hard on' comment and get him dressed. He goes, "Feels good down there. Thanks, man." We couldn't do this if he was a functioning gymnast because having shaved pubes would be awkward in the showers with the other gymnast gawking at his crotch, but he's only a spectator this year.

After I get dressed, we go out for brunch. On the way, Joey tells me he's always wanted to shave his pubes, but never had the balls. "It's some kind of a fetish I've had for years about shaved pubes, and now I finally have mine shaved. That's why I got a tad excited while you were doing it. And, haha, now that you started it, Oliver, you'll need to do it once or twice a week or else they'll get itchy and prickly." I chuckle, then mumble, "The things I do for you, Joey," wondering, 'If it's actually a fetish. If it is, maybe occasionally he'll spurt some cum when I'm shaving him. Ya know, without me even stroking his boner.' The next few days are just routine, meaning they're awesome, and the third day Joey hints around that his nuts are scratchy. He wants me to shave him again. All through the saving he grunts and makes hissing sounds sucking air through partially closed lips and sure enough, he's letting his fantasy take wings and his cock gets real hard.

I drag out the process feeling around with my fingers, purring, "Smooth as a baby," and he humps his hips, almost sliding off the edge of the tub, and shoots a long stream of spunks that arches upward over my shoulder... hot! When he's doing the spontaneous spunking he moans out my name, stretching it out, "Ooooolliver" and I stroke his boner for him finishing off his climax with spunk drooling down my fist. My boner throbs but doesn't spontaneously climax. I can't spontaneously have an orgasm. I need to pull by pud in the bathroom after cleaning Joey up and getting him in boxer shorts, and on the bed for homework. That night I have a vivid dream that I'm sucking Joey's cock and nuts and licking all around his belly and down in the shaved area. I wait up in the middle of the night startled and with another raging boner. Working with Joey's body is arousing me enormously with only my hand to relieve some of the pressure. Joey really turns me on and it's impossible he doesn't know I'm gay by now. He seems happy with the status quo, so I'll leave it at that, for now.

This Saturday we begin our weekend apart. Joey's doctor's visit and my Alexander visit. I'm gulping with excitement about a sexy time with Alexander, but I already miss Joey at the same time. Friday night, during his bath, Joey says, "Fuck, Oliver, I'm just realizing how much I'm going to miss you the next two days. You're the first gay friend I've ever had and I have to tell you, you've changed my mind about gays. You're the nicest guy I've ever met and you're so conscientious about my care it brings tears to my eyes sometimes. I just want to say thank you, and no joking around about it." Well, that's a random comment, one I let slide.

Okay, so he admits he knows I'm gay. I'll let that statement of his lie there.

Then when I'm shaving his pubic stubble he behind grunting again and he has another hard boner I'm holding in my left hand moving it away from the razor. When I'm almost done, Joey gasps and says ,"Shave it all down to my skin, Oliver." He's puffing out short bursts of air, then his body gets stiff and he groans, his face red as he climaxes. Two long creamy strings of cum shoot from his hard cock that I'm holding. The cum shoots sideways splashing at the end of the tub. I wait until he's breathing normally again, them mumble, "Nice orgasm," as I'm washing his shaved groin area. Picking up on his conversation before he shot off, I say, "It's very open-minded of you to allow a gay guy to do this for ya." He tells me he doesn't mind as long as the gay guy's me. As I'm drying his groin area, he goes on to tell me that all my hugging and little kisses make him feel good, almost as good as my hand jobs make him feel. By now we've become tight enough for him to express himself like this without feeling weird. There's still been no mention of a girlfriend in his life though, and me asking him point blank about it seems rude. It might also seem mean I'm fishing for information regarding his sexuality. He told me a few weeks ago that before his accident he was a world class jerk-off fanatic. Two three times a day at least. Well, that's not world class, but I don't burst his bubble. When he told me that me, stroking him off, is the hottest thing he'd experienced so far in life, I thought to myself, 'Maybe he's gay, but he just hasn't figured it out yet.'

Joey's mother picks Joey up Saturday morning. She looks at me suspiciously, and asks, "Are you keeping your word, Arthur? Are you taking care of Joseph's basic needs?" I go, "Oh, yes ma'am," and Joey grins, chirping, "It's the best care I've ever had." I push Joey's wheelchair to the car and help get him in his seat, then put the collapsible wheelchair in the trunk of the car. We say goodbye and I watch him as his mother drives away. He watches me watch him. He looks sad, but just before turning the corner he gives me a beautiful smile and a nod of his head. Damn, I like him! Later today, I'm driving down to Delaware for my rendezvous with Alexander North. I'm wickedly excited and a little nervous, not being at all sure how this adventure with him will turn out.

Chapter 4
Alexander

There was an email from Joey just as I'm about to leave for Delaware. He tells me he got home safely, although his mother grilled him about my care the whole way home. He's in the doctor's waiting room now thinking about how awkward it'll be having someone other than me helping him with his bathroom necessities, so he's decided to skip bathing until he gets back with me. Then he adds, 'I can't believe how much I'm missing my servant! I hope you don't think I'm giving you another weekend off until my casts come off.' I laugh at that. The email goes on to confirm he'll be back in the dorm Monday. No classes on Monday because of some professors' conference, which gives us students a welcome three-day weekend. It's to be missed by him, and I miss Joey too. I text him saying I'm just leaving and my fingers are crossed all goes well. Then, while throwing some stuff in my overnight bag, I think about how lucky both of us are that we're roommates. I keep changing my mind about Joey's sexuality, but recently I'm thinking he might have gay tendencies. How strong they are, who knows?

My sex life, so far, hasn't been a smooth trip. It's been mostly one shot deals, one and done, and with Frankie who knows? I've done it a couple of more times with Alexander, but that's my entire sexual portfolio in my nineteen years. I'm real anxious to expand upon it this trip. Seeing Alexander again is something I've been eagerly looking forward to for a few months now. We're young though, and things change quickly so I'm not sure what to expect. Putting my small satchel in the passenger seat of my Mini, I decide it's too chilly today to make the drive with the Mimi Cooper's top down. Then I decide, screw it, I'm putting the top down anyway. Top down, windows up, and the heat on, I drive off campus feeling kinda cool. Alexander emailed me directions, which is reassuring since I'd recently had that bad luck with MapQuest. I need a GPS though, and I'm gonna get one too. As I mentioned, I'm excited and a little nervous and it's understandable considering I'm spending a weekend with someone I met for only a week early last summer. We don't actually know each other, and like I said, things can change quickly with us teens. I'm thinking about that unique feeling getting sucked-off by Alexander that first time. Maybe I'm enhancing the memory, but I remember it resulting in an unbelievable orgasm. Well, that was the first time anyone's sucked my dick so it's understandable why I remember it so vividly.

I'd tried my best to duplicate Alexander's cock-sucking technique on Frankie's cock that time, but the truth is having Frankie's dick in my mouth forced all other thoughts out of my head. Now I begin thinking about Frankie again. Those little round eyeglasses and his pretty, cute face with his bright red hair and, of course, swapping spit with him. God damn, I love him so much and miss him so. His smell was on my arms that last time we were together. It's the time I maneuvered him into fucking me and I had my arms around his neck holding him tight for so long I could still smell his scent on my arm driving home. Naturally I couldn't stop smelling my arm which must have looked weird to other drivers. My heart hurts that I can't see Frankie and I still need to wait six more weeks before that bitch Darleen will even let him email me. I truly hate her with a passion. Then, trying to concentrate on positive things, I think about the weekend ahead of me. Alexander wants me to go directly to his barbershop and I'm to arrive right after the shop closes, which is why I didn't leave the campus until late Saturday afternoon. He wants me to see his barbershop and then I'll get a much needed haircut. After that we'll get cleaned up and go to the private gay club he belongs. Alexander's been a member since graduating high school. The club doesn't even open until nine o'clock so there isn't any rush. We'll have a fancy dinner with some of his friends and then he and I will spend the night in Alexander's condo that's over his barbershop. Nice to have rich parents. Alexander's a year older than me, but still not old enough to drink booze legally, although we can drink at his private club. Sounds like grown-up type fun, but the possibility for sex is what's monopolized my dreams about this trip.

I'd found fault with Alexander last summer because of his occasional feminine affectations and he isn't really a very good 'top', not that I'm very experienced myself. He's a sexy 'bottom' for me though, and like I said earlier, he's an expert at oral sex and he's a sweet, funny, likable guy too. At least he was that week in Wildwood. And his driving directions are perfect too as I arrive at his barbershop at twenty minutes to six, which is early so I'll walk around for a few minutes. Parking across the street, I check out at the barbershop from here. It doesn't look like any barbershops I'm familiar with. It looks, um, kinda classy, I'd have to say. Looks expensive in a brand new strip mall consisting of six attached businesses with condos above the shops. It's new, but built to look like something from a Charles Dickens story. Old fashioned lamp posts, shutters on the windows of the brick buildings, heavy paneled doors and it's very cool and, like I said, expensive looking. There's a Godiva chocolate shop, Wine and spirits shop, Coach leather shop, and others of that ilk. Alexander's parents are rich and I'm not sure how they got that way, but they've certainly set Alexander up in a very upscale location. Ya know, he's never acted like he's a rich kid with me. He seems like most kids I know, and they aren't rich.

Smoking a Marlboro lights, I gawk at my surroundings wondering if I'm worried about nothing. Spending a weekend with a friend is new to me, that's all. I need to be more confident! Experience new adventures while I learn about life. It's almost six o'clock now, so I walk back to my car and see a middle-aged man and his son walk out of the barbershop. Their haircuts look good, the man has a new regular haircut and the teenage boy is rocking a hot looking spiked haircut. A minute later, another fellow in his early twenties comes out in a bit of a hurry, putting on a windbreaker. He has that stylish faux hawk haircut that Alexander gave me way last summer. This guy's wearing a shirt with his name and the name of the barbershop embroidered over the pocket, and the shirt has epaulets on the shoulders. He must be the assistant Alexander told me he was having a difficult time training. Kind of a cute kid in a chunky sort of way, sort of like Myers. I watch him walk down the block till he turns up the next street. Nice ass! Then Alexander opens the door and looks around.

I smile because I know he sees my Mini Cooper with me standing next to it, but he does a theatrical shrug and pretends he'll lock up for the night. I call over, "Hey, mister barber dude, I'm not too late for a haircut, am I?" He ignores me for a second and then shows me his great smile and I relax thinking I worried for nothing. He comes over to me, smiling. I'm smiling too, muttering, "Hi Alexander, it's..." He says nothing, just kisses me on the lips and it reminds me of that first day when Alexander inhaled off his cigarette and kissed me as I was sitting on a stool in the North's Wildwood kitchen. It was after my haircut. Today, during our kiss, my exhale of cigarette smoke enveloped Alexander's head. I put my free arm around his neck and kiss him back. He's a very good kisser and my dick takes notice. Right here on the street Alexander sucks my tongue into his mouth and licks it while moaning, "Mmmmm mmmm." Man, it's so hot kissing with another guy, I swear I could cream my jeans. He pulls away and says, "I love you pretty white boys cause y'all taste so good." I go, "Never mind that boy, get my luggage and follow me." He goes, "Yessa, Massa," and he reaches in the Mini and carries my small satchel.

Laughing, we cross the street. Alexander does his 'step and fetch it' routine every now and then, but mostly he sounds like a polished public speaker. His father is of African descent, but Alexander's mother is a blond and as lily white as she can be without being an albino. His father's a very handsome man and his son takes after him. I'm told Alexander's father was a wide receiver for the NFL Dallas Cowboys back in the day. His mother, a beautiful Dallas Cowboy cheerleader back then, although I need to take their word for that because now she's fat and far from beautiful. Be that as it may, Alexander, a handsome boy with light brown skin with European facial features and large sparkling brown eyes, beautiful teeth and unique dark brown, very thick hair. Great body too. His father's athletic abilities show up in Alexander's golf game and his mother's artistic side shows up in Alexander's talent for styling hair. He has had boyfriends, but not many, and anyway he and I kinda think we're in love, although not really. We're in 'like' and that has a lot to do with sex. Last summer we had a lot of sex and fun together too, not just sex. We're sex buddies.

Alexander's rocking a new hair style from last summer. His hair's been straightened and cut real short all over his head with razor detail outlining his entire hairline. I use grab a handful of his soft dense hair pulling his head back while I fucked him. This stylish haircut of his now doesn't surprise me at all because he's in the business. If anything, Alexander's better looking and sexier than I remember. His handsome face with the warm smile and his lithe, tight body. YUM! I'm feeling aroused just looking at him, so I do a couple of fake coughs to cover it up. "Come on, Oliver, I can't wait to show you my cool barbershop. You look good enough to eat, by the way. That mop of hair is begging for a haircut though." I self-consciously run my fingers through my hair as he chuckles. I find I'm tongue-tied for the moment so I just grin as we walk across the street. Halfway across, Alexander takes my hand and pulls me with him, anxious for me to see the place he's so proud of. It makes me feel like a little boy in one way, but in another way, him holding my hand makes my dick move around in my tightie-whitie jockey shorts. The inside of the barbershop replicates the 1800s theme of the outside. There are two brand new old fashion barber chairs. You know, the ones with black leather backs and seats with white porcelain arm rest, and ornate steel foot rests. The chairs' backs crank down so that the customers' head can be over the sink that's behind each chair for shaving or shampooing purposes. Eight red upholstered waiting chairs with metal arms sit along the side wall. A lot of mirrors and period pieces for decoration. It's cool alright and as trendy as the rock music coming out of hidden speakers.

Alexander, still holding my hand, say, "Let's take all this luggage upstairs to the apartment, Oliver." He's carrying my small satchel with his free hand as he pulled me along with him, holding my hand with his other one. I stumble trying to keep up and he chuckles again, saying, "Aren't you the reluctant one. Don't worry, Oliver, I'm going to take good care of you." Scratching my head, not at all sure what he means by that, I trip on the step. It's all giving me a funny buzzing feeling in my stomach. I sense Alexander's in control and I'm in his world this weekend. This situation's a new one for me and I get a shiver from anticipation about the unknown, about what's coming next. It's a pleasurable sensation. Not wanting to be the little mouse, Oliver, of old, I force myself to relax and enjoy the ride. It's obvious Alexander's developed some confidence in the months since I last saw him, and apparently he's also eliminated the feminine routine entirely. I guess having your own condo and your own successful business will do that for ya.

The aura surrounding Alexander is different from last summer, Like, he's much more mature. I Follow him through a door which leads to a small room set-up with the same old-fashioned barber chair and mirrors, same as the main barbershop except private. The next room is obviously his office, with a half bath attached. Then he pulls me through yet another doorway and up the steps to his condo. Alexander is still leading me and holding my hand. Holding hands with another boy is a very erotic thing to do. It's so hot, but I rarely get the chance to do it. Alexander's hand is bigger than mine and this adds to that sensation I had of being a little boy with big boy Alexander. His palm against mine feels sexy and I sense myself slipping into that delicious trance-like state some guys can put me in, although it hasn't happened recently. They don't know they're doing it and I just let myself go and follow their lead. It makes for a dreamy, sexy, almost dizzy state of mind and it's quite pleasant.

Alexander drops my satchel as soon as we enter his apartment and then firmly pulls me into his tight body and hugs me with both arms. He's three or four inches taller than me so it's convenient for him to kiss the top of my head as he squeezes me tighter in his strong arms. Then he gives the side of my forehead a long wet kiss, murmuring, "I missed you, Oliver. We've only known each other for a short time so how did you manage to sneak inside my head like this? Huh?" Okay, my worries that Alexander lost interest in me can be put to rest. Another kiss on my cheek, as he says, "We're going to have a great time. Ooooh, you smell good." One last tight hug and he lets me go entirely, "Come on in the kitchen and I'll make us a vodka and tonic." I nod my head and follow him into the kitchen, wondering what a vodka and tonic will taste like. Not that it matters because Alexander's put me in a satisfying trance and I feel funny, but awesome. This is a new thing I'm experiencing. Alexander's in charge, I mean. It's what I was hoping for in Wildwood, but it seems he wanted inexperienced me to be the leader. I'm not good at that. With the beginnings of a boner in my pants, I marvel at how hot Alexander's body is. Working out at the gym is really paying off for him.

His apartment, or condo, is of course and very nice, although it pales in comparison to my brother's place. That condo is luxurious and probably cost ten times what this place cost. That being said, I much prefer Alexander's place because it's totally contemporary with brushed chrome appliances in the kitchen and off-white cushions on the seats and a number of earth-tone designer throw rugs here and there on the shiny hardwood floors. Everything gleams. Odd shaped floor lamps create shadows and bright spots that I suppose would be kind of creepy if it wasn't so cool.

Alexander mixes our drinks as I sit on one of three round counter stools, watching. He's very serious as he deliberately measures the vodka into a shot glass before pouring it into tall glasses with thick bottoms. Then he scoops in small squared clear ice cubes to fill the glass half-way, and then tonic and a squeeze from wedges of lime, finishes by dropping a small lime wedge in each glass. Everything Alexander does is unhurried and deliberate and that's exactly how he cut my hair last summer. It's the way he does everything. Done making the drinks, he wipes the counter with a clean dish towel and gives me the sexiest smile as hands me my drink. "Hope ya like it," he says, and lifts his glass for a toast. We click the rims of our glasses together and take a swallow. It's bitter, so I guess I don't like tonic, but I'm in this trance-like mood and don't want to break it by asking for orange juice instead of the tonic. He takes a long pull on his drink, and goes, "Mmmmm. I needed that. Long day, but now you're here and I'm getting my second wind. How ya been, Oliver?"

As soon as I speak, it breaks my spell somewhat, which is too bad. We reminisce our week at Wildwood, then do that thing where he tells me something that he thinks will be impressive, and then I try to top it by telling him something about Pennsylvania University, and so forth. We smoke and have a second drink and this time I do ask for orange juice. When we're done trying to impress each other, Alexander's staring at me so I look him in the eyes, grinning ask, "What?" This makes him chuckle, "You don't have any idea how special you are, do you?" I'm like, "Say what? Are you trying to break my balls again, Alexander?" I thought we're going to rag on each other for a while like we did in Wildwood, but he slowly shakes his head, "No, I'm serious, dude. I've never met anyone like you, Oliver, and I don't just mean how cute you are even though you are the cutest guy I ever dated, but it's also you're so, um, innocent I guess it is." With that he ruffles my hair and cups the back of my head pulling it to his and kisses me gently on my lips. Then he recreates the kiss he'd given me earlier when he greeted me on the sidewalk a half hour ago. A long kiss with both my arms going around the back his neck. He steps back as I take a deep breath reminding myself to be adventurous.

Lighting a cigarette, Alexander takes a drag and a big gulp of his drink right on top of the drag. Exhaling smoke from his nose, he's staring at me again and I'm drifting into another pleasant trance. He hands me the cigarette he'd just taken a drag off of and lights another one. When he has it lit, he goes, "Yeah, that's it, you appear innocent, Oliver. I know you're not all that innocent though from the way you fucked my brains out last summer, but you look innocent. Ya know, I jerked-off for a couple of months after that week we had together from just thinking about you fucking me. God, that was a hot time!" He takes another drag followed by another pull on his vodka and tonic, then for some reason, he laughs again, and says, "I know I keep repeating myself, but you're so fucking cute! Come on, I need to cut that mop of hair on your head." I try not to say anything so I can enjoy the dreamy trance I'm in again.

He comes around from behind the kitchen bar and takes my hand leading me downstairs to the smaller room with the single barber chair. He goes, "As long as I can remember I've had this fantasy about cutting hair while I'm completely naked." I give him a startled look, and then he says, "I know, I know, it's nuts! Anyway I'm still not ballsy enough to do it, how 'bout we do the haircut in just our boxer shorts?" and he pulls his shirt over his head and kicks off his Italian loafers. He isn't wearing socks. He drops his linen slacks and says with a laugh, "Get undressed, Oliver." His smooth body is so perfect I just stare at it for a moment. The manner in which he says everything, and the casual way he undressed in front of me, increases my dream-like state of mind. My balls are buzzing and that weird sexy feeling slithers around my stomach and groin. I need to take another deep breath and then do two fake coughs. Alexander goes, "Please, Oliver, it's my fantasy, but only with you. I wouldn't feel comfortable doing this with anybody else. If you really don't want to though, that's okay too." I pull my Polo golf shirt over my head as gives me a big beaming smile that makes me smile back at him. "Thanks, man" he mumbles, fiddling with a control panel changing the music. I take off everything except my jockey shorts, wishing I'd worn boxers today.

Alexander pats the seat of the barber chair, "Remember, Oliver, no talking so I can concentrate." I nod my head again. Staying in this trance, I nod my head and climb up into the old fashion barber chair. The leather seat is soft and very comfortable, but I feel silly sitting here almost naked. I'm trying to place the music that's playing. The guy's singing love songs I've never heard before. His guy's voice is smooth as can be, but kind of corny too. Alexander picks up a clean crisp white cape with black pin stripes and snaps it in the air opening it, then lets it float down around me. The whole scene is hypnotic to me. The cape feels cool on my bare skin as Alexander wraps a strip of tissue around my neck leaning close to my ear, whispering, "That's Johnny Mathias singing. He's from the fifties or sixties and he's gay. What do ya think?" As usual, I nod my head. He's chuckling as he pulls the cape up around my neck. "Sit up, Oliver," he says sternly while reaching around the back of the chair with both hands under the cape and grabbing either sides of my waist pulling me against the back of this big barber chair. "Stay like this, okay? Can ya do that, Oliver?" Of course I can, so I give my normal head nod as I feel my dick begin stiffening-up. For some reason my face gets red and I need to take a number of short breaths. The way he talks to me, as if I'm a little boy, is having a sexual effect. It's playing with something in my subconscious mind. The barber's cape now has a small tent at my lap where my semi-hard cock is located.

Everything Alexander does seems totally sensual to me, which is not at all what I'd expected or remembered from last summer. He cranks the back of the barber chair backwards and soon I'm almost lying flat on my back, which emphasizes the tent at my lap. He says nothing about my little tent, just turns on some water and I hear a bottle top pop off and I smell savory shampoo. Closing my eyes, enjoying being touched making me think of Joey. This must be how he feels when I'm bathing and taking care of him. Truly a pleasurable feeling, but I can't describe it exactly. Saying it's a dreamy and relaxing trance with serious sexual overtones with a scary feeling is the best I can do describing it. You know, scary because I'm never sure what's coming next.

That's part of the submissive attraction for me, 'What's he going to do next?' Guys like me relish that kind of thing. Submissive types get 'off' being temporarily under someone's control, but there's always that degree of apprehension of 'What's he going to do next?' It makes me wonder if Joey's submissive too. In any case, this kind of unplanned situation done correctly, like Alexander's doing it, works for me in a big way. That everything he does is unhurried and deliberate enhances the experience for me. Alexander begins by wetting and then washing my hair, massaging my scalp and the back of my neck with his fingers. Warm thick suds and strong, long fingers. I love the feeling, concentrating on every movement his finger tips make on my scalp and down near the back of my neck. It's so seductive. After doing that for a few luscious minutes, he rinses out the shampoo, and I think of the time I shampooed Frankie's hair in the shower of that little bathroom off my bedroom. Frankie closed his eyes and lulled his head this way and that while moaning his little moan. It's such a pleasurable thing to have a boy shampooing my hair and I realize that, just like Frankie, I'm lulling my head this way and that. It's like I'm indicating, 'Do whatever you want to do to me Alexander, this feels so fine.' Done rinsing, he works some nice manly smelling conditioner all through my longish hair and rinses that out too. The old time singer croons on in the smoothest sound I think I've ever heard and it's putting me further and further into a wonderful trance. And yes, the two vodka drinks help everything along too. Alexander quietly pumps the back of the chair up straight again and then pulled me up against the back of the chair like he did earlier. His long fingers on either side of my waist giving me goose bumps on my arms and shivers all around my belly. He whispers breathlessly, "Sit up straight, please." I put my shoulders back and sit as straight as I can, wanting to please him. Wanting to be a good boy.

From the moment I got up in this big barber's chair, I've had a fairly firm dick, one that went from firm to semi-hard during the shampoo. Sitting here after the shampoo, my dick's back to just being firm, but every stage it goes through feels sexy and warm. This is very sensual somehow and my balls are slowly churning sperm waiting for the signal to go into high gear. What a titillating experience. Then the sound of a hair dryer followed by Alexander running his fingers through my hair to help with the drying. When my hair is dry, he brushes it with a semi-stiff bristled brush that gets my scalp tingling all over. Now he's massaging the back of my head with his strong fingers. Then his fingers closing tightly along both my shoulders, he tightly grips my biceps simultaneously, and then a firm massage on both shoulders, and then up the back of my head again. My body's alive with shivers and shudders as I quietly blow out short bursts of air after each quick intake, all the time sitting up as straight as a Marine. It's making me slightly dizzy. The head massage becomes more of an upper body massage with his strong hands and fingers making me squirm in the chair, my eyes closed. It's almost like I'm getting too much stimulation so I need to cut off the visuals by closing my eyes. He now has both arms around the back of the chair and under my cape massaging my bare nipples, chest, and down low near my groin. I go, "Ohhh" and move away from the back of the chair as shivers zing around my body with Alexander saying, more sternly than last time, "Sit straight, Oliver"!

I slide back in the chair and up straight again as both his hands go inside my jockey shorts with his left hand cupping under my nuts and a finger pushing against my hole. I moan, "Mmmmm," as he pushes his finger tip in my hole while squeezing my balls. Pre-cum rolls down my six-inch bone-hard cock. Pushing his finger all the way up inside me causing my legs to stiffen and I made a hissing sound through my lips as my entire body shakes. Alexander's face is against the side of mine as he stands behind finger-fucking me. Our cheeks rub together and I smell his boyish aroma. I'm thinking how erotic this has become. It's kinda like what I do for Joey. I don't know which stimulation to concentrate on from one second to the next, the sensations in my hole or my squeezed nuts. I'm going, "Ohh," before he even squeezes my balls, just from anticipation. I'm very geared-up and fully turned-on and ready to go along with anything Alexander has in mind. He lets go of my nuts, adjust the waistband of my jockey shorts under my balls, and then stops everything pulling his finger out. While he washes his hands I'm making a long hissing sound as my shoulders shudder involuntarily, my head shaking back and forth in little quick jerks. In his usual deliberate way, Alexander comes around in front of me and lifts the cape exposing my throbbing boner. Moving my boner here and there he's using sing a pair of small barber's scissors cutting my pubic hairs. After a few cuts, he fakes cutting my cock and looks up at me with a pretend look of concern and mutters, "Oops." Everything's always fun to him. I stare back at him, hypnotized. Rubbing my nuts and ruffling through my pubes, combing them up with his fingers, he again takes hold of my boner and sucks the pre-cum off the head, then sticks the tip of his tongue in my pee slit for a few seconds. With a small giggle, he looks up at me again with his mischievous grin, then makes a face like, 'How'd ya like that?' I'm very aroused and all I can do is smile back at him and nod my head slightly. He's so good looking. Without further ado he casually and methodically goes back to cutting off my pubic hairs using only scissors.

Snip after snip after snip and it takes maybe a minute. When he's done it looks like my pubes were buzzed off with clippers to a quarter of an inch length all over. He held my boner all during the cutting and now that he's done, he squeezes it a little too hard and lets go of it. My boner's standing straight up from my crotch. I can't stop staring at his handsome face that's now has a bemused expression. I want to join him in his light-hearted mood, but in my mind I'm interpreting everything he does as erotic, not funny. My breathing is almost normal by now, watching Alexander get comfortable kneeling in front of me. He takes my boner in his fingers and sucks my nuts into his mouth. Again, totally unexpected, although in this case it shouldn't have been because he did basically the same thing last summer. Involuntarily, my ass lifts off the seat as I'm grunting, "Ahhh, ahhh, ah, ah," while he hums on my balls and licking them with his talented tongue. I'm holding myself off the seat with my forearms on the white porcelain arms of that barber chair, my feet firmly planted on the decorative foot rest. In his mouth my nuts are dripping wet and vibrating. Alexander's stimulation puts them into high gear real fast and that tantalizing feeling of sperm rolling around in my balls has me grunting through my tightly closed lips. When I'm right on the edge of blowing my load, Alexander abruptly pulls his mouth off my balls, scraping them against his upper and lower teeth as they exit that warm, juicy place. It's my boner's turn to go inside Alexander's warm wet mouth and he immediately swallows the head with the aid of some throat action. My cock throbs and expands and pulsates with pre-cum. I'm fully off the seat now making gagging sounds and blowing spit in a fine spay with each gagging sound I make. My chin's soon wet with saliva. He stimulates my cock in mysterious ways inside his mouth and throat. In less than a minute, I'm squealing some weird high pitched squeal as a huge load of cum shoots right down Alexander's throat. Tightening every muscle in my body, more cum flies down his throat as I'm hearing my own squeal, wondering, 'Who's sounding girlie now?' My third groin contraction quickly follows and this part of my orgasm feels just as intense as the first, and then another string of cum zips from my cock. The head of my boner's out of his throat now even as I'm continuing to tighten my groin muscles squeezing out drools of cum. He's sucking on my pee slit helping me get every drop of spunk up and out of my rotating nuts.

I try to turn the girly squealing sound I'd made into a sentence, but it comes out as high voiced gibberish, "Tha that. No, no, I mean, oh, oh no, oh, ah," I babble as Alexander continues to gently suck and tongue my cock milking my balls dry. He pulls my cock from his mouth entirely now and squeezes it to see if he can milk anymore spunk out, and then he licks from the base of my boner up to the head and all around the sides until it's slippery with spit. He continues holding my cock in his hand after he stops licking it, almost like it belongs to him, and maybe it does. I'm sitting back down on the seat trying not to pass out as aftershocks from that awesome climax are still zipping around my groin. The black streaming lines that filled my vision are fading and my heartbeat is calming down, but all kinds of pleasure sensations remain in my brain. The pleasure sensations during climax were so intense they almost became painful. Everything radiated out from my groin to my thighs and belly and ass, and even down to my feet, it was so intense they made my toes curl. It would be hard to imagine a wilder climax than the one I just had.

It's peaceful now though and my eyes close again as my head lulls back on the black leather cushion of that barber chair. I'm enjoying all of it again in my mind for a minute or so. When I open my eyes, Alexander's there with a big grin. There's a drop of my cum at the corner of his mouth, as he asks, "How'd ya like the shampoo and conditioner? They're called "Gents Only" and you can only buy them in upscale barbershops." I try giving a smart-ass reply, but I stutter instead, managing only, "Tha tha that wa was was ..oh my Ga God, awesome cum shot, dude!" Alexander pats the side of my ass gently and smiles, "Just for you, Oliver, just for you. Ya want another drink?" I go, "Sure," and as he turns, I notice his boner's poking out the front of his boxer shorts. I'd forgotten how long his cock was and it makes me grunt just glancing at it quickly. I ask for a rum and coke this time and Alexander gets himself another vodka and tonic. After a while he puts a Counting Crow's CD on the player. The song, "Round Here", one of my very favorite tunes, fills the room. I took off my jockey shorts entirely while he was making the new drinks. What the hell, might as well be naked. The cape's still covering my body anyway.

Alexander's looking very pleased with himself. I'm wondering what's next, but don't. He sure knows how to draw it out and extend the sexiness, and the end result was over the top. I feel so satisfied, so content. A concern enters my mind that I won't be able to fuck him hot enough after being so sexually satisfied, and it'll have to be after dinner in any case because I probably won't be able to get a boner up until then. We listen to maybe half the Counting Crows CD while drinking our drinks silently exchanging little grins and shrugs. I'm still in the big old-fashioned barber chair with the cape still around my neck covering my body, but now without a tent at my lap. It's covering my naked groin that now has quarter inch pubes, which I'm absently rubbing my fingers through under the cape. I'm feeling relaxed watching Alexander show off a few cool dance moves. It's a little after seven-thirty and the club we're going to won't open until nine o'clock so we were in good shape. When the CD's over, Alexander says, "Okay, Oliver, now for your haircut. Sit-up straight and please stay as quiet as you've been. Okay, boyfriend?" I nod and smile, liking him saying we're boyfriends. He leans over and kisses me on the lips, then switching CD's to the moody Van Morrison tunes we listened to when he gave me the first haircut in Wildwood. I don't know many Van Morrison songs, but the man is a one of a kind artist. His voice, low in the background, brings back memories of my first blow job too. This one was even better.

He does my entire haircut with scissors, comb, and his fingers, and like last summer, lots of my hair drops onto my cape. Alexander doesn't ask me how I want my hair cut, he cuts it the way he wants and that's cool, but so much of my hair is piling up on my lap it gets scary, and for some reason my limp dick actually moves. I check my reflection in the large mirror in front of me and need to stifle a gasp at how short my hair is. It looks almost as short as Frankie's, barely long enough so that it will lie on my head. Alexander takes a long time cutting it and it's obvious he loves cutting hair. I like to think he likes cutting my hair best. I know I have thick hair, but the follicles are fine but very numerous. When I think he's surely done, he combs it up and cuts off another half inch all over the top so the hairs at the crown of my head stand up like bristles. Then he deliberately cuts my already short bangs shorter, right up to my hairline. In short, he's giving me a haircut like his. Huh, and for some reason that gives me a sexual charge and my cock stirs in my pants enough that I want to stroke it. Satisfied my hair's short enough, Alexander uses a straight razor to alter my hairline to suit his idea of how it should look. The razor's so sharp he doesn't even need to wet my hair or use shaving cream. It takes about fifteen minutes to do the shaving and I watch him do it in the mirror from start to finish. His concentration is total and not a single nick from the razor. I gotta admit it looks so cool when he's done. He's an artist, a perfectionist. Finally he asks, "What do you think, Oliver?" I turn my head this way and that, and then say, "We're twins, and that's so cool. I love my haircut, Alexander, thank you." In reality, I think that it's way too short, but I couldn't hurt his feelings. And, it is cool, but probably too cool for me. Hair styling is Alexander's thing, not particularly mine. The thing about hair I like the best is that it grows back.

There's still a lot of fussing that Alexander needs to do, brushing every tiny piece of hair off me and carefully taking off the cape full of hair and putting a clean half cape back on me so he can make the slightest adjustment here and there. All the fussing around gets me back in a partial trance like state, peaceful and pleasant. I was sexually satisfied an hour ago from that amazing blow job, and now Alexander fussing over me is making me feel kind of sexy again. The room's warm and I'm used to being naked by now, so I'm quite comfortable. He finally says, "Alright," to himself, and pulls the little cape off me. I'm completely exposed sitting here up tight against the back of the chair. "Just stay there, Oliver," as he picks up a packet off the counter and sticks it in the waist band of his boxers shorts. "Relax, you'll enjoy this." I have that thrilling, scary feeling again wondering, 'What's he going to do?' Standing directly in front of me, he spread my legs and pulls on them so I slide down the seat towards him. When my rear-end is at the edge of the seat he pushes my right leg up and over the chair's porcelain arm rest, the underside of my knee resting on the arm, and then does the same with my left leg, hanging off the left arm rest.

My asshole is sort of looking at him now as he puts a small towel under each leg resting over the side of the barber's chair, asking, "Does that feel comfortable?" I'm looking at the ceiling mumbling, "Uh huh," then I feel his warm wet tongue on my buttocks. First the right cheek and then the left, lots of licking and sucking followed by a long lap up my ass crack, right over my anus. My whole body shudders and squirms in that big chair as he laps my ass again, this time pressing his tongue more firmly against my crack just below my anus, then right on it and the lips of my asshole quiver, then he presses his tongue up above my hole and right over the lips of my anus, five quick laps getting it quivering even more. He laps under my nut sack pulling my bag of nuts up away from my body and lets them flop back down dripping with spit against my ass. He repeats this entire lapping thing a half dozen times and I'm squirming in the chair thinking about the time I licked Frankie's hole and almost shot my cum load right then and there. My hands are all over Alexander's head rubbing his short hair and then pulling it as I'm gulping, trying not to cum.

I'd thought my cock was in a sexually satisfied state, but I guess I was wrong because Alexander's rimming has my cock very hard and all of a sudden I realize that I'm not going to be fucking him; he's going to be fucking me. And this whole unexpected scenario has me ridiculously aroused. More of that dominant/submissive thing I guess. He's doing exactly what he wants, when he wants. He's so sexually attractive and he's pushing so many of my buttons, including the submissive one making me extremely aroused. His rimming continues at Alexander's deliberate pace and it has me gulping and my asshole twitching. I moan quietly for a while highly aroused to an uncomfortable, almost desperate degree before whining, "Ohhh, mmmm, ooh, Alexander, fuck me, please." Sucking on the lips of my asshole, then he's darting the tip of his tongue inside me a half inch or so. Oh man, this is fucking hot! Shortly, I moan again, "Oooh, fuck me," but Alexander pays no attention. He continues in that infuriating manner of his, agonizingly deliberate. His tongue is getting in my hole two inches or so by now. My hips are doing little humps on their own. Everything feels wet, itchy, and squirmy and I want his boner inside me. "Please, Alexander, I'm ready." He does some more sucking and I do some more squirming around on the seat of that leather chair. The position he put me in prevents me from doing much other than squirm. I'm whining quietly, aroused and needing relief. My balls feel heavy and hard, and I don't believe I've ever felt this kind of immediate need before.

Alexander sees me squirming and whining and stands up, softly saying, "Shhh, be patient, Oliver, I want to do my best for you." As he speaks he takes the packet from the waistband of his boxer shorts. It's a condom of course, and holding it in his left hand he used his right to pull down and step out of his boxers. My face is hot and sweaty, my ass is hot and dripping wet with saliva, and my asshole's twitching and itching. I'm impatient and never stop squirming in the chair. Amazingly, Alexander's cock stands straight out from his buzzed pubic patch looking like it's ten inches long. Not fat though, the shaft a normal size, very straight with a head wider than the shaft. He unrolls a heavily lubed condom on that great boner of his and I let out a long sigh fantasizing how wonderful it will be having that boner up my ass. Alexander hears the sigh and misunderstanding it, says, "I know, Oliver. I'd love to do you bare-back too, but it's a foolish risk. This will be fine, I promise."

I can't talk because I want that boner in me so bad I feel like screaming. Alexander rubs both his thumbs in the condom's lube and his thumbs go in my anus Oooh, that feels good, I moan, "Ahhh, oh yeah, more." He rotates his thumb around my hole stretching it in all directions and it feels so good, I suck in a long breath and squeeze my anus muscle tightly on his thumbs. Looking through slits in my eyelashes, my eyes mostly closed at the pleasure his thrums gave my anus, I see Alexander smile to himself as he massages my hole from the inside for thirty seconds. He spreads my asshole until it hurts, but I don't care because it feels good too, like scratching an unbearable itch. Naked and immobilized with my back on the leather seat, sweat forming there, I don't want to move my legs off the arms of the chair because that would close off some access to my asshole. I want to make my hole fully accessible to Alexander. Both his long throbs are in my ass as far as they can go and my hips do three humps off the seat with Alexander soothingly saying, "Easy, Oliver. Just a minute, I want my big boner to slide in easily. I moan, "Uh, oh, oh," my back's squishy with sweat and spit's running down both sides of my mouth as I roll my head from side to side on the seat. Trying to sound composed, I grunt out, "I'm ready now, Alexander. Please...." He blurts out a chuckle, saying, "We're almost there. Are you jerking me around, or are you really this aroused?" I go, "Aroused? I'm far beyond aroused," and he laughs again. He's having fun.

Alexander moves his hard cock head against my hole and gently pulls my legs off the arm rests with a hand behind each knee. Pushing both legs back now, back until the tops of my thighs are against the seat on either side of me, my straight feet up in the air, which lifts my ass up off the seat a few inches. Maintaining pressure against my hole with the head of his boner with a flick of his hips, the head of that long boned-up cock slips inside me. I can't think of anything that's felt as good as this feels. I let out a long sigh followed by a moan of pleasure. Oh, how good it feels and absolutely no pain at all. Just pleasure. He chuckles again and says something so quietly I don't hear it as I try humping down on the head of his cock to get it farther inside me. He barks out another laugh at my futile effort, and goes, "You're a riot, Oliver, I know you're kidding me, you couldn't be this turned-on. My foreplay was like three minutes." What? Three minutes? It seemed like much longer." I shake my head, on the seat, but can't speak.

His boner goes up my ass two more inches and my back arches, as I'm thinking, 'Oh yeah, fuck me hard.' Pushing this boner in another two inches and doing little two to three-inch thrusts in and out, and then a five-inch thrust all the way up inside me until he bumps against my ass with his crotch. He humps against my butt cheeks with enough force that it picks my ass up further off the seat and he's able to get that extra half-inch of cock up my ass. No chuckling from Alexander now, just a quiet moan. He holds that long hard cock all the way up my ass, murmuring , "Oh yeah, baby," and pulls almost all the way out going. I go, "Ahhhhh," and he pushes it all the way back in before beginning a rhythmic fucking with me deliriously overcome with sexual pleasure. All the nerve endings in my rectum explode with intense sensations and my itch is being scratched deliciously. I can't stop moaning at the pleasure coming off my prostate and lips of my anus, as his long cock continually plows my rectum. He's into it now and the sounds of males fucking rings in my ear, "Slap, slap, slap, slap," as his crotch smacks into my buttocks with each incredible thrusts of his long hard boner.

My own boner's so hard it aches and it's only been about an hour and a half since I blew the load of my life down Alexander's throat. Even so I continue drooling pre-cum as my balls buzz while churning more spunk. It's, "Slap, slap, slap, slap," for five, six, seven minutes of ecstasy before my hard balls move up tightly against my groin feeling like big, solid glass marbles. Alexander's head is back and his eyes are closed. It's like his hips are on automatic pilot thrusting his big boner in my ass. He must be approaching climax as his humping hips are harder and faster pushing me back on the seat until the top of my head is against the back of the chair, sliding in my own sweat. Wet smacking sound each time

Alexander's crotch slaps into my lube dripping, sweaty ass with my feet flopping around above me. There's no way to describe how good it feels being fucked hard by a big cock like Alexander's. His face drips sweat droplets land on my stomach as he takes his hands off the back of my thighs and uses them stretch my butt cheeks apart almost painfully, but a sexy pain to go with the intense sexual pleasure coming from my rectum, anus and my incredibly hard boner that's so hard sticking straight up it barely moves.

Every thrust now lifts my buttocks off the seat. I can't hold out any longer, the need to cum is overwhelming so I get a tight hold of my boner and stroke my cock wickedly fast and almost immediately I feel a spray of watery cum fly out of my pee slit followed immediately by a decent string of cum shoots straight up and comes down on my chest. Not much volume, but I just about pass out from the explosion of sensation at the head of my cock as another string of cum flies out as firecrackers burst behind my eyes. Almost simultaneously to my climax, I hear Alexander make his only girlie sound of the night as my hole closes up the tight and with his loud gasp he fills his condom with creamy semen. Still humping his boner in my ass, he lets out another gasping sound as his shoulders shudder and I suppose he sent another load of creamy spunky sperm to die in the condom. There's nothing like a climax. Sensations buzz around my belly and then begin fading quickly leaving me sweaty and weak, but feeling so nice, so good. Alexander does some lazy thrusting in my sloppy rectum and then pulls that long cock out and strokes it a few times, getting lube on his hand while looking at me. Sweat on his face, taking deep breaths and then he slowly collapses on top of me squishing my cum between our bellies and chest. He's as sweaty as I am as I lick the side of his face like a cat.

Ha, I've got this funny feeling like I almost belong to him, or like I want to belong to him. Like his pet cat. I know it's a momentary fleeting feeling, but I enjoy it for the moment. Both my arms are around his strong neck, hugging him, keeping my ass off the seat an inch or so to maintain his cock up inside me at the fullest length possible. I start kissing his neck and, with my legs still around his waist, I hug into his hot sweaty body for all I'm worth. Alexander's grunting and snorting short shots of air as his heart hammers against my chest. I don't want to let go. After two minutes or so, he weakly mumbles, "Holy shit, that was awesome, Oliver. Nice tight hole ya got there. Whoa, one of the best fucks I've ever had, dude. And I'm serious." Then, with his breathing finally under control, he chuckles one of his easy chuckles, adding, "You, my friend, are some kind of male witch. What the fuck are they called anyway?" I quietly suggest, "Warlock?" He lazily replies, "No, that doesn't sound right. Oh, who the fuck cares. You get me crazy worked-up, that's all I know." He said the last part into the side of my head so low I can barely hear him and he follows it up with some more chuckling. Like I said, he's having a good ole time as usual.

I'm having myself a damn good time too. I continue hugging his muscular body against my slim one. For now, I'm concentrating on licking the sweat from Alexander's forehead. His cock's still firm all the way up inside me, which is exactly where I want it. I feel sorry for gay guys who never want to bottom, I mean... they have no idea how incredibly sexy it is to have a hot, big, strong cool dude fuck you. It's my favorite thing in life, getting fucked. And, Alexander just fucked me better than I've ever been fucked before, not that there's been many times so far. He says, "We're all sweaty. You want to take a shower?" I go, "Um, not yet. I like this." Alexander laughingly goes, "You are one hot tamale, Oliver. I better mark you so the guys at the club know you belong to me." With that, he gently puts his fingers on my chin to push the side of my head away from his face and he begins sucking on my neck right under my jaw as he lowers me to my back on the barber chair again. It feels weird and then warm and then itchy and finally a little raw. He's giving me a world-class hickey and after a while, it doesn't feel too good and I start whining about it and moving my head away, but Alexander continues sucking and licking on the same spot and it becomes kind of hypnotic after a while and I lay docile in his arms. This must be what it's like being dominated. And I like it. Everything he does to me is carnal and earthy and very sensuous.

I lie under him with my legs around his waist, my arms loosely around his neck and his cock up my ass while he continues to lightly suck on the hickey and it feels good now because I want his mark. I want everyone to know I'm Alexander's and I'll bet there'll be some jealous boys at the club. His cock begins to grow inside me and get very hard again and my smaller cock is twitching again too. The whole package Alexander had laid on me from the shampoo, the rimming and blow job, the haircut and the fuck, including the making out and this long hickey deal, it all has me moaning and feeling mighty fine, and his scent is sexy as hell too. Sure, every step has been the way Alexander wanted it, when he wanted it, but I don't care. I like being submissive to him. He'll stop sucking on my hickey when he's ready to stop. It's more than okay with me 'cause I feel so creamy and smooth and satisfied. I lay relaxed under him thinking back almost two hours when we were coming up the stairs and Alexander said something about. 'Don't worry, he'd be taking good care of me,' meaning sexually, and he sure has done that. I'm feeling my dreamy contended best.

He stops the hickey-licking, lifts his head a little to look at it, and says with a laugh, "Oh my God, Oliver, that's the biggest hickey I ever saw," and he laughs with his shoulders shaking so I start to laugh too, and I talk through my laughing, "You asshole, Alexander. I'm going to look like I have two fucking heads tonight." He says he's sorry, he didn't realize a hickey could swell up like that. Kissing him just because I feel like it, and he goes, "Oh jeez, I just got and idea. Hold on tight, I'm going to straighten up with you impaled on my rod. Hold on!" I tighten my grip around his waist with my legs and around his neck with my arms and he gets a hold of me around the back, and stands up with amazing ease. "Jesus Christ, Oliver. How much do you weight? You're light as a feather." He carries me into the main barber shop, then turns around to sit back in one of the customer's waiting chairs. He wants me to ride his boner. He jokes that he's had to do all the work up till now, so it's my turn to hump up and down on that steel rod of his. Good idea, but trying to sit back with me wrapped around his torso doesn't work out too well. His ass hits the edge of the seat and we both go sprawling on the tile floor with me sliding off his boner and Alexander yelling, "My dick, my dick," as he grabs at his still hard cock that's once again sticking straight out from his crotch. I'd slid off of it and cracked my knees on the floor. My boner, such as it was, goes down now that my hole's empty and gaping open. Alexander's stroking his boner and laughing, then I start laughing. It's contagious. This tall, fit, handsome, naked boy sitting on the floor, holding his cock and calling out, "My dick, my dick!" I can't catch my breath from laughing so hard. Never mind the cool breeze flying up my gaping asshole.

We take awhile to get ourselves together. We've been at this sex play for quite some time and we had the three hard liquor drinks so we're both in really silly ass moods. Finally, we get up and Alexander pulls out the rest of the condom that's hanging half out of my ass making a strange sound when it plops out which started us laughing again. I didn't know it was there. He mumbles something about, "I need another kiss," and we start a nice French kiss, which grows and grows. We're nuts or something and I'm trying to swallow his tongue and he's groping my ass with both hands. Wild things, that's what we are. Our boners return and it's just crazy. I feel the pre-cum from his boner on my hip and a stream of it runs down the outside of my leg. He's making noises in his throat and all of a sudden he stops sucking on my mouth and grabs my bicep and just about drags me into his office. I'm again panting with desire watching him roll on a new condom, my eyes big as saucers.

The condom's on and he briskly turns me around, pushing the back of my head down so I lean on his desk, holding on to the edge of it with both hands, bending over at the waist. No more laughing, we're aroused and it's like we haven't had sex for weeks. He hurriedly and roughly spreads my legs and then grabs onto my hips with both hands and pulls me backward onto his cock. I go, "Ahhh, ohh," and as he pulls me further onto that hard boner of his until my feet leave the ground and the pressure on my arms increases significantly. He's grunting and puffing as he humps his hips and the entire eight inches is once again inside me. Not taking his time to do it in his usual deliberate way, he just rams his boned-up cock roughly inside me and sighs a long sigh, moaning, "God damn this feels good." His voice is strained, holding me by the waist, keeping my feet just off the floor. Alexander does a number of circular grinds against my buttocks, in effect, rotating my hole with his boner and it feels so awesome.

He drops my feet back on the floor and, pushing at the back of my head with one hand while keeping my head down and my ass up, he used his other arm to hold me under my belly and humps fast and hard for six or seven minutes. No variation in the speed just thrust, thrust, thrust. With every thrust I moaned out, "Ooh, ooh, ooh." Alexander is taller than me and therefore his thrust into my hole are more downward than straight forward and each downward jab rubs tightly over my prostate gland. It's thrust thrust thrust! "Ooh, ooh, ooh." He squeezes my belly hard before doing two last big rough humps, grunting as he's climaxing into the condom, his second climax of the evening. The last big thrust knocks me into the side of his desk and he quickly wraps both arms around my chest now and hugs my back up against his chest still humping his boner inside my sore asshole. It's very noticeably sore now and I need to grit my teeth. And sore ass or not, I squeal, "Eeeee," as two spurts of almost clear cum splat from my cock. My third orgasm of the night, but it felt almost as good as the others. Right after that I notice how sore my ass actually is.

Neither of us has anything to say for a few minutes. We're taking deep breaths with our hearts pounding. I'm not experiencing the normal sexy after affects I usually get right after climaxing and that's maybe because my hole is so sore. Alexander pulls out of me slowly and says real low, "Man, I'm sorry about that, Oliver. I didn't mean to be so rough with you. Don't know what the hell came over me? You okay?" I tell him my asshole is wicked sore, but I'm good other than that. He sort of pats me on my head like maybe I am his cat, "Well, my bad, and I am sorry." Both of us are still naked of course, as he takes my hand and leads me over to the office sofa where we both sit, his arm going across my shoulders. Pulling off his second condom, he tosses it toward the wastebasket, but misses and it sticks to the side. We both stared at the condom on the side of the wastebasket waiting for it to lose its stickiness and fall to the floor. Finally I say, "You're supposed to be good at basketball, ain't ya? I mean, being a black dude and all." I'm pointing at the condom, "So what's that all about?" I ask the question with mock concern in my voice. Alexander says, "Fuck you talking about now, you honky motherfucker?" We laugh, then he adds, "Anyway, I'm brown." Looking at him, I'm like, "You're tan and handsome." He nods his head, grinning, "Yeah, I know," and gives my shoulders a hug.

Alexander glances at me now, then touches the hickey he gave me, chuckling, "That's a beauty of a hickey ya got going for ya, buddy," and we both shake our heads giggling. Basically we're like two twelve-year-olds with the giggles. When we run out of giggles, Alexander leads me upstairs and we take a long shower together with absolutely no sex involved. Neither of us wants or needs anymore sex at the moment, nor are we capable of any. My asshole is still sore so I'm walking oddly and Alexander burst out laughing, then says how sorry he is for laughing. I do look so funny walking bow-legged. Grinning, I call him an asshole when he laughs at me, but every time he laughs, I can't help but laugh too. We put on boxer shorts and Alexander makes us another drink while I stand next to the stool watching him. I won't be sitting down for a while. We smoke and look at each other, both of us pleased with ourselves. I'm pleased to have gotten the fuck of my life, and feeling completely sexually satisfied. It's a pleasant, relaxed state of mind I'm in right now. For his part, Alexander seems pleased to have been able to provide such an extensive sexual experience for us both. Breaking the silence, I ask what I should wear to his club tonight. Alexander smirks, then says, "It's sports coat Saturday night for members. Guests, you in this case, wear whatever the member sponsor, that would be me in your case, wants him to wear." It's a little weird the way he put that, "Um, well what do you want me to wear?" He takes a big drag of his cigarette and looks a little mischievous, saying, "That's something I wanted to talk to you about." Then he says, "Bring your drink and come into the bedroom for a second." When we're there, he mumbles, "Would you sit here, Oliver?" indicating a straight back chair next to his desk. I sit my sore ass on the bed instead, real curious now. Alexander blurts out, "Okay, how to start? Hmmm, maybe by saying, please, please, please do me a favor and let me put eyeliner on you?" I go, "What?" He explains that he and his three best gay buds are all bringing guests tonight and the hottest/cutest guest wins fifty bucks from each of the other three. Plus, bragging rights. In other words, he wants me to be part of some kind of half-ass beauty contest. Well, at least it wasn't a dog-pound contest where guys try to bring the biggest dog of a date they can find. He goes on to tell me that one of the requirements in the contest is that the guest needs to have some make-up on, and another requirement is that he needs to be gay. The second part is no problem, but I've never worn make-up in my life. That reminds me of Pattie's brother, Miles, with his make-up. Alexander's going to have eyeliner on too and, with our identical haircuts, and with both of us with the same eye make-up, well it might be kinda hot. Then, to butter me up, he adds, "Plus, you being cuter than any boy my three buds could ever hope to pick-up, you'll win hands down." I give him a funny look and he goes, "Not only do I beat them on the golf course, but I'll win the pick-up department too. What do ya say, buddy?" Laughing again, he goes, "It's cool, don't ya think? I've kind of made you look like a smaller version of me with the haircut." I stare at him blankly as he explains the rest of the club's members aren't in the contest, just him and his buds.

It isn't cool of Alexander not to have mentioned this little contest to me earlier, and it's slightly humiliating for me to be one of these contestants, particularly if it turns out I'm one of the three losers. There are other disappointing aspects of this whole thing, such as Alexander being more than a little disingenuous about why I couldn't visit him earlier. Now I know he wanted me up here the night of the contest. Also, this indicates a self-centered, insensitive side of Alexander that isn't very attractive and it surprises me. I never realized how competitive he is, but I promised myself recently to be more open to new experiences and also, being a little self-centered myself, I want to have sex with Alexander again, so I'm like, "Sure, what's the big deal. Go for it, dude." Alexander's full of thank you, thank you, Oliver. Without hesitating, he looks in a mirror and does his own eyes with eyeliner. It's just a thin eyeliner pencil, I guess you'd call it. When he does my eyes, he puts on a much thicker outlining, but I'm committed and don't want to seem like a prude so I let it slide. Alexander's very up-beat now and explains that eyeliner is the least intrusive make-up he could think of. He doesn't like make-up on guys, it's just for this contest. Done with the eye lining, he pulls on some black slacks, explaining, "One more little favor, Oliver. Please put on that T-shirt and those shorts there on the chair." The so-called T-shirt is made of black silk that clings to my body, it's sleeveless and doesn't extend down as far as my belly button. I put it on staring at him, but he won't look back at me. He's busy putting on those beautiful black slacks and a long sleeve, silk fitted-shirt. He looks hot alright. My shorts are actually shorty-shorts of the same black material that Alexander's slacks are made from. A skinny replica of Alexander's belt completes my outfit. With the shorty shorts being barely longer than my dick, they make my thin, smooth legs look extra long. I stare at them in the full length mirror and I think they look nice, even if I do say so myself. I hope the club is worth this humiliation! It's the booze Alexander's been feeding me that's reduced my inhibition enough to go through with this. I only hope there's no more surprises.

Chapter 5
Alexander

These fucking shorts barely reach down to my balls, never mind my dick. Good thing I'm wearing tighty/whitey jockey shorts. Also, there's no chance in the world I'll know a single soul at this gay club in Delaware. Looking at myself in the full length mirror, I sarcastically ask Alexander, "How do I look?" He takes a long drink from his forth gin and tonic, finishing it off, then stalling for time asks, "What was that, Oliver?" He's trying not to laugh, and then I burst out with a laugh at myself and Alexander chuckles along with me giving me a hug. With the shorty-shorts, I'm to wear black Converse high-tops sneakers socks. He says, "I guessed your foot size." He got it close enough and after putting the sneakers on, I look at my reflection in the full length mirror again. My extreme haircut and my black eyeliner eyes made me look slightly like an ancient Egyptian boy pharaoh. Weird! My next thought is that my whole appearance looks more like an expensive boy prostitute than anything else. Alexander put on a light gray cashmere sport coat, saying, "You look hot, Oliver," then he steps into black leather loafers. He's so handsome I find myself staring at him again. In a semi-joking manner, he goes, "I knew you'd be a good sport about this, Oliver. You're so sexy looking, and so cute I could eat you." Who doesn't like compliments? I shrug, mumbling, "Thanks," and he says, "Let's go, cutie, I need to go and collect my hundred and fifty bucks off those suckers." I smile at him. He gets excited about things acting like a little kid… he makes me laugh.

I follow him down two flights of stairs to his basement that connects to his garage. In there is his brand new titanium silver BMW 3 series hardtop convertible and what a beautiful car it is too. He leaves the top up because it's cool outside and I'm not really dressed for cool weather. The gay club's not downtown like I imagined it would be, but rather it's a free standing stone building in the suburbs near an eighteen-hole golf course. The building over-looks a man-made lake. We come to a stop under a stone archway fifty yards in trot of the club. Alexander enters his password into a keypad at the guard house there and the barrier bar raises allowing us to pass through. He drives up the long driveway stopping in front of the building that's illuminated by bright spot lights. I can't help but marvel at how some privileged people get to belong to these exclusive places, and assume eventually take it all for granted as their due. The club's an impressive and very expensive looking building in a gorgeous landscaped setting with huge old trees all around it, the leaves just now beginning to change to fall colors. Of course there's valet parking and a uniformed doorman. We get out and Alexander tips the man, who motions with his hand for a young gut to park the car. "Yes, Sirs. Good to see you gentlemen tonight," and like that. All of the employees are busy pretending that I'm wearing a very appropriate outfit this evening. A young man with a ponytail, who's apparently in charge of cataloging each car's set of keys is staring at the hickey on my neck.

I look over at him and see his big robin-egg blue eyes that he never seems to blink. He also has a bad case of acne, but looking past the acne I see that he's in fact beautiful. What a waste if he's straight. I'm self-conscious now that we're actually out in public dressed the way I am. Even Alexander seems anxious for us to get inside. There's a metal detector to walk through and then Alexander enters his club membership password into another keypad and a uniformed doorman opens the door to the main foyer. It's a big foyer, the decor fairly understated. At the main restaurant, down a side hallway, the maitre d' is dealing with some older men. Then there are five other middle-aged men waiting to be seated. I noticed a husky guy in his twenties walking briskly toward Alexander and me, followed closely by a short teenager type. The teenager is wearing dark red lipstick and he has a fake beauty mark on his cheek. He's not a beauty though. His wide mouth and nose, small eyes and long brown hair eliminate the description of beauty for this lad. The long hair reminds me of a middle-aged woman's hairdo, but what do I know. Can't help but think, 'This is my competition? Ho hum'. When the husky guy gets a couple of feet from us Alexander looks up and says, "Well if it isn't my favorite busboy. Wussup, Dennis?" Dennis says, "Busboy my ass. I'm running that fucking restaurant and you know it." He points at me and says to Alexander, in an exasperated manner, "He's your boy?" Everything Dennis does or says screams homosexual. Alexander gives him a smirk and asks, "What do you think?" Without saying anything else, Dennis reaches in his pocket and pulls out a wad of money. He peels off a fifty-dollar bill and gives it to Alexander, who takes it grinning. Dennis laughs nodding his head at me, saying, "Get real! Tunes or Roger aren't coming up with anyone who can compete with him?" Alexander shrugs, "Yeah, I love my boy, Oliver. Cute isn't he?" and he rubs my head, "And he's got the same haircut I have too." Dennis is shaking his head, "Fuck, I told the guys you suckered us into this bet. Jesus, a little twin Alexander. You're too much, dude."

Then Dennis, looking passed Alexander and me, shouts out, "Just get your fifty dollars out gentlemen, and let's not talk about this ever again." I turn around and four young guys are coming down the hall together. The first guy's nice looking, but he has one of those trendy beards that he purposely keeps looking like he hasn't shaved the last two days. He's athleticlooking too, like Alexander. Alexander says to him, "Hi, Tunes. Don't pay any attention to Dennis, I'm sure your boy is very hot." Tunes looks at me, frowns, blinks twice dramatically, then looks back at Alexander, and says, "Or not" and he hands over his fifty dollar bill. I try to look blank. It isn't hard. Dennis' boy just stares at me with furrowed eyebrows, and then mumbles, "Nice hickey." I pretend not to hear him. The last of Alexander's friends is talking with an older man at the door before joining us. His boy, trailing behind him has red hair like Frankie's, but the comparison abruptly ends there. He isn't bad looking, but not really cute either. Frankly, except for the red hair, none of these boys would catch my eye if I saw them on the street. If I had to choose one, Tunes' boy would be the one because he's at least interesting to look at. Very sharp features with bright green eyes and spiked blond hair. He's wearing black lipstick, which is a sharp contrast to his light complexion and the blond hair. Now, if I'm included in the contest, Dennis is correct, forget about it. Just being honest. Alexander pockets the third fifty dollar bill and the maitre d' leads us to a round table for eight with a view of the fake lake. The other three guys are doing their best to break Alexander's balls about the extent he went to making me a mini him. Tunes is saying, "Seriously, if you're hurting for money I can let ya have some." Then to Dennis he says in a mock whisper, "How the fuck he thinks he can support himself cutting hair... it's laughable." Alexander's saying things like, "You boys are really good losers, ain't ya? No sour grapes here." They're having fun anyway. After everyone orders drinks, Alexander introduces me all around and the other members introduce their boys and themselves. That's the end of conversation with us boys. The other three members are Alexanders' golfing partners. They golf together at the country club all the time, and as far as I can tell from their conversation, when they aren't actually playing golf they're talking about the last time they did play golf. Boring.

Alexander's step-dad is a partner in the group that owns the golf/country club so Alexander and his friends have a free run of the place. Their course isn't the one near this private gay club though. It's much nicer than this one if I can believe what they're saying about it. Dennis' parents own a fancy restaurant that he manages for them. Tunes is a 22-year-old stock broker, and Roger's a writer who hasn't been published yet. All these boys come from money and they'd all gone to the same prep school, but not in the same class, although they met and become friends in the prep school's gay and lesbian outreach club. Two of the contest boys that the members rounded-up are actually hired from a dating service and therefore are getting paid for this nonsense, and the red-haired boy is a busboy at the restaurant Dennis manages. I'm here because I like having sex with Alexander. So, that's everyone's history, or all of it that I find slightly interesting anyway. Oh yeah, Tunes' real name is Tommy Tooney and he's apparently, 'the man', as far as this little clique is concerned. Everyone seems to follow his lead. Alexander's the youngest as well as the best golfer. Both Tunes and Alexander are very straight-acting gays while Dennis and Roger are not straight-acting. They're all okay as far as I'm concerned and they seemed to like each other a lot. Not sexually, they're friends. The members order dinner for us boys which had us boys exchanging looks and shaking our heads a little bit. The food the members ordered for us turns out to be very good though. Tunes has a way of acting like he's maybe a tiny bit better than everyone else. It doesn't bother me, particularly because I'm never going to see him again after tonight, and to his credit he does have a funny way about him. Funny ha ha I mean, not funny as in odd. He went on a rant about his sister who's apparently addicted to clothes shopping and he says if she'd been on the Titanic she would surely have stopped at the ship's apparel shop for the half-price ship-sinking sale on her way to the lifeboats. He says everything in a flat, bored voice. I laugh out loud when he said that Titanic comment, and everyone stopped eating to look at me. I look back at them one by one and give each of them my killer smile which they all somehow resist. I'd been drinking maybe a tiny bit too much since getting to Alexander's.

Alexander follows-up the story about Tunes' sister with another story about her. He tells us about the time the sister, Denise, who's extremely pushy and bossy, in addition to being a clothes junky, insisted on going with Tunes and Alexander to shoot pool one night last summer. He says, looking at the other three members in turn as he recites the story, "Tunes is in the head taking a leek, so I'm racking the balls. I lift up the rack after racking the balls and say to Denise, 'Since you're such a ball-breaker, sweetie, it's only right that you should break first.'" Alexander chuckles at his witty comment as Roger lisps, "Oh no you didn't, Alexander. You're just as scared of her as I am. What'd you really say?" Alexander looks down smiling, muttering, "I told her, 'after you, ma'dam,' but I almost said that ball-breaker thing." They all laugh as us four boys again exchange frowning looks, like, 'Are these guys for real?' We'd all had before-dinner hard liquor drinks and then wine with dinner! After dinner, all of us sit around the table and drink beer, except for Tunes who has brandy and coffee. All the guys smoke cigars and us so-called boys smoke cigarettes. It's very smoky at our table.

After dinner some of us are starting to slur our words. It's eleven o'clock by the time we're through with desert. Roger and Dennis are talking quietly to each other and although I can't hear them, I'm pretty sure they're engaged in witty conversation bordering on the banal. I say that because all night those two tried for witty, but only got as far as banal. As we drink more beers the conversation turns to sports other than golf. Someone begins playing footsy with me under the table and I look over and decide it's the red-haired boy, who's looking a little cuter to me now after all the mixed drinks, wine, and beer have altered reality for me a bit. He stares defiantly back at me and makes a kissing motion with his lip. I look behind me pretending he's doing that for someone else. When I look back at him he shoots me his middle finger. I switch my attention to Tunes again who's now into serious science shit. He goes, "This gigantic black hole in the center of the galaxy, called Cygnus X-1, has swallowed 100 suns and compressed them into a mathematical point like the point of a pencil. You, Roger, have the audacity to think you can understand the true nature of God? You're absurd, my friend." The red haired boy says to one of the hired boys, "What da fuck's he talking about?" We all looked at the redhead and then Alexander says, "You're getting all pompous on us, Tunes. Nobody gives a shit about any of that." Tunes does a face like he's confused by that comment and finishes the last of his drink waving at our waiter to order another round of beers for us and another brandy for himself.

During a lull in their conversation, I say to no one in particular, "I'm going to take a piss," and the redhead says, "I'll come with ya, Oliver." Red's name is Spunky, that's how he was introduced and the only name I heard him called. He knows where the lavatory is and at the urinals with our dicks out, he does an exaggerated look over to check out mine, and says, "At least something about you is average." I think that was some kind of back-handed compliment so I look over at him giving him a little grin. He says, "That haircut you got is way cool. How much did it cost ya?" I say, "A hundred and five dollars plus a twenty dollar tip, why?" Spunky zips up and sighs, "Every fucking body has money but me. That sucks." I tell him the truth about the haircut and confess I too have no money. He doesn't seem to hear me, as he asks, "Can I zip you up, Oliver?" I go, "Sure thing, Spunky." I'm fairly drunk. He zips my short zipper and rubs the palm of his hand all around my naked belly. After all, we're just a couple of the member's boys. He points at my hickey and says, "I wish I could give you one of those." That's a random thought.

He's still rubbing the palm of his hand on my belly button so I say, "You can give me my hickey, but for now are you almost done rubbing my belly button?" He nods his head that he's done, then asks, "Would you suck me off? I politely decline that request and then decline, "Um, can I suck you off then?" After the second rejection, he mumbles, "I guess asking if I can fuck you is out of the question?" and I tell him he's correct. "Well can I have a kiss at least?" When he asks, he looks so pathetic, and in the bright light of that rest room, he appears so young too. "How old are you, Spunky?" and he tells me he'd just turned eighteen. I'm shaking my head, grinning, then asks, "Can I see your driver's license?" He takes his wallet out of his back pocket and hands me his driver's license. I go, "Nice phony ID, Spunky." He takes it back, "It's not phony and I know I look young, but I turned eighteen almost month ago." Then he tells me he quit high school in his junior year to wok work full-time at the restaurant.

We're still standing in the lavatory with nobody else here, and Spunky seems so naive and he's very young looking, so I shrug, saying, "Yeah, okay, one kiss because we're all in the same boat tonight, aren't we?" and he goes, "You mean the Titanic that he was talking about earlier, Oliver?" and he's serious too. Not the sharpest knife in the drawer and my heart kind of feels for him, him being so clueless and all. He sure looks a lot cuter now than earlier and so I get a paper towel and spit on it to wet it a little. Then, putting my left hand behind his head, I wipe the remaining lipstick off his lips. He stands here like a good boy, his face tilted up, while I do it. When his lips are free of lipstick and just glistening slightly with my spit from the paper towel, I take hold of his head in both my hands and kiss his nice full lips as he pushes his tongue in my mouth. I keep running my fingers all through his bright red hair thinking that this is how Frankie's hair would feel if he ever lets it grow out. I'm swooning with the thought of Frankie, and from the hot kiss from this eighteen-year-old Mensa candidate too, and all the booze I'd drank tonight, it's a sexy time sharing some spit with Spunky. He has both his arms wrapped around my waist and he's humping his hips into my crotch fast, like a rabbit. I feel his hard spike hit my hip with every thrust. This boy is hot. "Please jerk me off, Oliver. Please, you make me so hot just looking at you." This kid doesn't seem to let pride get in the way of something he wants, so he's fine with begging for it. Why the hell not jerk him off? So we go into a toilet stall and he drops his pants. No underwear, of course. Nice normal size uncut penis that's already fairly hard, and to complete the package, he's got himself a pair of oversized nuts hanging low. Big nut! I might as well mention he has very nice well-defined legs too. Legs that he's obviously shaved, but they looked excellent.

It's awkward at first, but I get him turned around so his back's against my chest with my left arm around the front of him just under his chin. He holds onto my forearm with both his hands as I take his firm cock in my fist. As soon as I start stroking his cock, he's very excited and moves a lot, stepping on my toes repeatedly, pushing back so we're both bouncing against the metal panel separating the stalls. The top of his head reaching to just under my nose and as he's bucking his bubble-butt ass into my crotch, his red Frankie-like hair smells real nice. It's fun pulling his pud and seeing how excited he gets, but maybe it's closer to a wrestling match than it needs to be. Spunky's five-inch fat cock sure gets hard. It gets fat too and just before he climaxes, the head swells and, WOW, this boy can shoot out some spunk. Holy shit, it pours straight out hard from the gaping pee slit at the end of the swollen head. Whoa, that's something to see, this kid can shoot off some cum. It's splattered all over the other opposite metal panel. Oh my God, he's squealing this banshee screech and I swear to God he shoots another fat load of cum. I think I've got a pretty good idea why he got the nickname, 'Spunky'. He follows up those first two streams with some short shots with him moaning contentedly. Jeez, if my ass wasn't sore I'd like to feel that fat cock up my ass.

Luckily, most of the diners are in the bar area now and no one used this lavatory while we did our three-minute jerk off. I don't imagine two guys in a stall is all that uncommon in a gay club anyway. Spunky swallowed some spit down his wind pipe during his initial super cum shot and he's coughing now trying to force that drop of spit back up. While he's doing that, I taste some of his spunk from my fingers and find it's a neutral taste but surprisingly creamy considering the volume. When he gets his coughing controlled, with me patting him on the back hard, he turns around and hugs me asking where I live. Maybe he wants to move in with me. It makes me laugh because the thought comes to mind that I'm the king of teens. Myers, lil Pete, and now my latest conquest, Spunky. I'm still a teen myself, but not for long.

I hug his neck and kiss the side of his face and get a bit of a hard-on. I haven't had a semblance of a boner since that last fucking Alexander laid on me hours ago. Thinking about that makes me remember my sore ass and I say, "Come on, Spunky, let's get back before they send a search party looking for us." He asks, "Why would they do that, Oliver. You said you was gonna take a piss." I go, "It's just a figure of speech, but yeah, Spunk." We make our way back and they all are in the bar, them and about a hundred other men. There's karaoke tonight with some old gay guy doing The Killers "Read My Mind". Um, it's not working out real well for him. Some of the older guys are hissing at his singing, but hopefully it's all in fun. Everyone here appears to be feeling no pain. Gazing around, I'd guess about two thirds of the men are over forty, but there's a decent size crew of guys in their twenties and thirties too. Our group has a number of under twenty-year-olds, but I don't see any others. Then there are the real old gay guys looking all around, remembering when they were the deal, when they had their day.

Huh, I feel comfortable being with all gay guys. It's a new experience and everyone seems to enjoy being themselves here where in other parts of their lives they probably all can't be themselves totally. Alexander buys Spunky and me another drink, cranberry juice, with something else, and vodka. It's called a sea breeze I think. Spunky's like a gum on my shoe now. I can't turn around without bumping into him. He's kinda cute though so I don't mind. At the moment he's shoulder to shoulder with me while we drink our sea breeze and then we dance a fast dance together and I don't know who's a worse dancer, him or me. He's very clingy and he sneaks in kisses on my neck and on my lips whenever he can. Hell, I don't mind that either, he's got Frankie's hair, ha ha. I love thinking about Frankie and Spunky's hair reminds me of him. Spunk and me do two slow dances and get another drink from Alexander, who's been dancing with the sharp featured boy, the one with those bright green eyes and the spiked blond hair. That kid looks wicked hot too, especially after all the drinks I've had. Before the next dance, Alexander asks me if I'm doing okay and I assure him I am, and realize I actually am okay and I am having a good time. It isn't anything fabulous, but it's fun. After my last drink, I put my name on line for the Karaoke machine. When my name's called, I hop up on stage and sing the Plain White T's "Hey There Delilah". Maybe not quite as good as Tom Higgenson can sing it, but it stops the show. I look down and see Alexander with his mouth hanging open. Spunky's clapping and cheering for me and I have to do the song again by popular demand. Oh man, it's great being a big star in a little world for a couple of minutes.

None of the guys knew I can sing and while singing I thought of Cristobal... and Tyler. It makes me kinda sad so I sneak away from Spunky and go to the restroom for a good cry. All that booze has me melancholy. Spunky finds me there after my tears, when I'm washing my face. I'm not sure how it started but Spunk and me have a hot ten-minute make-out. Then the lights start blinking telling everyone the club's closing. Spunky's groping my crotch like mad during our make-out and my boner's very hard. Thank God for the blinking lights or I might have gotten involved in something I'd regret. Spunky and I have a hot goodnight kiss around two-thirty in the morning with no one paying us much attention, everyone's drunk and hugging everybody they can grab hold of and then Alexander and I are finally in the car and on our way to his condo.

We're pretty drunk, but he drives safely and we get back without killing ourselves. "One last nightcap, Oliver," mutters Alexander, and we have another vodka drink that we both need like we need electric shock treatment. A few more cigarettes along with the drink as we have a drunken conversation about how cool both of us are, and how cool all the guys are, and what a great singer everyone thinks I am, and on and on till after four o'clock. We crash with me holding onto Alexander like he's my binky blanket. The next conscious thing I'm aware of is me stumbling around the condo just after nine o'clock in the morning looking for a bathroom, and not remembering where one is. I need to take the piss of my life and I finally bumble into a small bathroom in a spare bedroom. The relief floods over me as I'm letting that pee come pouring out. My eyes close and my mouth hangs open. When I woke up a few minutes ago, I was confused wondering who's bed I am in. I stared stupidly at the back of Alexander's head and it was scary for a second 'cause I didn't know who he was. I'm making a solemn promise to myself, right now, to never drink that much booze ever again. I feel like shit and I'm still drunk! How bad will the hangover be when I'm sober? Oh my God, I don't want to even think about that. And, why am I still wearing this ridiculous outfit Alexander dressed me in last night? At least I took off my sneakers before falling in bed. Done the piss and finding my way back to the big master bedroom, I get out of my silly clothes and I crawl back in bed wearing only my underwear, then nuzzle up against Alexander's unbelievably hot body and fall right back to sleep.

The hangover I have when I wake up around one o'clock, sitting on the side of the bed, is unbelievable. Then a shattering sound makes my headache spike as Alexander howls because he'd stubbed his toe. I haven't had many, but this, by far, is the worst hangover of my young life. Rationalizing my stupid behavior last night, I tell myself it's worth it because I've learned my lesson. From now on, I'm never ever going to smoke or drink anything alcoholic. I'm giving up smoking and drinking totally... done with that shit forever. Both Alexander and I are very grumpy all day. We aren't even able to eat anything until around four o'clock at a diner. After drinking two large fountain Cokes along with a bowl of chicken soup and a chicken salad sandwich, I initially feel better, but then back at the condo the food made me feel sick and I have to lie down again. Alexander mumbled a couple of times how lucky we are that his parents are in France buying art work. If they'd been home we'd have to go over for Sunday dinner. That thought scares me so I finally joined Alexander and have a Bloody Mary with just a little bit of vodka, and after two of those, we both light up cigarettes.

The vodka, along with the Tylenol I'd taken during the day, cured my headache, but the cigarette brought it right back. Alexander cooked soup around eight o'clock but it boiled over and one thing led to another and we settled for another Bloody Mary chuckling about who knows what. We're back in bed before ten o'clock and sleeping shortly after that. No sex. I swear, I didn't even think about it. After almost twelve hours sleep though, I'm lying awake in bed Monday morning thinking about just that. Specifically sex with the twenty-year-old boy sleeping next to me. I have the urge to fuck him because my asshole is still a little sore, but the primary reason I have an urge to fuck him is I don't want to leave without doing it at least once. I've been fantasizing about fucking Alexander from the day I left Wildwood last summer and I probably won't have a better chance to fulfill my fantasy than this. And after all, fucking Alexander is my main reason for this trip in the first place. During the past two days I've had every other kind of sex one might want except the one where I fuck Alexander.

I'll wait for him to wake up, but five minutes later, my patience runs out, so I slowly rub Alexander's ass through his boxers. After a minute or so of that, I let my hand slip into his boxers and finger up his butt crack. This boy's a sound sleeper though so I begin pushing on his hole and he finally groans and rolls away from me. Giggling like a little kid, I shimmy over to him again. He's facing away from me, lying on his side so I massage the butt cheek he isn't laying on. It's real firm, but not as firm as Joey's. When this activity doesn't get the results I'm looking for, I begin grabbing handful after handful of his ass squeezing each handful tightly. This is pretty sexy and I feel myself getting hard so I get my arm under his neck and pull the back of his head against my face blowing into his short dense hair while gently humping my boner into the back of his thigh. In a sleepy voice Alexander says, "You are giving me the hardest boner, Oliver. Let me guess, you want me to do you again before you go." I chuckle, then mumble, "You're close." He goes, "Oh, goody, Oliver is going to do me this morning," and he really does sound happy about that. After a little more messing around, he hops out of bed saying he needs to take care of some bathroom stuff necessities, but that I'm not to go anywhere. Ignoring that, I get up too and brush my teeth in the little bathroom I peed in last night. Then I pee again, wash my face and hands and go back to the bedroom. Alexander doesn't work on Mondays and I have no classes today, so it's cool. Later this morning, I'm driving up to say hello during a quick visit with the twins, who also have school off today. It's a two-hour drive and then an hour and a half from there to the University, so a lot of driving for me. The twins want me to at least say hello since I'm this close. The idea of teaching the twins about gay sex has never come up again.

Back in bed, smelling Alexander's pillow, I hear the toilet flush and the shower go on so I get out of bed, dropping my shorts as I walk into the bathroom, and get in the shower with Alexander. He goes, "No hanky panky in here, Oliver, someone could slip and break off a boner." That gets us laughing again. We're happy to be over most of our hangovers. Stuff seems funnier today than it did yesterday. Washing Alexander's cock and balls with soapy hands, my fist goes around that long cock of his and slide my fist from his nuts to the head of his cock a few times brings back his long boner. I kinda want it up inside me again, and except for still being sore back there, that's where it would wind up too. He has a great cock, but then I can't think of a cock I haven't liked. We manage to get clean and dry without anybody getting fucked. Still naked, we get back in bed to make out a little. As I've said, Alexander is a fabulous kisser and he can lick and suck pretty good too. It doesn't take him long to get me moaning with pleasure, and my cock as rock hard. He goes down on it and sucks it, then licks my balls and after ten minutes or so of foreplay, he reaches into the drawer of the bedside stand and comes out with an extra lubed condom that he rips open and rolls on my dripping boner. We're both red in the face and short of breath with pounding hearts and vibrating boners.

Condom snugly on, I look at him, and he asks, "How do you want to do me?" I just slide over to him and he turns around, both of us lying on our side. Alexander brings his knees up towards his chest as I position my boner to just spread the lips of his anus. The head of my cock feels good so I put a little more pressure and the head almost disappears inside him. Now I need to stop and get control of my breathing. It's been so long since I fucked Alexander. I've been fantasying doing this for months, so I'm overly excited. Alexander looks back, I grin at him, saying, "Don't be impatient," then a strong hump of my hips and my cock goes five inches up his ass with both of us exclaiming, "Ohhh!" we both like gay sex quite a bit. Steadily pushing the last inch in, I almost climax. Gasping at the sensations sizzling around my joint and coming off my hard penis, blinking my eyes rapidly and concentrating on being calm and the feeling of climax subsides. That would have been embarrassing!

Leaving my boner fully impaling him for a few seconds while I take a deep breath, Alexander mutters, "Damn, that feels good, Oliver." With that endorsement, I begin fucking him fast, my arm over his side, my fingers spread on his chest hold him against me. My hips are in a nice rhythm and my boner's sliding tightly in and out creating awesome sensations on a number of sensitive spots on my cock. The head of a penis has so many nerve endings all firing off pleasure sensations at the same time it makes me dizzy. Humping my hips steadily, fucking him deep and hard gets my balls bouncing off his butt with every thrust. The unmistakable slapping sound of my crotch smacking into his ass, "Slap, slap, slap, slap," fills the room along with my grunting and Alexander's, "Ah, ah, ah," sounds of pleasure. I know very well how good it feels being fucked in the ass. My favorite pastime of all time. I'm remembering how good it feels to be doing the fucking too. Oooh, it's sexy! My balls are buzzing and my cock sizzling with awesome sensation, I feel my climax building as my grunts turn into desperate whimpers with each thrusts of my swollen cock inside Alexander's tight rectum. His anus muscle squeezing my boner with each penetration as I bury my face in the short hairs on the back of this hot boy's head. Oh, the scent of Alexander, and his sounds of pleasure are increasing the erotic sensations I'm feeling.

I want these feelings to last a long time but my orgasm's building. Dropping my hand from his chest, I get my fist around his hard cock and stroke it in time with my thrusts up his ass. More moans of pleasure from both of us as sweat forms between us so the slapping sounds of our colliding bodies is louder. Another frantic minute of fucking his ass hard and fast gets a squeal out of Alexander, a girlie squeal no less as cum flies from his cock and splatters against the back of the straight back chair. His sphincter contracts even more when he fires cum from his nuts and I blow my load into the condom as a second string of cum shoots from Alexander's cock, then three more smaller streaks of cum. Drools of it wet my fist and I stoke his cock. I moan and shoot more cum into the condom feeling lightheaded, but fantastic. There's electricity buzzing around my balls and my cock seems to glow with pleasure. My shoulders shudder as sensations fade, I'm still lazily stroking his cock to milk out a few drools of cum and continue thrusting slowly until all the sensations quiet down. Sweat drips from my forehead as a last wave of pleasure drifts around my stomach and the inside of my thighs. Stopping to take deep breaths, I realize this was kinda quick, but for me the first one usually is. I'm hoping for another fuck, one that will be slow and that awhile extending the juicy pleasure of anal intercourse.

We're both breathing heavily coming down off our climaxes when his phone rings. "Who the fuck is that?' Alexander mutters as he looks at the caller ID, then jumps out of bed saying, "Oh damn, I forgot. I promised to show Anthony the secrets of double accounting today. He's downstairs right now. Double accounting? Alexander's quickly throwing some clothes on as I laid here in his bed. He comes over and gives me a big kiss mumbling, "Um, Oliver, me and Anthony are sort of fucking each other too. You know, while he learns the business and all. Um, he's not as sophisticated as you are, so he'll freak out if he knows I just spent the weekend with another boy. So, ah, this is awkward, but could you sneak out the back door while I'm keeping Anthony occupied in my office? Pleeeeeze!" I'm frowning at him, trying to grasp what he means. Is he serious? He rubs my barbered head, grinning and saying, "I know I'm being a dick, but please do this for me." Obviously I'm disappointed, maybe a little shocked at the ballsiness of what he's saying, but it's not like we're going steady or anything. I make a face, but mutter, "Sure, I understand, no problem." He gives me another kiss muttering it was an awesome weekend.

He hurries down to his employee/sex partner. Huh! Abrupt end to our weekend date. Oh well, I get out of bed and slowly get dressed.

Collecting my stuff, I walk down the outside steps at the back of his condo, then cross the street to my car. It was a good time although we wasted all day yesterday with hangovers. This is far from the ideal way to end the weekend, but what the hell. Driving away with the top down in fifty-eight degree weather, I'm chuckling to myself because I can't believe the balls on Alexander to pull a stunt like this. The top's down because I want the fresh air to help clear my head. Going to the same diner we ate at last night, I have a late breakfast and then head west to St. John's Prep for my visit with the twins. I guess Alexander is a bit of a shit when I think about it, but I still like him. Alexander and I both agree we're not lovers. We're sex buddies and he didn't short change me in the sex department, but I wish he was slightly more honorable. Oh well, he's fine for a sex buddy. Hell, we're close sex buddies and I'll settle for that between him and me. I'd be lying if I didn't admit I'm somewhat disappointed in him though for my awkward exit, maybe more than a little disappointed. Damn, why does the reality part of life always suck?

Then it hits me, I don't feel like seeing Alexander's brother. Maybe I catch the twins another trip to Delaware. I put on a Killers CD and crank up the volume. Singing along with the songs, flying down the highway at seventy-five miles an hour, I'm thinking about Joey.

Chapter 6
Randy

On my way back to school I keep feeling the very short haircut Alexander gave me. It's too short for my taste, but he didn't ask, he gave me whatever haircut he wanted me to have. Ballsy and dominant at that. Strangely, almost everything he did this weekend had a dominant aura to it. Alexander's had a big personality turn-around since I last saw him in Wildwood and in a nice sexy way he made me want to be submissive to him. It was a weird but sexy couple of days in Delaware. Somewhere he's acquired a confident take-charge attitude that makes him even sexier than before. It took me by surprise, although I liked the new Alexander even more than the previous one. This weekend he had no trouble getting me to do pretty much everything he wanted, but at the same time I enjoyed myself so I'm not complaining. His metamorphosis into this confident personality is almost the last thing I expected. It's like he charmed me right out of my pants, not that he had to work up much of a sweat doing it.

It wasn't only his choice of haircut, I've also got his hickey on my neck the size of a radish, plus I have a sore asshole, compliments of him, and I'm still dealing with the memory of being dressed-up like a boy prostitute for all to see. The saving grace to all this is the fact I didn't know a single person at the club, and it's unlikely I'll ever see any of them again, so there really wasn't a need for me to be embarrassed. With all the booze I had to drink, I wasn't bothered by anything to a great degree, but now I'm going back to where I do know people and I still have this Marine haircut. I can't get too mad at Alexander because he made me feel wicked hot and sexy, and he fucks really good, too. He's now in a different league than me. He transformed himself into a confident and dominant sex partner. Maybe he gained the confidence from owning his own business and living on his own in that cool condo with the BMW and his rich friends living a playboy's life. Good for him. The thing is, his changes in personality and lifestyle cost him the sweet side of his nature, a side of him which he probably won't get back any time soon. He used to be kind of innocently bumbling along trying to find his way with gay boy sex, just like me. Now I guess he's suave or something. Oh what the fuck, he is a cool dude and I wish him well, but any dreams I had about falling in love with him are gone. We're good sex buddies living in different worlds and I'm back to hoping Frankie falls in love with me. I think I'm in love with him, so that's half the battle.

Frankie is actually in my dreams every once in a while. It's almost like he's sending me telepathic messages or something. I really missed him. I yearn to suck his cock and swap spit with him again, and run my fingers through his red burr haircut. Hell, the truth is I'm helplessly in love with Frankie but I don't like to admit that to myself very often because he's not in love with me. Well, actually I think he is, but he won't admit it. And, no matter how hard I try not to picture that bitch Darleen in my head, there she is! Oh man, I hate her for stealing Frankie from me. Why would he prefer her to me anyway? I'd do anything for him and she bullies him…. I better start thinking about something else or I'll get depressed.

Here's a cheery thought: soon I'll be picking up Joey! What would I do without Joey? It's been three nights since the last time I did his bathroom routine for him. That'll to be fun to do again, and thinking about it starts my dick slipping into the early stages of a boner. So what, all my boners feel good. I am a little concerned though, Joey didn't sound like himself on the phone when I talked to him yesterday. I'll cheer him up when I see him. It makes me smile to think about him, him and his fabulous gymnast body naked and wet and slippery with me bathing and shampooing him. Ooooh, and putting the ointment on that rash up his hole. That usually leads to me jerking him off. Ha ha, a big snake on that kid too. It still amazes me how comfortable he is with me doing all that stuff for him. Guess he has very little choice since he can't do any of it for himself. Yeah but he won't be wearing casts on both arms and a leg forever. Still, even after his bones heal there will be a lot of rehab to go through.

Thinking about Joey brightens my outlook quite a bit as I fly down the highway towards the University Of Massachusetts. Finally, back in the city, then onto the campus, I park in front of the gymnast seniors' dorm. Inside I spot Joey's wheelchair, but no Joey. "Over here, Oliver" and there he is sitting at a table with some guy I don't recognize. They're playing cribbage. The first thing he comments on is my haircut, "Oh, um, ya got a haircut rom your friend, huh?" Ooh, that doesn't sound like an endorsement. One of the guys he's with, mumbles, "What kind of a fucked up barber you going to, dude? He smoking crack while cutting your hair?" I want to say, "Go fuck yourself," but I do my fake cough instead, as Joey asks, "Do ya mind if I finish this match, Oliver? We're playing best of three." I mutter, "Sure, no sweat," not that I have a clue what cribbage is. I notice his bright new casts, and exclaim, "Wow, Joey. Your new casts are thinner, and where's the harness?" He still can't use his arms, but the new casts are lighter, and looking much more comfortable for him. He explains they're partially soft casts for the next four to six weeks. And no more shoulder rig. Even with these new lighter casts, he still can't reach below his belly button because the casts are bent at the elbow. Still, everything will be easier to do and he can wear regular shirts now too. There's something else going on though. Joey's trying to act excited about the new casts and about seeing me, but his emotions seem flat. Not like him at all, and he doesn't look all that well.

After watching for a while and still not knowing what they're doing, I ask, "You okay, Joey?" and he tell me he's fine and suggests I kill some time checking out the new wide screen TV in the common room. Huh, he wants me to stop staring at him I guess. Wandering downstairs to the common area where there's only one other guy in the whole place. He's sitting in a chair reading something with his back to me. I know who it is even though I can only see the back of him. A guy with a short, slim and toned body, slightly wavy light red hair. It can only be one person, Randy Rider. When I clear my throat he turns to look at me, so I say, "Wassup, Randy?" He casually replies, "Oliver, my favorite freshman. Are you looking for the wheelchair boy?" He talks as if he and I have been buds for years, which gives me a good feeling. We easily slide into some small talk with me mentioning my trip to Delaware, leaving out all the sex except the part about Spunky. He laughs and tells me I'm lucky hooking up with him. Huh, is Randy being upfront about being gay? I jokingly ask him, and comes right out and tells me he's always felt he was gay. I reply, "Weird, but that's my exact history too."

Randy wants to know if I have a boyfriend and I go, "Well, almost. I think of him as my boyfriend and now all I need is for him to think that way too." We both laugh a little and he says he knows all about those one-sided deals. Randy's easy to talk to. Feeling comfortable with him, I'm sitting on the arm of the chair right next him. He's telling me this long unrequited love tale while I study his face and marvel that I've been thinking about the extraordinarily cute Frankie, and now I'm staring at another one of those one-in-a-million cute faces. Randy's probably twenty-one years old and he's as tall as he'll ever be, but his sexiness makes up for him being height challenged. Most gymnasts are short. Joey, at five foot nine inches is one of the taller gymnasts. In addition to Randy's extraordinary hair, he has a peaches and cream blemish-free complexion that gives him an ultra-clean look at all times. His eyes are bright in different shades of brown with a look of intelligence in them. It seems that everything Randy says is either intelligent or smart-ass, but always compelling. He's funny, and even though he's a big-shot junior, he puts me at ease and makes me feel like a friend.

I don't know, but there's something about his cheekbone structure in conjunction with his mouth and lips that complement each other just right. That nose of his is so cute I'd like to bite it. He also has that perfect imperfection, as I call it; a slight separation between his two front, brilliantly white teeth giving him a boyish mischievous look all the time. When the boy smiles, everything lights up too, highlighted by those fabulous dimples next to his kissable lips. It's not fair really, but he's got it all. Frankie's got the looks too, his cuteness factor is off the charts, but I'm not so sure he's all that smart. Hey, I've been cataloging boys' looks in my head for nine or ten years now, so I know what I'm talking about. Intruding on my daydreaming, I realize Randy's asked me a question so I say, "Excuse me, dude, what was that?" He chuckles and mutters, "Good answer." Instead of letting it go, curiosity gets the best of me, "No, what'd you want to know?" Randy gets up and walks over to stand in front of me a little too close for comfort. He runs the back of his fingers through my short hair, saying, "I asked if you'd like to mess around in my room a little." I try doing my fake cough, but it gets caught in my throat and comes out as a gasp. He ignores that and grins at me.

I'm four or five inches taller than Randy, but with me sitting on the arm of the chair and Randy standing between my legs, his head's a little above mine and I'm looking up at him as he stares back at me calmly. He casually puts his hand behind my head and this time rubs his knuckles through my hair slowly, mumbling, "I wasn't suggesting you get your hair cut this short when I told you need a haircut the other day." I go, "What?" then remember when he pushed my long hair up off my forehead saying I'd look even cuter with the hair off my forehead. He thinks I'm cute! His face gets so close to mine that I can smell spearmint gum on his breath when he says, "This haircut is too sexy for you, Oliver. You're plenty cute and hot enough with a normal haircut." By the time he finishes saying that, our lips are touching and I gulp, trying again to say something. Randy closes his lips on mine and I open my mouth a little so he pushed his spearmint gum from his mouth into mine and then does his version of a French kiss. I'm already way over stimulated when Randy demonstrates the difference between making-out with beginners and with him, an experienced university junior. Soon there's a boner in each of our pants as I go over backwards off the arm of the chair landing on my back on the seat with Randy and his boner on top of me.

The fall breaks our kiss and makes Randy laugh, saying, "You taste good, Oliver. I knew you would." He's lying comfortably on top of me with his sexy distinctive personal scent unlike any I've noticed on a boy before. And I say that even though he's sweaty from gymnastic practice. With our face almost touching, I quietly ask, "You want your gum back?" He kisses me on the cheek and with a chuckle, says, "What I'd rather have is you sucking me off. That's what I asked you that you claim you didn't hear. So, will you?" I mutter, "Okay," and we struggle to get up out of the chair, and mostly because of Randy's efforts we succeed in doing that. "Let's go to my room, Oliver," and just like that I follow him, thinking to myself, 'I'm so scared.' Yeah, but if I ever hope to be confident, I have to be decisive first. Plus, there isn't any reason I can't have some casual, playful sex with a hot kid like this. A kid who thinks I'm cute. Nothing wrong with that."

Because he's the co-captain of the wrestling team, he's allowed to room in the senior's dorm even though he's a junior. The senior dorms are the newest on campus and I hope to be in one of them in a few years. His roommate won't be back for at least an hour according to Randy. Inside the room he drops his gym shorts while apologizing for his sweaty condition. Then leaves his jockstrap on, asking, "Would you mind getting on your knees, Oliver? It's hot having someone blow me on their knees." As I'm getting down in front of him, feeling hypnotized or something, he mumbles, "I've had this funny thing for you ever since that first day we took you guys to lunch. You were sneaking glances at me all the whole time we were eating." He's rubbing my head with both his hands as he talks. It feels nice and adds to the casual confidence Randy seems to bring to everything. It's also a bit dominant of him and the kind of thing that puts me in a trance. He's taking for granted I'll do what he wants, and I get the sense he feels he can do with me what he wants. Now he's holding my head loosely in both hands, saying, "It would be fabulous if you could start by licking through my jockstrap. Why don't you start doing that now and later I'll let you taste my big cock. Okay?" Without waiting for me to agree, he pulls my head towards him until my face is tight up against his sweaty jockstrap. Randy talks in a normal conversational tone of voice, saying, "Just start tonguing under my jock and see if you can clean it with your tongue, really get my jock saturated with your saliva. Go ahead, Oliver." I'm in a trance staring into Randy's eyes, but I still notice the strong odor coming off his crotch, and it isn't an especially pleasant one. His jock smells pretty much like you'd think a sweaty jockstrap would smell. I like sucking a young guys cock though, so I ignore the smell convincing myself it's sexy. I began lapping just under his jockstrap near his hole.

I'm licking his jockstrap with fast licks and Randy goes, "Oh yeah, freshman, that's nice but try doing longer licks. Get your tongue way out. Let me see how much tongue you can get out of that cute mouth." My cock gets tight as I push my tongue out until it hurts and do long licks from his asshole over his nuts and cock encased in the jockstrap. Randy coos, "Ohh, good." It doesn't deem to surprise Randy I'm doing this, and it doesn't surprise me either. His ass is pretty much hairless like most of the rest of his body, including his legs. With an arm around each of his thighs, for something to hold on to, I continue doing long licks with my tongue all over his jockstrap's enclosed pubic area. Some pubic hairs peek out the sides of the jock looking more like regular hair than pubic hair. He pushes my head further under him until my head's between his muscle-bound thighs and they hold my head in place as I'm rimming him. It's unpleasant initially, but the more I lick his asshole the better I like it. The foul taste and smell quickly gets replaced with my spearmint gum saliva smell and after a short time his asshole is slippery with my spit and I'm lapping long licks all over his butt crack.

All the time I'm doing this, the gum from Randy's mouth is between my cheek and back teeth. He has me rimming him for at least five minutes until my cock is so hard it aches. My neck begins aching too from being bent backwards too long. I can't hear anything during this entire time because his thighs are flat against my ears holding my head in place. He gets two pinches of my short hair and pulls my head forward, face to face with his sweaty jockstrap again. His cock is now very hard and pointed up past the jockstrap's waistband. Randy's breathing is a short, fast burst of air as he says, "Now the jock again." I'm totally under his control and want so much to please him. I'm lapping at that stinky jock until it's saturated with my spit. Randy moans, "Ohhh shit, whoa. Wait a second, let me get this off," and with that he holds my head in place with another pinch of my hair, and with me helping, he finally steps out of his jock. His breathing is raspy as he strokes his long fat hard boner a half dozen times before murmuring, "Jesus, I'm glad you showed up, dude. I needed this." He's pulling on my hair again making me grimace, as he goes, "Be patient, I'll let you suck it." Then, positioned my face against his naked groin, I start hungrily lapping under his big balls. For a guy his size, he's really hung. Not quite as big as Pete, the mailroom kid, but almost. I try remembering some of the things Alexander did when sucking me off, but mostly I just do long laps all around his sweaty balls and then take one ball at a time into my mouth to tongue and suck. Done that, I lick his scrotum some more. It hangs kind of low and I can feel his large nuts rolling around in there.

Randy breathlessly grunts, "Get my pubes now, and use more tongue." I'm licking fast long licks in his pubes with random ones sticking inside my mouth, but it doesn't bother me now because my own cock is hard and throbbing and that's got a lot of my attention. When his pubic hairs are full of saliva and plastered to his shin, I begin lapping under his balls again before working my way up one side of his big boner, over the head, sucking off a big pre-cum bubble, and down the other side. It gets to be incredibly sexy licking Randy's private parts. "Oh, you're good, Oliver. Now lick all over my cock like it's a big lollypop." I lap up the outside of that long cock and around the sides, and up and down dragging my nose against his fat cock and on the way down, then my chin drags on it on my way up. My tongue is stretched way out of my mouth, flat against his great boner. After a few minutes of that big tongue action he grunts out, "Oh fuck ohhh," and he roughly pulls my head away slightly so he can get his cock in my mouth and I suck on the expanding head with my lips, and lap it with my tongue. This the best part for me.

While sucking the head of his cock, I stroke the shaft with my fist, stroking his wet stone-hard cock tightly. My cock is painfully hard so I unzip, pull it out and wildly jerk myself off continuing to suck of Randy's. It's so awesomely sexy... sucking Randy Rider's cock and fisting of my own boner in a blur of motion and, ohhhh, everything feels so good. All day I've been sexually stimulated by one thing or another and I desperately need an orgasm. Sloppy wet sucking sounds from my mouth as I'm making sounds in my throat of intense sexual pleasure and arousal. Randy moans, then says in a strangled voice, "I'm fucking close now, get ready to swallow my load," and he holds my head in both hands again and forces his fat cock head into my throat. I'm gagging until he pulls back and runs the head of his cock along the roof of my mouth as I'm gasping for oxygen, then in one smooth movement he forces it down my throat all the way, all the way down to my Adam's apple pressing his spit soaked crotch tight against my lips and teeth while he grinds his hip on my face, my nose squishing against his spit and sweat wet belly. Moaning openly now, he pulls his cock head up and then my throat, it goes again.

I'm on the verge of climax when he pulls his boner out of my throat a third time and it lays heavily on my tongue. Randy's rasping breathing sounds desperate now as his cock head begin expanding disturbingly large and he goes, "Eeeeeee, ooooh," contracting his stomach muscles forcing a long stream of creamy cum against the back of my throat, then a shot of cum at the roof of my mouth. He pulls his cock out entirely out of my mouth stroking it like crazy. It's a race who's stroking themselves faster, Randy or me. I need to swallow three times before all the cum in my mouth and throat. Randy's chewing gum gets swallowed too. The third stream of cum from Randy's long boner hits me right in my face as my back arches and I see stars as my orgasm flies out of my hard boner in a thin creamy stream of cum splattering against Randy's legs as I'm going, "Ohhhh fuck! Aghhhh, ooooh yeah." My second shot hits his legs too and Randy's smaller spurts of cum land in my hair, then we both pull tightly on our peckers milking drools of cum until our nuts are drained.

The big pitched squeaking and squealing sounds I made at climax cause Randy to give me an expression, like, "What the fuck...?" I shrug and we both have to chuckle at how goofy I sounded while climaxing. We're out of breath, but we have to laugh. Randy gives me a hug around my neck and then bends down to kiss me on the side of my face, exclaiming, "Oh my God, Oliver, that was freaking awesome! You rock, dude! I'm going to be following you around like your fucking dog begging you to suck me off again. That was something." I'm smiling at the compliment as he helps me up. We go into the bathroom to clean up. Picking up a used washcloth from the side of the sink, used by someone earlier, Randy washes my face with it and cleans the cum out of my hair, all the time telling me what a fantastic blow job it was. That's nice to hear, but the washcloth smells funky! When I'm relatively cum-free, he uses the same washcloth to clean the cum off his legs and then rubs his crotch and under his ass with it. After drying himself with paper towels, he checks out a pile of dirty clothes. Finding the cleanest dirty pair of boxer shorts, he puts it on, saying, "You're an expert at giving head, Oliver. You've had a lot of experience, haven't you?" He say this a neutral way, like he's sincerely interested. I tell him the truth, "I've done it only three or four times, but a thousand times in my head." Randy's surprised, as he says, "Wow, you're a natural! I hope you'll let me return the favor sometime. I'd really love to." I go, "Sure, Randy."

Getting a comb out of a drawer and while combing his hair, he goes, "My boyfriend, Danny, dumped me after all these months together so I'm single again." When he said that he sounded sad. I ask, "He dropped you?" Randy chuckles, mumbling, "Yeah, hard to imagine ain't it?" He takes me to the dorm's vending machine area where he buys both of us an ice cold bottle of water. I'm feeling so good. Getting my rocks off did wonders for my outlook. Randy says, "Ya know, I could fall for you, dude. Ya wanna be my boyfriend?" Smiling at him because I can tell he's just goofing around. I say, "Well what about my half a boyfriend? What am I going to do about him?" Randy finishes his water and goes, "It doesn't sound like he'd even know you dumped him since he doesn't know you two are boyfriends in the first place." I thought about that and mumble, "Oh yeah, that's a good point. Okay, let's get married...our children are going to be cute, don't ya think?" He squeezes the back of my neck and tells me that my half a boyfriend is a fool.

As we're walking together back to the common area, we talk about the University and then I tell him about my hot convertible Mini Cooper, which he thinks is way cool. Then I hear Joey call out, "Any time you're ready, Oliver. I'm just watching these guys play now." Randy and I bump fists and say, "See ya around the campus, dude," as he gets his book and goes back to his room. Someone has helped Joey hop over to his wheelchair. I've got a smile on my face, thinking, 'Not only am I fitting in at college, I've had a fabulously sexy weekend, made a great friend in Joey, and we're both almost straight As students. Plus, I've just had a hot and fun blow job with the hottest thing I've seen in college so far, so everything is coming up roses in Oliver's world.' Pushing Joey's wheelchair to my car, I stop behind a van, lean over and kiss Joey on the cheek, saying, "I really missed my master." Joey gives me a small smile and goes, "Get me in the car, slave. I need to pee like mad!" He always has to pee, and he always waits for me to help him do it, which is nice.

Putting the top down so the collapsible wheelchair will fit in the little back seat, we drive to our dorm and go directly to the bathroom where I plopped Joey on the toilet and hold his penis for him. He takes a sixty-second pee with me standing in front of him bending over holding his dick so he pees in the water and not on himself. My forehead rests on his shoulder and he leans the side of his head against mine, and says, "I missed you more than you missed me, I'll bet." He must be referring to me taking care of him, especially the hygiene stuff and the hand jobs. I mutter, "I'm the gay kid, so I missed you more," and he chuckles, "Yeah, but I'm the kid who can't reach my own dick." I ask, "You hungry?" I'm starving again and anxious to get to the dining hall, but Joey's much less enthusiastic about it, although he agrees to go. All he wants is a cup of chicken soup while I get the full pot roast dinner with ice cream and a brownie for dessert.

Joey looks away for most of the meal so finally I say, "Apparently, you're not going to tell me on your own, so I'm asking you point plank, what's wrong?" He beats around the bush for a bit, but finally admits he hasn't taking a crap for three days. He was too embarrassed to ask his mother to wipe his ass. He tries to make a joke of it by saying, "You're the only person I trust wiping my ass." Relieved that the only thing wrong is he's constipated, I say, "No problem, dude. This dorm room of ours has all kinds of first aid stuff including a couple of those Fleet enema bottles. We'll go back and I'll give you one of them right now." Joey says, "Just like that?" and I go, "Yep, just like that." He's shaking his head, muttering, "You're really a good friend, Oliver. Thanks, man." I was worried him being out of sorts might have had something to do with me. Like he'd been thinking about me being gay and taking care of him and maybe was feeling uncomfortable about it.

I'm determined to see that Joey feels better. Constipation isn't something I've had much experience with, but the few times I've been constipated it made me feel sluggish and slightly sick. Putting a straight-back chair in the bathroom next to the toilet, I get both Fleet enema bottles out of their boxes. Then, with a bit of difficulty, I get Joey naked and laying across my lap as I sit in the chair. First I lube his hole with creamy Vaseline, enjoying fingering him for a couple minutes. Not a peep out of Joey. Pushing my finger in his hole a couple of inches, I feel a hard stoppage. So, into his hole goes the nozzle of the Fleet enema tube and I squeeze in the solution steadily. Shortly, Joey complains of cramps, but I haven't even finished the first bottle. The instructions say one bottle will usually be more than enough for a two-hundred-pound person, but what the hell, we have two bottles so we might as well do it twice as good. What gives me pause though is Joey's about a hundred and thirty pounds. Then I figure, let's really clean his insides out once and for all... we'll use them both bottles.

Massaging under his belly low down near his dick, I'm hoping to relieve some of the cramping as I continue pumping the enema inside him figuring it'll get the solution up further into his bowels. I hear the growling inside him, sounding kind of like my stomach growling when I'm hungry. The cramping is still there, but it's enough so I can finish off the first bottle, and then the nozzle of the new one goes in his ass. Joey moans, "Oh my God this sucks." Squeezing in some more from the second enema bottle, I massage Joey's muscular buttocks, hoping it helps push the liquid inside him quicker. It startles the hell out of me when some brown water drools out his hole around the nozzle of the enema tube, "Hey, you're leaking, Joey. Hold it in so it can loosen everything up inside there." I dab at the smelly brown water, then give the enema bottle a big squeeze with Joey complaining, "It really hurts, I have bad cramps and I don't know how much longer I can hold it in. I'm straining my ass off as it is."

Doing some tough love for his benefit, I go, "Hmmmm. Try a little harder, dude. Work with me here. This isn't my idea of fun either, ya know." I'm a little disappointed he isn't more grateful I'm going through all this trouble for him. His voice is very strained, so feeling a sense of urgency to get the remainder of this second bottle inside him, I squeezed it all in him real fast. Proud of myself, I pull the nozzle out of his hole and just like that, a six-inch hard stream of shitty water follows the nozzle out of his asshole. "God damnit! Hold it in, Joey!" I shout, barely making out his groaning, "I can't hold it in any longer." Well, obviously I've got to get him on the toilet quickly, so I swing his legs around off my lap as a stream of shitty water is now coming out in a pressurized ten-inch spray and going all over everything, including me. "God damn it!" I yell again, getting him up on his one good leg, but he's disoriented, hopping around in a circle with that hose of shitty brown water shooting out of his hole covering everything in its path. He's going, "Ahhhhh," as he hops in that stupid circle. Grabbing his shoulders, I sit his ass down hard on the toilet seat and immediately hear clumps of waste matter hit the water. Good grief, just in the nick of time.

His stream of brown water crossed the toilet seat too so he's sitting in shitty water even as he evacuates his bowels. Taking all my clothes off except my underpants, muttering the whole time, I get out the bathroom cleaner and begin the clean-up. First, all the shitty water is wiped up using three large bath towels and then the Lysol disinfectant cleaner, the whole freaking container is sprayed around that bathroom and more clean towels are used to absorb the disinfectant. Then clean wet towels and finally clean dry towels soak the clean water up. All during the clean-up, Joey's groaning as he shits out four days worth of fecal matter. Gross smell all around us. I use all our towels so it's going to be a hell of a laundry load tomorrow and bleach is definitely gonna be a part of the wash. Joey keeps shitting periodically as I'm searching through the bathroom cabinets for other towels and I find two clean ones in Joey's cabinet under the sink. I'll use these for our bath. Sitting on the edge of the tub trying not to show Joey how distasteful this ordeal is to me, I watch him shit for fifteen minutes, then help him stand while I disinfected the toilet seat and clean his ass and the back of his legs with washcloths. He, me, and the entire bathroom are very clean when I've finished. Sweat's dripping off my face and glistening on my chest, I say, "Ta da! Nothing to it."

Joey's sitting on the clean toilet seat, again moaning and in between grunting out the last of the enema water, he gives me a goofy look and says in his pretend serious voice, "That went very well, don't ya thing, Oliver?" and we start laughing. It's so preposterous and silly I can't stop laughing thinking of Joey hopping in a circle while a stream of shitty water flies out his ass. For a second there, the laughing almost make me a pee my pants. Tears are running down our faces from laughing so hard. Snickering goes on for awhile with one of us twirling our index finger in a circle imitating Joey hoping around with that hose of brown shitty water firing out his ass hole and we get laughing again. By the time we're over the laughing, Joey's over his shitting and I wipe his ass real good for him as he mutters, "I'm so friggin' weak from shitting, but I feel so much better, Oliver. My ass hurts and my belly hurts, and I'm wicked tired, but other than that I'm great." I know how he feels, but we still need a bath so I get the water running and remove the soft casts from both arms. He holds his arms against his stomach and clasps his hands together to prevent sudden movement. The cast on his knee still needs the plastic cover. When he's situated in the warm water he goes, "Oh yeah Oliver, you were right, this bath feels good. How about you getting in with me like you did last Friday?"

Chapter 7
Phil

Joey asking me to join him in his bath is an unexpected request, so for fun, I act flabbergasted, "Are you inviting a self-proclaimed gay boy to share a bathtub with you? You're not drunk are you?" He laughs, "If the gay boy in question is my slave then it's okay by me, drunk or not." I go, "Oh, yes, my master, of course." The drunk comment refers to Joey's bath after the gymnasts' party when I shared the tub with him from necessity. Anyway, like most things with Joey and me, it's all light banter and doesn't necessarily mean anything. He may have been trying to do me a favor. That would be just like Joey. He knows I get aroused touching and taking care of him. I mean, he's seen my many boners as proof of that. He's also grateful for all my caregiving and especially the specialized stuff, so maybe he wants to return the favor.

I'm only wearing boxer shorts, which come right off and I step in the bathtub behind Joey and sit down behind him. As soon as I'm situated, he leans back against my chest and rests the back of his head on my shoulder. "Okay, now take care of me, slave," as he closes his eyes and his body completely relaxes against me. Quite quickly my boner grows and Joey mumbles, "I can feel that damn boner of yours. You better put a leash on it." I go, "You should probably close your eyes and mouth tightly now, Joey, because here comes a soapy sponge," and I wash his face, ears, neck and shoulders. Gee, he feels good against my chest. Taking my time, I slowly wash Joey's arms, hands, underarms, and then push him forward to wash his back. With an arm around his chest, I pull him back against me and wash the front of his torso. It's soothing and we both slip into a dreamy lazy mood, neither of us talking. Except for an occasional bit of noisy breathing from both of us, the only sounds in the bathroom are the subtle sounds of dripping water and a soapy sponge on slippery skin. By the time I get down to his belly button, the sponge is bumping into Joey's long fat boner and he doesn't have a leash on his either.

You don't need to be gay to get a boner from bodily contact. I've seen many boners on Joey so it doesn't surprise me that he has one now, but it does leave open the possibility that he's either bisexual or maybe even gay. I'll bet no one has touched his penis since the last time I touched it almost four days ago. For damn sure Joey hasn't touched it, he couldn't get his arms extended that far down, poor boy. Moving into a tight position in the tub, almost next to him, I wash his legs and feet. Joey still has his eyes lightly closed with a peaceful look on his face. Supporting him with my left arm around the back of his neck, holding his side against my chest, I go over his chest and stomach again, down close to his cock. This position wouldn't even be possible in most modern bathtub, but this old tub is huge. Joey's becoming a very clean boy as I scrub and scrub with that big bath sponge. The gel's lathered into thick creamy bubbles and helps me get Joey squeaky clean. Before washing his feet, I stare at them, so perfectly formed. Joey has rather small feet, and by the way, the misguided wisdom that small feet equal small penis definitely does not apply in Joey's case.

After soaping his feet, I let the sponge float in the water and use my hand to massage the soap into each foot because I like touching them. I don't think I'll ever take feet for granted again once I learned they're people who have a foot fetish and get sexually aroused by feet. Wish I had the fetish because in my mind, there's never enough ways to get sexually aroused. Finished with his lower extremities, I maneuvered in the tub until I'm sitting behind him again and begin sponging his private parts. We both remain very quiet as I wash his boner, balls, and all around his crotch, and then under his buttock. Joey raises one buttock and then the other to allow me access. We're familiar with the process by now. When he's up on his right buttock, I clean his left one and get the soapy sponge scrubbing all along his crack, and then using the corner of the sponge, a tiny bit up his hole too. Then I push the tip of my finger inside him for just a few seconds. He's so relaxed it goes in easily, but once inside, he closes his sphincter muscle tightly on my finger, holding it there briefly. There's a long windy sound from Joey as he whistles air quietly through his clenched teeth.

When I finished the bathing, I toss the sponge in the direction of the laundry basket and just relax in that warm soapy water with Joey, leaning back against me and my arms wrapped around his chest.

My cock is hard as steel pointing left up against his butt cheek. After a bit I ask, "You want your hair shampooed, Joey?" He's tired and in a quiet voice, he asks, "Can we do it tomorrow morning, Oliver? You know what I really need though, don't ya?" I mumble, "Sure, master," and I get some bath gel on my right hand and stroke that long cock of his while peeking around his shoulder so I can watch the uncut foreskin slide on and off his swollen cock head. It becomes so full of blood it's dark red. Only the top half of his cock head is out of the water up out of the water and probably leaking pre-cum by now. It's hard to tell because the bath water keeps sloshing up on it. Joey moan, "Oh yeah, tighter, Oliver, faster." He doesn't last two minutes before climaxing an amazing amount of creamy spunk that goes up, then over to splash against the side of the tub. Joey starts jerking around so much during his climax that he's gotten himself twisted sideways and his last cum shots, in short spurts, fire against the side of the tub. Really fast moving spunk. He climaxed too quickly to bring on my orgasm, but my sex play with Randy took care of my horniness for now.

Joey's still gulping and grunting at the after effects of his orgasm. I pull him back against my chest and sneak a kiss on his cheek. He told me once that before the accident, he was jerking himself off three or four times a day. A boy after my own heart, but I wonder what he thinks about while he's doing all that wanking. The days he was home over the weekend without even one climax must have been stressful for him, the poor horny boy. Nothing to do now except drain the tub and then use the hose with the shower head attachment to thoroughly rinse us both off. The water's very warm and feels so nice and relaxing that we lay together in the tub. I keep the shower head on us until the water starts to get cool. Then we struggle a bit getting out of that big, old tub and I dry us both. I'm standing in front of Joey and him sitting on that straight back chair I'd brought in earlier for the enema. That chair really helps the process along so I decide to leave it right here in the bathroom. See, the experience curve is kicking in. We're learning about shit like that in our business management course.

When I've dried Joey, I get a pair of clean boxer underwear, pull them up past his leg cast, put his light-weight cast back on his arms, and with Joey's help, I get him in his bed. Then, with me sitting next to him, we spent an hour going over course materials for tomorrow's classes. At the end of that, Joey gets comfortable under the covers ready for sleep. I'm about to turn off the lights when he complains that his rear-end feels raw from all the crapping he did earlier with the enema. Pulling the covers down and helping Joey get on his stomach, I pull down the back of his boxers and use creamy Vaseline to finger his hole pushing lots of creamy Vaseline into his ass with him quietly moaning with pleasure again. His hole doesn't look at all raw to me, but I know what this drill is about. It takes about ten minutes of fingering his hole and then another five minutes of fingering him while stroking his new boner before he finally has his second climax of the evening. It's a small one, but he does a lot of pleasure moaning along the way. Smiling to myself, I wipe up the spurt of cum as Joey collapses on his pillow and is asleep before I even finish cleaning the Vaseline off my finger. Back in the bedroom I climb in bed leaving only the night light on. It shines weakly on Joey's face so I study his looks for awhile.

If I go by my imaginary cute-o-meter, which assigned ratings of ten for Frankie and Randy, I guess I'll have to be honest and accept the fact that Joey isn't at their level. Joey actually only registers maybe an eight-minus. Hmmm, I really do like his olive complexion and his short dark curly hair is very nice too. He's a bean pole for sure, but a very fit bean pole, and then I think about his eyes. They're closed now but I can picture them in my head as dark blue eyes with long black curved eyelashes and a fine line of dark eyebrows. Whoa, his eyes are sex and go so nicely with that special smooth creamy olive complexion. I always want to lick his face. Okay, maybe he's not a ten per se, but he definitely has pedigree looks, no doubt about that, and he's sexy too. Striking looks surely must qualify him for a cute category of some kind, and so what if his nose is a little too big for his face. I love that nose 'cause it's Joey's nose. I see fuzz on his upper lip that will someday soon grow into whiskers and the same for the fuzz along his sideburns. Baby soft just beginning beards on young guys are the sexiest thing imaginable. He has nice pink lips and kinda small white teeth. Oh what the fuck was I thinking? He's cute! The hell with my cute-o-meter, Joey's cute in a special way. He's cute and pretty too, actually. And then I think again of his bean-pole, gymnast body with the muscle-packed buttocks and, oh jeez, it's exciting stuff! Just imagine being able to put my slippery boner between those two hard buttocks. Lord have mercy, I squirm under the covers groping my dick.

Somewhere along the line I fall asleep because the next thing I'm aware of is the alarm going off. First thing I do is look at Joey and see the night light still shining where Joey's face use to be. He's on his side now and doesn't seem to be noticing the light or the alarm. He must have had a terrible weekend. I feel bad for him because my three-day weekend was great. It's back to class now though. Classes, the drudgery of homework, and studying for exams. I'd set the alarm for a half hour earlier than normal so we'd have time to shampoo Joey's hair. It obviously hasn't been shampooed since the last time I did it. Getting out of bed, I gently shake Joey's shoulder and he says in his sleepy voice, "Good morning, Oliver, would you please help me get to the bathroom. I need to pee." Well, whats new about that? Getting him on the toilet and holding his dick, then getting him situated on the recently added bathroom chair, I can take a nice pee of my own. Joey looks away making some kind of sound in his throat, but he's seen my dick any number of times so I don't really know why he did the exaggerated look-away. After washing my hands and face and brushing my teeth, I do the same for Joey. Next is Joey's shampoo and massage routine, including his shoulder exercises. When all of that's done I pull off Joey's boxes and lay a soaking-wet, warm, washcloth on his pubic area to soften his pubic hair stubble. Joey claims ii's itching. Lathering his pubic stubble with shaving cream gets Joey biting his upper lip while experiencing shortness of breath. When I take out the safety razor, his cock begins boning up because of his fetish for shaved pubic hair.

Joey goes, "Ohh, wait a second Oliver. I can't catch my breath and my heart is going to beat itself out of my chest. This shaved pubes deal gets me kinda excited." I squeeze the back of his neck and he bends his head back to rub his head against my hand and I run my fingers through his hair, then massages his scalp. Joey murmurs, "That feels nice, Oliver. I think I'm okay now." What he means is I can shave his pubes without him spontaneously climaxing and shooting spunk all over the place. He hasn't been able to hold it off in the past, but we'll see how he does this time. Maybe the shaving will lose its sexual allure as we do it more and more. Holding his boner in my fist, I move it out of harm's way and carefully shave his lower belly and under his balls. Almost with the first scrape of the razor though, he goes, "Ahhh, oh my God," and squirms in the chair. Guess the allure is still there for him. I need to be alert to his squirming because I don't want to nick his skin with the razor. His boner's in my hand and I feel it getting harder and harder with each pass of the razor. Now there's some pre-cum drooling over my fist. Joey's a very sensual boy. He's squeezing his eyes closed, moaning with pleasure, and it's more than a little sexy for both of us. Each scrape of the razor is followed by a sexually turned-on moan from Joey as his fetish takes over his brain.

Funny thing about fetishes, there's no way to control your emotions when involved in one. Last time I did this his boner spurted spunk almost as soon as I began shaving him. Not this time though, so maybe he's getting used to it like I thought might happen. Finished shaving him as clean and hairless as a baby's ass, I'm verifying that I haven't missed a spot by rubbing my fingers all around his groin and somehow this triggers something and Joey goes "Agggh," as the first squirt of cum blurbs two inches out of his pee slit and joins the pre-cum already drooling over my fingers. Joey goes, "Oh, agggh, Oliver!" and I know he desperately wants me to stroke him off so he can get the full impact of his climax. Standing behind him now, I do my best to help him out. A few quick strokes pulling the uncut foreskin on and off the head of his boner causes a foot long string of creamy cum to fire out of that seven-inch boner with Joey making odd humming sounds. Next a fat, two-foot high spurt joins the previous one pooling on his belly and the humming sound changes to a funny squeal as Joey's shoulders shudder. I'm trying not to laugh, but come on, this is unusual. The remainder of the orgasm is creamy drools as I slowly stroke his cock milking his nuts dry. Joey was squirming so much I needed to wrap my arm around his narrow waist and hold him tight against the back of the chair. Then, when he's docile in the chair, I let go of him and use the same warm damp washcloth from earlier to clean up his cum. He moans quietly and contentedly with his head lulling forward.

It's actually very arousing for me being in control of his climaxes like this. Mostly though, it gives me a good feeling to be helping him get through his recovery period after the car wreck. Finished cleaning him, I rest my forehead on the top of his head and then, unable to stop myself, I give him a longish kiss on the side of his forehead and another one on his cheek. Joey's use to these kisses by now. As long as I don't overdo it, he doesn't seem to mind. The one time I tried kissing the side of his lips, he protested quietly so I haven't tried that again, but I'm very attached to him by now. There's some kind of special bond that's formed between us and I feel very protective of him. In a way I even love him. Not romantically I guess, but I feel love for Joey.

Ignoring my kisses, Joey laughs at himself, saying, "This crazy fetish of mine! Huh, Oliver? How do you figure fetishes? I should be so embarrassed about climaxing like that my face gets so red and hot it breaks out in flames, but your manner is so kind I sometimes forget how weird I am." I mutter, "You're not weird. Many people have fetishes, and a lot of them are way more bizarre than yours." He mumblers, "I guess you're right, Oliver. There are some off the chain bizarre fetishes out there. I read about some of them on Google, although mine didn't get mentioned." Earlier, while I was shampooing his hair, he told me how much better he felt this morning, referring to his bowels and his ass because of the enema last night. So now he feels great in that other special area too. His climaxes have taken care of his horniness for the moment and he's back to his nice smiley self.

He's a year younger than me because I'd taken a year off from middle school after my friend died, so I'm a nineteen-year-old freshman and Joey's the usual freshman age of eighteen. The thing is, I've come to kind of think of Joey as my younger brother, the one I never had, and I'm determined to be just as good a big brother to Joey as Christian always was to me. I get us both dressed and we make it to class on time. Things started off good this morning and the entire day goes very well too. Especially the last period because the professor taped a note on the door saying he had to go home early to deal with a family emergency. Ha! We're done for the day early. It's an unusually nice day for fall in the northeast so Joey and I enjoy some sun outside while we smoke a few cigarettes. Frankie Nerney got me hooked on cigarettes and Joey tells me his friend who died in the car accident got him hooked on smoking when they were juniors in high school. He's chokes up discussing his friend's death and sheds a few tears without being embarrassed about it. I listen as he tells me how often he thinks about his dead friend, making me think of Tyler so many years ago. Joey and I have a lot in common. As we talk, I hold the cigarette to Joey's lips and he drags on it, then I take a drag feeling a little dampness from his saliva and I like that. This is how we smoke, sharing the same cigarette. I leave some of my saliva on the filter for him. After a bit, we laugh about that, which is good because it gets Joey thinking about something besides the accident.

I ask about his doctor's appointment and he tells me how well that went and how excited he'll have the casts off permanently over the Thanksgiving break. Joey's voice gets a little emotional again, but this time from anticipating being free of his casts at last. I go, "Just think how happy I'll be not to need to wipe your ass after your frequent craps." Joey goes, "You love doing that so I'm gonna have you do it for me even after the casts come off, and the same when I need to take a piss. You'll hold my dick for me. Whaddaya say?" I mutter, "Put down the crack pipe and get sober. You're delusional, master." We goof around with no sense like that as we're taking our time getting to gymnastics practice. Joey is helping arrange the gymnasts' floor exercises. He's become sort of an unofficial assistant coach, which keeps him busy and involved with the team. It's obvious he's popular and appears to have natural leadership skills. Hanging around practice for a while, I spot Randy who nods his head at me. Casually sauntering over to where he's working out, I watch him practice with his coach, amazed at how athletic gymnasts are.

Ten minutes later, he's done working with his coach, who moves on to the next gymnast. Randy's looking so cool as he glides over to me, his feet barely touching the floor. When he gets near me, his cute face brakes out in this awesome smile, which he seemed to be trying to hold back. He sits down on the bleacher row in front of me and turns around to go, "Bow wow," and we chuckled at that because yesterday, he said he'd probably follow me around like my dog begging me to blow him again. I mutter, "Any time, dude" and he's like, "No, my turn next time, but you're a tough act to follow." We try agreeing on a time to hook up, but he decides he needs to check the team's schedule first so he tells me to look him up tomorrow at practice. He's more or less telling me what to do, but he's a junior so I don't mind. He's established that he's the dominant one between us and I'm fine with that. Hell, he's interested in me and I'm feeling good about myself because of that. Randy Rider's the hottest guy I've seen at the university, and he's got a thing for little ole Oliver Nickerson and that's a big deal to me.

Monday was a good day, but of course there's always a little crap in everyone's life, and Tuesdays usually provides some for me. It's laundry day and today I have all those shit stained towels to wash in addition to the regular weekly wash for Joey and me. Add to that Richards' and Phil's laundry too. So balls! Oh well, a lot of things are going my way lately so I'm not going to dwell on this one negative. Even though this Tuesday's an extra-large wash load, it can be done in less than two hours. That includes washed, dried, folded, and delivered. I might as well get started, but my mind's still mostly on Randy Rider. He told me yesterday he wants to suck me off. Sweet! As I'm gathering up the shitty towels, stuffing them into two large plastic trash bags, I think how I'd rather be enjoying this beautiful day outside and just leave the laundry for tomorrow. I can't because Richard insists on me doing his laundry on Tuesdays, and that bully, Phil, will smack my ass silly if I try to change it. What a prick Phil is. I haven't even seen the other prick, Richard, since he handed the job of supervising my laundry chores to Phil. Richard is clever too, he's covering Phil's and his ass by paying for the cost of Joey and my laundromat including the cost of the dryers. If I ever complained to someone about having to do their laundry, it will look like I'm earning money doing it. It's a paying job, so what am I bitching about, right? They're seniors so I'm not about to complain anyway. No one ever believes a freshman about anything. Oh and there's one other thing, they'd kick my ass if I told anyone.

Carrying the shitty towels down first, I get them going on the heavy cycle with bleach, extra detergent, and a second rinse. Then I hurry up to get Phil and Richard's laundry on the third floor. Phil doesn't like it if I'm late because he has to stay in the room until I get there. The thing about this chain of command, from Richard to Phil to me, is that if something gets screwed up with their laundry, Phil, not me, endures Richard's wrath. Phil's scared of Richard and I guess so am I because he can't control his temper, and he doesn't know his own strength. If only I hadn't bumped into that prick when I first got here, he'd never even know I was alive. Then, to make matters worse, later I also knocked his clean clothes on the dirty floor in the laundromat. Shit-terrible luck! So, now I either do his laundry or get beat-up. There's a side benefit to this though and it's that none of the senior wrestlers fuck with me at all because they know I'm Richard's flunky and everyone thinks Richard is nuts. All the other freshman in our dorm have had unpleasant experiences with the third floor bullies. Senior wrestlers, what a bunch of assholes they are.

Oh well, here goes. Knocking twice on Phil's door, I need to wait as much as five minutes some days. I'm nervous as I always am when picking up their laundry. That's because Phil has this thing about smacking my ass. He yells, "Come in, ya dumb ass, it's open." When I step inside, he says, "I told ya before, just come the fuck in. You're the laundry boy, ya don't have to knock!" He never fucking told me that. He's lying on his bed, "Oh, something else, dumb ass, there's an extra duffel bag of stuff I want laundered today. I brought it back with me from home after our three day weekend. It's some of my winter stuff. You'll need to make two trips probably." I'm frowning and he yells, "Well, what the fuck are you staring at? Get moving." Phil seems very edgy today. Edgy and scary so I make sure not to say anything. Even so, apparently my frown at the mention of extra laundry struck him the wrong way.

I could see it coming from his expression. Without a word, he storms off his bed and does some kind of wrestling move so fast it's like it never happened, but I'm on my ass looking up at the ceiling. I don't even know if I'm hurt. Phil's face is bright red as all of these maniacs are on something, steroids or God knows what, but they're unbalanced and borderline crazy. Phil snarls, "I do not intend to put up with any shit from you today, girlie-boy. No annoyed faces, no back talk, no nothing! Just do what you're fucking told. Ya got that?" I'm beginning to realize my left wrist has been sprained, probably when I tried to break my fall. I hold it in my right hand and massage it, trying to determine the extent of my injury. It doesn't seem too bad. Phil blurts out, "You skinny shit! I asked you a question," and with that, he yanks me to my feet and pushes me to bend me over onto his desk top. His left hand at the back of my neck, pinning my face against an open book. The button on my jeans pops off when he violently pulled my jeans and underpants down. Then the palm of his right hand is snapping off slap after slap on my bare ass.

I'm helpless against this brute and while I should probably be humiliated to have my pants pulled down with my cock swinging against the desk with each loud slap on my bare ass, mostly I concentrate on not peeing myself. That's mostly what I concentrated on the last time he spanked me too. Didn't work though. It's never obvious to me what sets this maniac off. He smacks my ass until he's out of breath. As soon as he stops, I start begging him that I've had enough because the pain just builds and builds. "Please Phil, I'm sorry. I'll get all your stuff and do it all first. I promise it'll be done right. I didn't mean to ignore your question." I can hear his heavy breathing and only some of it's from exertion because he appears to get sexually aroused spanking me. I've seen and even felt his boner from time to time, but always inside his pants as he's never exposed himself. Breathlessly, Phil says, "You are a maggot and the next time you disrespect me it will be much worse. Got it, maggot?" I mumble, "Yes, I'm sorry. Please, I learned my lesson" With me begging in the background, he gives my ass a dozen more deliberate smacks, each one harder than the one before it, and even through I'm squeezing it closed with all my might my bladder spurts out a few squirts of pee as tears break out from my eyes. So much for begging. The pee is on my thigh and down on my crumpled pants hanging just under my limp dick.

Still pressing my face against his desktop, he grunts out, "Get all the fucking clothes, clean the fucking clothes, dry the fucking clothes, fold 'em and get them back up here fucking fast. Got it?" I say real quick, "Yes Phil, right away". He backs away breathing hard and says, "Don't move, pussy, stay on that desk, I'm not done with you. When you bring the clean, folded clothes back up here, not a single word from you. Keep your head down, don't you dare make eye contact with me. Put the clothes away, and then come in here and drop your drawers and lean over this desk just like you're doing right now. You wait like that while I inspect the job you did and decide if you need another smack or two on your ass. Got it?" I quickly say, "Yes, Phil." He tells me to go ahead then and do what I'm told. Straightening up from his desk, quickly pulling up my wet underwear and jeans, I walk quickly into the utility room to get his duffel bag and place it outside the dorm room door, then back in to get the overflowing laundry basket. Keeping my head humbly down all the time, but he never looked up anyway, which I'm grateful for because he'd see the big pee stain on the front of my jeans. My buttocks are burning and sore as hell and it hurts to walk, but I'm doing everything quickly just the same. Holding the laundry in front of me to hide the pee stain, I hurry from the room. Going down the stairs there's no fooling myself, Phil totally dominates me and I'm going to be a little scared mouse whenever I see him. He's twice my size and a senior who's also a wrestler. Next time, I'm doing what he just said. I'm keeping my head humbly down and quickly doing whatever he says, keeping my mouth shut. No one else sees me like that but Phil. It's something I need to live with. It's only once a week for a short period of time and from now on, I'm going to be totally submissive and cooperative with him. It's the best way to avoid a spanking and he really hurts me with those spankings.

In the laundromat, there are a few other kids doing laundry, none I know and thank God for that. It's necessary to keep something in front of me at all times to hide my pee stained pants in the laundromat too. I get the washing machines going and then back to my room to clean myself up and change clothes. I'm feeling sorry for myself the whole time. All the good feelings I'd had just a little while ago vanish into oblivion. I know I'm acting like a coward, but what options do I realistically have? Doing what I'm told will elicit the least bad consequences. Being a hero won't work like it does in movies. Fuck it! It's my dirty secret.

In my bathroom, I run cold water in the tub, fold two hand towels as a cushion and sit on them bare ass in the cold water. The stinging pain from my butt cheeks makes my eyes water, but I'm not crying. That's one battle I'm winning. All my efforts now go into not crying. I've got to conquer that urge I've had since, well since Tyler's death. I've been a crybaby at times and I'm too old for that shit. At first all I care about is relieving the burning stinging on my ass cheeks, but when they feel a bit better, I spend all my energy hating on Phil and to a lesser degree, Richard. After exhausting my hate energy, I try to understand it all and I still can't come up with any better explanation then, wicked bad luck on my part to get myself involved with a sadist like Phil. Richard almost seems normal compared to Phil. Phil's one sick motherfucker alright. Then I wonder why I accept the wicked good luck I experience as what I deserved, but wicked bad luck is not what I deserved at all. After trying to analyze that I feel a headache coming on so I drag my smacked ass out of the tub and get dressed.

Back in the laundromat, I switch everything from the washing machines to the dryers and then go into the vending area for a Snapple. My ass is still hurts and stings, but it's not throbbing like earlier. It's still bad enough that I don't want to sit down. Only worked in the tub because of the cold water and the folded towel. Walking outside with my drink, I have a cigarette still trying to figure out some fucking solution to my troubles with Phil. He can't be reasoned with though, and he told me just last week that Richard's rougher on him that he, Phil, is on me. In any case, he doesn't want to hear any whining from me. They're animals, there fucking animals and they deserve each other, but do I deserve this treatment for bumping accidentally into Richard twice? I don't think so. Fucking animals. I don't even care that much about the humiliation Phil puts me through because, like I said, no one ever witnesses it but him.

As these thoughts swish around in my brain, I absently do one of my favorite things, which is boy-watching. Evaluating a guy's looks as they walk past. It goes like this: nothing special about him, nothing special again, Oh my god, ugh! Nothing special, nice hair, hot bod but goofy face, nothing special and then, yes very cute. Ha ha! Not many winners, that's for sure. Dumping my empty bottle in a recycle bin, I casually sauntered over to get a better look at this one cute boy out of ten. I haven't seen him on campus before. Light brown hair, medium complexion, with big alert shining blue eyes. Jeez, nice body and my type too. Thin, well maybe this guy, he's skinny. He's wearing a tight sleeveless T-shirt, laughing with an older version of himself. Frowning, I'm thinking, 'They can't be twins,' and then it's obvious; the super cute boy is too young to be in college so he's got to be the other kid's little brother visiting him in college. That's cool. The older kid puts his arm around his younger brother's shoulder and off they go. I think of Joey, then feel all warm inside. Never mind asshole Phil, I'll concentrate on all the positive things that are happening in my life. I have to deal with Phil in about fifteen minutes a week but that piece of shit has to be with himself twenty-four hours a day every day of his miserable life. Thinking about that makes me feel better. Fuck you, Phil, ya sick bastard. Back in the laundromat, I carefully fold Phil's clothing and then Richard's. After going back over every piece to be sure none of Phil's is mixed in with Richard's, I carried half of them upstairs. Then, like I was told, without knocking, I cautiously open the door. As soon as I turn the knob, my heart starts pounding with fear, apprehension, whatever. I walk in and go directly to Phil's dresser and put his regular clothes away and his new winter ones stacked neatly on his bed. Then, without a word, I go right back down to get Richard's clothes and do the same with them. One last look to see everything's correctly in order. Satisfied, I go over to Phil's desk, pull down my jeans and underwear and lean over with my chest flat against his desk top, my bare ass sticking out and my dick and nuts shriveling up.

I saw Phil out of the corner of my eye watching me from the second I walked in. He looks up from the body builder magazine he was pretending to read. He's sitting in a big over-stuffed chair. Closing the magazine and dropping it next to the chair, he says, "Stay just like that, you pussy," and he goes over to verify I'd gotten everything put away correctly. I'm nervous as hell, sweat on my forehead, my breathing is too quick and my heart's pounding away like a hummingbird's heart. It's at least two humiliating minutes bent over on his deal with my bare ass and privates on display. My dick's shriveling up like I've been in a swimming pool and my nuts are the size of raisins. Phil slowly walks over and lightly rubs both my ass cheeks, which makes them sting again, but I don't utter a sound. "Jesus, hehe heh. I spanked these butt cheeks a nice bright cherry red color," Phil mumbles to himself with a snicker.

He smacks each butt cheek twice, very hard, "SMACK! SMACK" then "SMACK!SMACK!" and says, "Stand up and turn around." I do that with both my hands behind me rubbing my ass. Phil looks at my package, says, "Turn around again," pulls one of my hands away and rubs the pad of a finger up my ass crack hesitating at my asshole before completing the short journey. "Pull your pants up, pussy, and get the fuck outtta here. Next week you better have a happy look on that girlie face of yours. All ya gotta do is what you're told to do for fuck sake. That shouldn't be too hard even for a maggot like you." Those last smacks start the hot burning stinging all over again. My head down, making sure not to have eye contact, I pull up my pants and scurry out the door before even buttoning up the front of my jeans and I almost run into Richard who's coming in. He says, "Oh yeah, laundry day, Oliver. Phil treating ya okay?" I say, "Yes, it's laundry day. How are you, Richard?" He mumbles, "Whatever," and goes inside as I hurry back to the laundromat to finish Joey's and my stuff, plus all our towels.

Just knowing I won't have to see Phil for a whole week makes my eyes water with glee. The treatment I get from Phil isn't right, fair, or in any way justified, but it's over with for another week so I'm putting it out of my mind completely. Next Tuesday, I'll make sure I don't say anything unless I'm spoken to, and I'll make damn sure I have a pleasant expression on my face so I can avoid the spanking. And, oh yes, avoid eye contact with Phil. There's a lot to remember so I go over these things a few times in my head, and then drop the topic from my brain. It doesn't take long to finish up the rest of my laundry and soon I'm outside in the beautiful, unseasonably warm sunny day with a stinging red smacked ass and a shattered self-image, but it is what it is. Lighting a cigarette, I'm enjoying the sunshine while not thinking about anything in particular, just walking slowly to nowhere when from nowhere, tears burst out of my eyes and I start crying hard.

Dropping the cigarette and covering my face with my hands and slump down on the grass leaning against a huge oak tree. No one seems to notice as my shoulders shake like a six-year-old and I bawl uncontrollably. Of course this crying jag is because of Phil's humiliating and painful treatment, but I'm shocked at the severity of my emotional breakdown. The feeling of being powerless and of being afraid, and I guess it's also disturbing to think that maybe I'm a coward in the way I cower to him. Oh hell, the injustice of the entire laundry debacle overwhelms me and it's all so depressing that this wild crying jag has completely taken over. Crying this hard takes a tremendous amount of energy. Mostly it's over in a few minutes, but I'm exhausted from it just the same. Lying down completely on the grass now, my forearm across my eyes, I take deep breaths ignoring the stinging on my ass. Feeling a bit more in control, I wipe my face and nose with the bottom part of my T-shirt, then light another cigarette, sitting up again. This is where cigarettes come in handy, offering something to do to keep you occupied and keep your mind numb. It's not as if this is the first time I've felt all those kinds of negative emotions. I felt them from my first encounter with Richard too. Actually I've felt them before him, too. I've experienced the same type emotion with every bully who's bullied me throughout my entire life and, ya know, there have been too goddamn many of them for it to be a coincidence. In high school whenever a bully was having a bad day, he'd start asking around for that Dickerson kid. I'm doing something that attracts bullies, but what?

No answer comes to mind, but there has to be some reason other than just bad luck. Getting on my feet, feeling ridiculous for crying like that, I'm glancing around to see if anyone I know witnessed my breakdown. That makes me realize how few people I actually know here at the University. Who the hell did I think I'd see who knows me? My responsibilities in taking care of Joey limit my opportunity to mingle with kids other than the gymnast, and they're mostly interested in other gymnast. I'm just a necessary temporary outsider as far as they're concerned, except maybe for Randy. Feeling down in the dumps again, I'm worrying that maybe I suffer from depression, huh?

I don't need to pick up Joey for over an hour so, down in the dumps or not, I'm determined not to waste this free time outside in the sun. What to do though? Okay, I've got the time so I'll walk over to the Campus Mall where I'd first saw Cristobal four or five months ago. Thinking of him makes me daydream about my first gay kiss, my first dance with a boy, and my first gay sex. All with Cristobal of course. Somehow, if he were here everything would be different. That's what I tell myself anyway, this is just rationalizing though because why would it be better even if he were here. Well, maybe I wouldn't have run into Richard for one thing. At the street mall I notice there's only one street singer today and he's no Cristobal. An overweight kid with a full beard and a flat voice. For some reason the beard makes me think of my neighbor Edward, who fucked me when I was younger . That memory was buried in my sub-conscious mind until the trip to Seattle visiting Christian. Hmmm, so technically Christobal wasn't my first gay sex, but I can't see how thinking along weird stuff like that helps anything, so I decide to keep Cristobal as my official first time. I'm in this weird frame of mind walking the street with all these strangers around me which just intensified my feelings of loneliness. I try doing some boy-watching, staring quickly at every face of interest, but don't see a single one that qualifies as cute. Wandering to Cristobal's old dorm thinking about how much nicer my dorm is then the one he had last year. While this walk isn't improving my mood, on the positive side, my ass is feeling a lot better.

It's just about time to pick up Joey so I try getting myself fired up about that. Hey, and maybe Randy and I are actually becoming a couple too. Nah, I can't make myself take that seriously. Thinking about

Frankie and all the issues he has with Darlene, and with himself too. Ya know, with his denial of his true sexuality. What future is there for me with Frankie, I mean if I'm honest with myself? And Alexander has turned into a bit of a dick although a fun dick. He's a good sex buddy anyway. But there's no future for me with him. Spunky, Myers, Pete are also no, no, and no, future-wise. Then I'm thinking: for fuck sake, I'm only nineteen years old, I've got my whole life ahead of me. I'll eventually meet the right guy to have a future with. My frame of mind had been excellent before that animal Phil beat me up, so I tell myself to think about the hot fun things that have been going on in your life lately. I'm lucky in my sex life! Then, just like that, I realize I've talked myself in a complete circle and I'm on my way back to feeling upbeat again. I mean, I hate being a pussy with all this whining and feeling sorry for myself. Enjoy yourself! That's my latest motto. Hey, that motto is really catchy and wicked original too. Enjoy yourself!

College is the best time in our lives, right? Feeling proud of myself for working out of the funk so quickly, and doing it by myself too. It used to be I'd run to Christian with every problem that came up, but now I'm learning how to deal with my problems myself. Gee, I better be careful not to pull a muscle patting myself on the back. Checking my watch as I walk into the gymnasium, I still have half an hour before practice is over, so I'll watch some hot gymnastics till then. Gymnasts are amazing athletes. Walking by the equipment room on my way to the gym, someone grabs me from behind and pulls me inside. The special sexy odor of Randy Rider gives him away though, not to mention his little chuckles as I stagger before falling backward into his arms. Inside he says, "Hi, ya sexy hottie. We got ten minutes to screw around if ya want to. Do ya?" While turning around I go, "Oh, okay," and we both go for each other's lips. Randy's a good make-out, and his strong hands and arms are all over my body giving me shivers and goose bumps and tiny electric shocks. It seems strange to say that I look up to Randy because he's actually four inches shorter than me, but even so I always do feel like I am looking up to him. He's kind of my idol, I guess.

His wet sloppy kisses and sucking on my lips and tongue gets me so hard, so fast, it's scary and exciting. Sort of like a thrill ride at an amusement park. Plus, the way he smells, that natural sexy odor of his augmented by a hot sexy perspiration smell which threatens to override everything, but adds to my attraction to him. He's been practicing hard for two hours and his whole body's sweaty damp, but he has me swooning and moaning in spite of it. Almost immediately, Randy has his hand inside the back of my jeans grabbing my bare ass. Stinging ass or not, it's such a turn-on having a guy's bare hand fondling my bare ass. If it's Randy giving me a spanking, well that might be sexy. Randy's special as I moan into his mouth and hump my hips into his belly just above his crotch. He's in the process of giving me his own quick version of a hickey when he pushes his finger up inside me. My hole burns initially as he finger-fucks me with little strokes, but then it gets slippery and feels good! I mutter, "Do you think we have time for the real thing?" Randy goes, "Nah, not this time, but we'll make time soon." Then he begins thrusting up my hole using his middle finger and I go up on my toes with each thrust going, "Ahhh," with each penetration.

My boner's soon dripping inside my pants pressed into Randy's side. He finishes with the hickey and pulls his finger out of me to begin massaging both my buttocks using his strong hands, squeezing them too hard and it hurts my spanked ass. He's almost picking me off the floor, pulling up on my buttocks and there's an extra sexy something I'm sensing, maybe because Randy has no idea I'd gotten that hard spanking a few hours ago, but because it's Randy doing it, I'm incredibly turned-on. I grunt, "Um, it hurts, Randy." He puts his lips to my ear, "Some pain with sex heightens the pleasure. They'll be pain when I fuck you. I just want to see if you can take it." Oh, I can take it alright. His tongue goes back in my ear and squishes around, then his tongue's in my mouth again and I'm close to cuming as I hear myself making little squealing noises and saying Randy's name. I feel like such a dork doing that but I can't stop. His fingers in my ass again and he has me bent over finger-fucking me hard now, I'm soon red-faced, out of breath, and partially hypnotized. When he's satisfied, he's gotten me as hot as I need to be, he pulls his finger out, straightens me up holding my head with a hand on either side of my face and looks me in the eyes, saying, "I know I said it's my turn to do you, but I want you to suck me off real quick right now and then I'll owe you two." The shit smell from his middle finger is close to my nose as he speaks, but I numbly nod my head and get down on my knees in front of him.

Same deal as last time, only quicker. Randy's much sweatier this time too, but I swear I don't mind. I'm flattered he wants me sucking him off and I'm so hot and horny from all his attention, it's surreal. This time while rimming him, I try impressing him by getting the tip of my tongue further inside his asshole and I think I have some success. He's saying "Oh yeah, Oliver, push harder, oh yeah." It's a little gross down here at first, but it's Randy so I don't mind and I'll get used to it with practice. I lap his sweat-soaked jockstrap for a bit, but Randy's short on time so he takes his jock off and presses my face into his sweaty crotch. His cock's very hard, sticking straight up his belly, drooling pre-cum. It presses against my forehead and his balls hang underneath my chin. I never stop licking and lapping for a second, my tongue's aching from the effort but I keep at it with Randy encouraging me to keep it up, "You're doing great, Oliver, oh yeah. Lick more there, more Oliver, use longer laps." My tongue is licking his crotch clean and before I know it, Randy's deep-throating me again. He manipulates my head in his strong hands and really goes at fucking my mouth and throat with his long fat boner going down my throat further than it did the first time and me gagging with every thrust. For me it's truly awesome to be sexually dominated so fully and my balls tighten up against my belly so I undo the front of my pants to get at my cock. Almost immediately, those hard nuts send my spunk flying up and out of my boner. I'd only stroked it three times and the head of my cock burns as the cum flies out. Actually, I would have climaxed without touching my cock at all except the urge was strong and made me grab it and stroke it. Randy got me so sexually alive I feel like electricity is making my whole body vibrate.

The last sensations of orgasm sizzle away and then Randy's climax goes off like a supernova with an avalanche of spunk shooting up and out of those big balls of his. Lots and lots of creamy spunk down my throat, in my mouth, and on my face and neck when he pulls his cock from my mouth and strokes it. It's too much too fast down my throat and I hiccup cum up my sinuses and some spurt out my nose where it drools around the outside of my mouth with me catching some on my tongue. After blasting his major load in my throat and mouth like last time, he pulls his boner out and strokes it in a frenzy and that's now I've gotten his cum drooling down my face, and like I said, out of my nose.

I'm gulping and hawking up his cum from my sinuses and he uses his cock to smear his cum around my face as I sit back on my ankles in a trance. Randy's breathing deeply while using his hand now to wipe the cum in my hair. I see a mean streak in him as I'm coming down off the high of climaxing.

In a fog, I notice my own cum shots had miraculously gone through the narrow opening between Randy's legs. He's grinning now, mumbling, "You'd let me do whatever I want with you, wouldn't you?" In a daze, not sure what he means, I nod my head and he says, "Get the fuck up, Oliver, and let's clean you up. Come on, get up!" When I stand, he smirks and says, "You like a little abuse, don't ya?" He sounds out of breath as he talks while pulling up his pants. I'm not sure what he means by abuse, but I do what he says and get up. He takes a small sweaty towel that's hanging out the back pocket of his gym shorts and wipes his own sweaty face with it first, then reaching up, he uses it to try wiping the cum off my face. After each swipe of the towel, he spits on it then wipes my face. His spit smells nice and reminds me of the same thing when I cleaned Spunky's lipstick off. I used my spit on a handkerchief as a cleaning fluid. And like Spunky did for me, I stand still for Randy.

When he's got most of the cum off my face and hair, Randy cups the back of my head with his left hand and holding that funky smelling towel against my nose with his other hand, he says, "Blow hard, Oliver, you've got some of my cum up your nose." He makes me blow hard three times before he's satisfied and I feel like I'm a six-year-old as I submissively stand here and do what he tells me. As Randy's treating me like his kid, he's whining about how much he misses his boyfriend. He claims he's relieving his pent-up sexual needs on me and, "I just want to say thanks for being here for me, Oliver. You're helping me get through this break-up. Now I owe you two blow jobs." I'm staring back, coming out of my trance. He looks puzzled now, asking, "You're really getting off on me dominating you, aren't you?" Again I'm not sure what he means. He nods his head grinning, saying, "Yeah, you do. Open your mouth." When I do, he puts the finger he had up my hole and he tells me to suck it clean. Surprising myself, I do it and yuck, what an unpleasant acrid taste. Thirty seconds of sucking his finger and the taste miraculously is gone. Randy pulls it out and rubs it up the front of my nose with some of my spit going up my nostrils, as he asks, "Smell okay?" I nod my head, still in my usual trance. Randy smiles, saying, "I'm still a little fucked-up about Danny dumping me at the moment, but I've got some ideas for you that I'm thinking you're gonna love. You might not even know it, but you are a very naively submissive boy. I'm gonna put my big boy dominant pants on and have myself some fun with my very own slave boy. Would you like that?" I shrug, again not at all sure what he means." He grins again, patting my cheek, saying, "Yeah, this is gonna be fun, but for right now, I gotta go," and he sprints out the door to go wherever it is he needs to go.

Standing here, still in a bit of a trance-like state of mind, I'm absently wiping the palm of my hand over my face wondering what he meant by all that. It sounded like he wants us to have a closer relationship, which I'm definitely in favor of. I can feel some cum shot still in my hair and around my face so I shake my head getting back to reality and head for the lavatory to wash up. Wow, talk about the unexpected though! I already said it's surreal that Randy's interested in me and now he seems even more interested than before. Fantasizing about me and Randy spending a night together in bed sometime, I go in the lavatory and look in the mirror. Ha ha, Randy did a lousy job of cleaning his cum off my face. I wash my face and hands really well, then my head. After drying myself with paper towels, I went off looking for Joey. Realistically spending a night with Randy can't happen until Joey is able to take care of himself. You know, when he can be on his own for the night. Then I think, 'Whoa Oliver, you're getting way ahead of yourself! You need to calm down.' He never said anything about spending the night together. He said something about doing something I'd love. It was awkward listening to him confess how broken-up he is over being dumped. He wears his heart on his sleeve but I do not want to get involved in their break-up.

I find Joey, who gives me that sweet smile of his, so I rub his hair, "How ya doing, Joey?" and off we go to the dorm. We'll drop off our backpacks, and then to the dining hall. Joey's in a good mood and that helps me stay upbeat too. It's been a rollercoaster ride of emotions for me today, but I'm feeling good now. My mind keeps drifting to that last quickie with Randy and the way he's taking more and more interest in me every time we get together. He's so confident and in-charge, even bossy, but he's nice too. It's so cool being with him and doing what he tells me. Thinking about that gives me a semi-boner and I'm not sure why. I try to understand through most of my dinner why I get a submissive feeling when I'm with certain sexy guys. I like when they're bossy, and I think I first noticed that on the boardwalk when that cool guy, Mike Sullivan, dominated me. And we didn't even have sex. Man, there's a fun fantasy right there. Mike would be a hell of a dominant sex partner. I'm letting my imagination run away with me, but wouldn't it be hot if Mike's cute friend Richie were gay too? Jeez, haha! I'd like to make it a threesome. Unfortunately reality doesn't for things to work out that perfectly. Sigh....

Chapter 8
Randy

As the days drift by routinely, October of my freshman year at University of Pennsylvania comes to an end, and we're halfway through November with more of the same. Meaning, business as usual with the Joey's baths and boners. At times I wonder if I might be falling in love with him, but I don't know how to tell if I am. I've grown close to him because of all the intimate touching necessary in taking care of his hygiene and horny needs. My fantasies that he might be a closeted gay or bisexual are fading. Our daily schedule doesn't fluctuate much, and I can't say I have a social life because of Joey's extensive needs for help with everything. Fortunately, we do a lot of laughing together so it's mostly fun, not drudgery. We have a lot of studying every night which would be drudgery except we do it together, often side by side on his bed. Joey seems to enjoy being with me too, although it's not like he tells me as much. Our physical closeness, much of the time, we take for granted by now. I'm gay and very fond of him so it's not surprising I accept the level of care he needs, including wiping his ass. His comfort level with things like that is harder to understand if he's straight. Early in our relationship, we've been honest with each other about everything, at least I know I have. Our situation is beyond unique and I personally think it's kind of a beautiful thing too. So Joey and me are closer than close, but the only actual sex we do together is me jerking him off once or twice a day. Okay, it's pretty much twice a day now. We have affection for one another and I'm sure we'll be friends all through our college years, but I've pretty much given up hope of anything beyond that. There are times when it seems Joey has things on his mind and he can be quiet for a few hours at a time. I assume it's something to do with the loss of his friend in the accident so I don't intrude on his thoughts. My quiet time I mostly spend worrying that I think about sex too much. Who knows what's normal in that regard anyway, but I think about sex a lot.

Everything considered, we're doing about as good as one could hope for, but we're both looking forward to Thanksgiving break. We need a holiday from college. For Joey, the most important aspect of Thanksgiving break is he'll be getting all three casts removed. Maybe as soon as the very first day he's home. In any case, Thanksgiving break is still a couple of weeks away. Randy and I still haven't spent a night together. He's been my sole sexual outlet at random times he feels like it. I see him at practice and we talk, but other than that, Randy being a junior and me being a freshman limits the opportunities for us to be at same place at the same time. Ten days after the equipment room blow job, Randy had a break in practice. It's rare that the equipment room isn't a busy place, but on that day all the planets were aligned just right and we got together, sort of. Randy arranged, as co-captain of the team, for the room to be off limits while he's allegedly doing inventory of the equipment. He nods his head at me and I let myself get excited. I want to fuck with him so badly, it's sick. Casually making my way over to the equipment room, and then Randy grabbed me. No kissing though, which I missed. No, he was rough with me, pushing my face against his crotch. He's so fucking strong! He told me to pull his gym shorts down and lick his jock strap until he told me to stop. Basically, I ended up recreating the cock-sucking and rimming. Before he let me suck his cock though, he roughly finger-fucked me while giving me another stinging hickey on my neck. I became very docile for him and he moved me around where he wanted me easily.

That's the first time I acknowledged from the start that he was dominant and I was submissive and he gave me the hardest boner I've ever had. There was no mention of the two blow jobs he owed me. He milked my balls by finger-fucking me and I almost passed out at the force of my climax. When I had his jockstrap saturated with saliva and sucked on his asshole and licked all the salty sweat from his ass and crotch, he let me suck his cock and by then, I was so aroused I gobbled it into my mouth and he smacked the back of my head, saying, "NO! Suck it right." I've never felt so submissive to anyone before in my life… and I loved it. He deep-throated me in the end, did it so long I thought I'd die from loss of oxygen but he had a nice orgasm and the sent me on my way. I gave that experience a lot of thought afterwards and decided I liked it. Can't wait till next time.

Randy's got the blond hair and blue eyes, he's exceptionally attractive and cute in a macho way, and he says I'm his sex toy… haha.

Who better to be a sex toy for than him. It's little bit of a thrill him being a junior and me, a freshman. At this university, that's a big deal. So that was our second equipment room sex and now it's three days later. I'm helping Joey hop on his good leg from his wheelchair to sit at a table with the coaches when I spot Randy doing that thing with his index finger, wiggling it for me to go to him. Oh boy! Trying to be casual about it, I walk around the perimeter of the gym and follow him to the hall. He gets a vice-like grip on the back of my neck, making me hunch my shoulders as he walks me down the hall, quietly saying, "My roommate's already left for our weekend competition at Yale, soooo, I've got some time in my dorm room. I'll tell you I'm feeling generous today, so if my sex-toy boy rims my ass the right way, I just might reward you by fucking your brains out," and he squeezes the back of my neck harder. I go, "Ow, Randy, ooow!" He says, "What'd I say about pain with sex?

Swallowing, I mutter, "That hurts." Chuckling, he says, "Don't you dare disappoint me, Oliver, I need a submissive boy toy, not just a cute one. So behave yourself!" He shakes my head and lets it go, mumbling and chuckling, "Just a little friendly neck-squeeze. Hey, I've thought up some surprises for you 'cause you need a little bit of control in your sex life, and I'm just the guy to provide it." Okay, fuck the sore neck, I'm excited now. Not wanting to stutter, like I do when I get excited sometimes, I say each word carefully, "I do need you to dominate me, Randy. I'll be the best boy toy you ever had." Randy goes, "I'll be the judge of that, boy. You know where my room is, I'll see ya there about five o'clock." I'm excited, yes, but also nervous and a little scared. All the things I usually feel about any new experience, but I managed to say, "Can't wait." Randy squeezes my ass this time and then he's off and running. It's exciting to know Randy's been planning this with me in mind, but I'm disappointed it's not now. I'll be thinking about it for two full hours. Damn, Randy Rider fucking me, oh my God. Walking back down the hall, I think about it. My first fuck since the Delaware trip almost a month ago and I'm horny for it. Then, walking back into the gym, something makes me look up and from the other side of the gym, Joey's staring at me. He was probably the only one in the gym who noticed Randy and me walking out together. The gym's a beehive of activity, everyone fully engaged in what they're doing, except Joey. Doing a dumb nervous smile at him, Joey just stares back at me. He looks confused or angry maybe, and then he turns his back on me to watch a gymnast doing a floor exercise. Hmmmm?

That look from Joey is disconcerting. He knows I'm gay and everyone in gymnastics knows Randy's gay, so if Randy talks to me, why should Joey care? You know what? I'll ask him, it's that simple. For now I've got two hours all to myself. What a luxury. Fridays are always the best day of the week anyway because I only have one course scheduled and then it's the weekend. Sweet! I'm going to get a haircut now because Randy told me Alexander's are too exotic for me. It's growing ragged-looking and I want it to look neat, and what the hell, maybe it'll please Randy. I drive my Mini to the campus barbershop thinking about me and Randy. I'm going to try being less 'Gee whizz' with him. Try thinking like a junior and be more blasé like I've been there, done that. After parking the car, I walk inside the barbershop checking out the guys waiting for haircuts. Huh, zero cute guys here. I read an old People magazine while waiting and when it's my turn, I ask the barber to just neaten up my hair, cutting off as little as possible. He does an okay job of it and afterwards, I check out the street mall and don't see any cute guys there either. It never ceases to amaze me how rare really cute guys are. That fact makes me appreciate the boys qualifying for a ten in cuteness with Randy being right there in that select group.

I buy a coffee from a pastry shop and then taking it outside to drink while I smoke a cigarette, 'cause coffee and cigarettes go good together. Sitting on a bench enjoying the thought of getting fucked later this afternoon, I have a nice time imagining Randy plugging my ass with his big cock. I've got some nice boner action going for me from thinking about being controlled sexually by him. With a hand in my pocket, playing with myself, I think more about my favorite topic, which is gay sex. Alexander fucked me real good and exactly the way he wanted to do it too. But, like I said, that was like a month ago now and until today, I thought I'd have to wait until I saw Alexander over the Thanksgiving holiday before experiencing that particular sexy thrill again. Then my mind goes to something I've wondered about... am I some kind of sex fiend? Do I need sex more often than everybody else? Not that I'm getting it. I've gotten laid exactly once since last June.

We've emailed each other, Alexander and me, and made plans for a night together when I'm home for Thanksgiving. He wants me to go with him to some kind of a costume party at the private gay club. Maybe I'll even see Spunky again, and I'd like to. It'll be great having Alexander to do me again. I can compare it with the way Randy does me. Now I'll have something to compare to Alexander's fucking. As I finished my coffee, I think, 'Hmmm, maybe thinking about sex all the time qualifies as being over-sexed even if I've only been fucked once since June. Nah, that's stupid, I'm fine.'

Finishing my second cigarette, my cell phone rings. It's Bob Numan, one of the gymnasts, who tells me Joey is not feeling good and he's taking him back to our dorm room. Joey asked him to call me so I can meet them there. I'm concerned about this because it's so unlike Joey. I mean, he always perseveres through all kinds of unpleasant aches and pains without a whimper. Whatever this latest problem is, it must be serious, especially since he asked to leave gymnastics practice. I run all the way and get there before they do. Sitting on the steps outside, I'm feeling apprehensive trying to remember what my Ass Group instructional booklet said about emergency medical care. Then Joey's wheelchair comes around the corner and I walk down to meet them. "Hi, Bob. Thanks for bringing Joey over here. What's up Joey? How ya feeling?" Joey's looking down as he mutters, "Can we just get inside, please." Bob tells me Joey complained of being sick to his stomach and dizzy.

Inside, Joey says, "I think I just need to lie down. Will you lie with me, Oliver?" I get him in bed on top of the covers and lay on my side next to him. On a twin bed, you pretty much have to be next to whoever you're on the bed with. Joey doesn't want to talk right now, but he wiggles right up next to me, his back against my chest. His body's tense and stiff and that worries me. What the hell should I do? Concerned for sure, but I also have this creepy feeling that something isn't right here. I only say that because Joey's acting differently than ever before. So, something new is up, but what? As I'm contemplating that, I doze off for a while and then snapping awake and checking the time, it's ten minutes to five and I'm supposed to meet Randy at five. Joey's still right up against me as I ask, "You awake, Joey?" He mutters, "Please stay with me, Oliver. I'm still feeling strange." Well, what the fuck can I do, he needs me so I put my arm over his chest and he snuggles in even tighter. Damn, just feeling that hard ass of his up against me is hot and I'm getting another frigging boner. A boner's the last thing Joey needs to feel right now. Yeah, except he seems to be pressing against it. Letting out a long, quiet wheezy breath, I try to think how I can get a message to Randy. The last thing I need is for Randy to think I stood him up intentionally. Maybe he saw Bob wheeling Joey out of the gym earlier. No, Randy wouldn't see that because he works out with the seniors at another part of the gym. Fuck! Randy's probably waiting in his dorm getting madder and madder at me. Why does this stuff always happen to me? I'm frustrated, then furious, and then I feel guilty because Joey's sick; he is sick, right? Now why would I question that? Probably because I'm disappointed about missing out on this golden opportunity with Randy.

I haven't met many college students who aren't always tired because of all the studying we do and, yeah, a lot of them do too much partying. Partying is an unwritten obligation for most college students. Sleep gets pushed aside, but with Joey and me, it isn't so much that we party a lot, but rather that the gymnastics team takes up so much of our free time we're always up late studying and doing assignments. Anyway, a college student lying in bed at any time of the day or night will fall asleep. Next time I wake-up, it's quarter to six. I can't tell if Joey's still sleeping or not, he's right up against me and not moving so he's probably sleeping. If I can somehow get over to Randy's dorm before six, I'd be able to explain why I missed our date. "You asleep, Joey?" I ask quietly. He rustles around and mumbles, "I was." I ask if he'd be alright for fifteen minutes so I can run over to tell Randy Rider something. Joey asks the time and when I tell him, he goes, "Oh, it's almost six o'clock. I'll be okay, but don't be long because I'm still a little dizzy." Carefully, I slide off Joey's bed and into the bathroom to hurriedly try straightening up my appearance.

My hair's still short of course, but now it's more of a normal short haircut. The shaved outline around my hairline had grown out and after today's haircut, it blends in with the rest of my hair. Looking in the mirror at myself, I do a double take realizing my haircut's pretty much like Frankie's because it's sticking up on top . Isn't that a coincidence? It makes me want to see my red-headed friend again. Brushing my hair up like the barber did it. Huh, it's basically a flat top. Huh, but I gotta get going. Telling Joey I'll be right back, I leave the dorm and run the short distance to Randy's dorm and get there a little before six. Joey isn't going with the gymnastics team on this overnight trip, but the rest of the gymnastics team are leaving on buses before seven o'clock. Randy's roommate is a team manager and he left earlier today to be there to arrange something or other. I knocked on Randy's door, then after a full minute, knocked again. Nothing but silence. I missed him, but going downstairs, I get the idea to check the equipment room. Running to the gymnasium and going inside, I hear something and when I look in the room, there's Randy standing on a stool reaching to get a duffel bag off a shelf. I say, "Randy, I'm so sorry I didn't make it at five o'clock, my roommate got sick and I don't have your cellphone number. I ran over here as soon as I could to explain. I mean, um, well, you know, why I couldn't make it." Randy looks over his shoulder, "Yeah, I heard about it, Oliver. No problem, come on over here." He looks so cute standing on that stool wearing a sleeveless T-shirt, gym shorts, and sneakers. His body's so perfect I want to wrap it up in my arms. He's wearing a baseball cap turned backwards. When I walk over, he says, "Closer, Oliver. I want a hug." It's odd because standing on that little stool, he's now a couple of inches taller than me, instead of the other way around. He hugs me wrapping his strong arms around me, pinning my arms to my side as he whispers in my ear, "I like your new haircut." His lips move against my ear, then he licks my ear and it gives me shivers all over.

Randy's voice is low and sexy as he continues whispering in a breathless manner, his lips are still caressing my ear, "You need to be under a little bit of control to enjoy sex to the fullest, don't you, Oliver? You like to be told what to do, don't ya?" As I try to think of an appropriate response to that, I discover it's difficult to breathe all of a sudden. He's being so hypnotic I'm only able to sputter, "What?" which I always say when I can't think how I should respond to something. He smells so good and so sexy as I stand motionless, wrapped in his arms. Randy whispers, "Don't you, Oliver?" and I nod my head up and down once. He goes, "You're going to be my secret boyfriend, who I'm going teach some sexy stuff. It'll get you so hot you'll have a hard time believing it, and I do mean *hard* time. Do you want me to do that, Oliver?" What I want is to stay wrapped in his arms listening to him whisper dirty sexy stuff in my ear while I'm inhaling his aroma and pressing my thigh against his cock. It isn't a new thing for me to get mesmerized by a hot sexy guy. I like being submissive to certain types, and Randy's certainly one of those types. I mean a tattooed leather freak with chains and whips would have me running for my life, but someone like Randy, who I know isn't dangerous, can have his way with me. It's my dream to have a controlling gay lover. If that someone turns out to be Randy Rider, so much the better because I can't even fantasize anyone hotter than him.

In a voice so low I can barely hear him, Randy says, "I have to meet for a captains' meeting in ten minutes so I can't do it now, but when I get back, we'll find a time and a place for me to fuck you like nobody's fucked you before. You're going to experience sexual feelings you don't even knew exists. You'll be whimpering my name and begging me to do you again." He licks all the way across my forehead. I'm panting, pressing my forehead against his lips, "Lift your face, Oliver," and when I do, he sucks on my mouth, then just with my top lip and I feel my wet boner move in my shorts and all ten of my toes curl up tight in my sneakers. Randy holds me against him with one arm and with the other, he forces his hand inside the waistband at the back of my pants and cups my bare buttock, then squeezes it with his strong hand. I moan, "Ohhhh," then, "Ow, that hurts." He squeezes once more and then just holds my buttock with his finger at my asshole as he sucks on my neck at a spot under my chin. Pushing his finger inside me, my toes straightened out and I go up on them as Randy roughly finger-fucks me and as soon as the one finger is smoothly going in and out of me, he forces in a second. I sputter, "Ah, ahh, oh, that hurts too...".

His methodical penetration of my hole creates sweat as a natural lubricant and he's soon penetrating deeper inside me with both fingers going right over my prostate. Every few thrusts, he stops and massages right on my prostate gland, "Ohh, ahh, oh that feels good." A minute later, I mumble, "I'm going to cum, Randy," and right after that, my back arches and my hips buck as cum shoots from my pulsating cock flooding my underpants. He continues thrusting his fingers far up my hole while sucking on my neck. Another long moan from me as more cum pumps up from my nuts and my shoulders shudder as my pants absorb another spurt of spunk and I almost black out. Shooting my climax, I'm standing on my toes making quiet squeals as I squeeze out drools of cum filling up my shorts with my creamy spunk. Oh, so hot and it felt so good, I'm still moaning quietly leaning into Randy as if my life depended on it. Such an excellent feeling, but I'm jittery now as the waves of pleasure drift away.

Randy pulls his shorts and underwear down on his thighs, and says, "Suck me off quick, boy" I get on my knees, rubbing my face around his crotch that smells sexy. He's had a shower recently, it's his personal scent, not soap and not sweat, just him. His cock's already hard as mine as I lick his balls a few times, then bend my head way back getting between his legs rimming his asshole, getting my tongue up inside his hole about an inch. Randy groans, "Oh fuck, yeah," and a minute later "Suck my cock." And that's what I did until it's sloppy with spit and he pulls my head, pressing my face against he's pubic hair, then he fucks my throat hard and fast in almost a frenzy with me almost losing consciousness from lack of oxygen. He thrusts his boner in my throat until he cums and it's a big, long load of spunk choking me. I'm gagging like last time and his cum is again sucked in my sinuses and out my nose. Thrusting roughly, recklessly ramming his cock down my throat, back and forth shooting shorter spurts of cum as he's noisily taking rasping breaths. My nose is stuffed with Randy's spunk when he withdraws his cock, stroking it. I'm blowing through my nose real hard, stopping at my ears as cum sprays out from both nostrils. When my airway's clear, I inhale delicious oxygen. Everything sounds like it's coming from far, far away until my ears pop and I can hear clearly again.

Randy's hyperventilating, taking fast little breaths for maybe a minute as I sit back on my heels and look up at his cute face. His breathing slows down and his body relaxes, "Well, Oliver, you're quite the cock-sucker. Looks like you've earned yourself a hard fucking. I'm gonna be rough with you because I can see you crave it like that. Right now though, I gotta take off. Enjoy the taste of my cum." I stare at him while wiping his cum off my lips and chin with the back of my hand. He goes, "Oh, by the way, Danny's taking me back as his boyfriend, but don't worry, I'm gonna have me a cute freshman on the side. "Then he takes a used Kleenex from his pocket and wipes at my face and nose with it, mumbling, "You and I are going to have us some fun. Like I said before, you need a controlling influence in your sex life and I'm gonna take care of that for you. Wait till I put a dog collar on you then tie you up tight, and fuck you hard you'll be walking bowlegged when I'm done with you. Think about that. You have no idea how hot I'm going to get you." I'm in a daze, hypnotized by his confident manner. He tells me to pull his shorts up and when I do that, he sucks on the hickey and then smacks the back of my head, muttering, "Later, cock sucker."

Still in some kind of trance, I watch him leave. Then I sit on the stool Randy stood on and try clearing my head. I honestly feel like I'm hypnotized. It's the dreamiest feeling and it has everything to do with Randy whispering to me and holding me so tightly in those strong arms of his. My hole's burning a little now and my hickey stings, but I'm in a sexy, dreamy mood just the same. Soon the fog begins to lift and I notice the wet cum in my pants has cooled off, and think, 'Boyfriend on the side? Is that what he said?' Standing now, I walk unsteadily over to the lavatory at the end of the hall. Checking my watch, I've been gone a half hour. Washing my face and hands quickly, I run back to the room, Randy's cum squishing in my pants, hoping Joey's sleeping again. He isn't sleeping. He's lying on his side staring at the door as I walk in. "I've had to take a piss for quite some time, Oliver. Where you been?"

He has watery eyes and that crying-whine in his voice. What the hell's going on with Joey? I tell him I'm sorry to hear that. "Randy was telling me about his gymnastics team's competition at Yale and I lost track of time." Joey has this funny expression on his face. He says nothing, so I'm feeling guilty for lying and babble something about I'm hoping Randy and I can be friends, "You know, Joey, like gay friends." He sputters out, "Don't tell me about your fag stuff. I don't want to hear it and please don't be so fucking obvious and gross. Put a bandage over that disgusting hickey and change your pants." Looking down, I see that the wet cum stain has soaked through my right thigh. Joey finishes with, "But, before any of that, I need to take a piss!" He's never been in this bad of a mood before. It's probably best if I keep quiet and help him pee. I assist him, hopping on one foot to the toilet and get him sitting on the toilet. Holding his dick for him so he doesn't pee outside the toilet bowel, like I always do, but this time we don't rest our heads next to each other. He's very tense, his body's like a taut wire. "Do you want to get some dinner, Joey?" I ask in a quiet voice. He answers in an annoyed one, "If you can spare the time, yes I would. Haven't eaten all day." After he finished his piss, I put a bandage on my hickey, changed my underwear and jeans, then, in silence, push Joey's wheelchair through the chilly evening to the dining hall. He had breakfast with me this morning and he'd said he wasn't hungry at lunch, but what would it accomplish reminding him of that?

We have a quick, silent dinner and then back to the room. I ask if he wants to go to an open mixer a fraternity on campus is throwing. Joey mumbles something about preferring to go online because he needs to connect with real friends. The way he said it implies he doesn't have a real friend here. Not wanting to fight with him, I mutter, "Okay, sure." Why's he mad at me? I don't want to go to the mixer alone and I can't leave him anyway, so what the fuck, I'll go outside to smoke, but it's gotten too chilly to enjoy sitting on the step smoking. I can't come up with anything better to do and I don't want to be in the room with him while he's in this miserable mood. While smoking my second cigarette, my cellphone rings and I see it's Frankie. So, Frankie's calling me. That's odd because Darleen forbids him to even email me, never mind call me. Hmmm.

"Hello. I know a guy named Frankie Nerney although this couldn't be him because his girlfriend won't allow him to communicate with the likes of me. The Frankie Nerney I know has the brightest, shiniest red hair I've ever seen and he wears round glasses. He is so cute I can't even tell ya. I got my haircut just like his, so what do ya think about that? What color's your hair, stranger?" Frankie says, "Are you done you're rant, Oliver? I'm your Frankie and I called to tell you that… And to say you've been right about everything from the start and that the girl you mentioned is now really, really, really history. That bitch is yesterday's news and she's outta my life for good! I swear to you it's true. It's you and me now, Oliver, you and me. Is that okay with you?" I go, "This sounds familiar, Frankie," and he goes, "You got your haircut like mine, really?" Frankie has a cute voice. I probably mentioned that thing about a boy's voice before. Yeah, seriously, guys can have a cute-sounding voice, and I don't mean cartoon-character cute, but youthful and boyish and excited and maybe a little squeak in it if he gets nervous or speaks too quickly. Frankie always sounds cute, in person or on the phone. I bite my lip and squint my eyes because Frankie wiggled his way into my heart early on. Ya can't turn love on and off. I learned what I think being in love is from the way I feel about him, that's what I call love. He also has caused me more heartache than any other person on the planet 'cause love hurts too, ya know.

Remaining calm, because I'm maturing a little now, and because Frankie has built my hopes up a number of times before, then sends them crashing down the next day. Keeping it light, I go, "This is my Frankie, you say? The boy who I worked with on the loading dock and swapped spit with and the one whose pubes I had to cut off to get to a splinter near his nuts so I could save his life? That Frankie? Is that what you're telling me?" I'm a little nervous, but my voice doesn't sound nervous. My fingers are shaking, my stomach's turning over and I pretty much don't know what to do or say, but my voice doesn't sound nervous. Frankie is always catching me totally off guard and that holds true for as long as I've known him. He doesn't do it on purpose, I don't think, it's just him. I want to start the whole conversation over from the beginning and stop trying to be funny. I want to say, 'Thank God, Frankie, I love you,' but it isn't so easy to do after being disappointed in the past with him. He says, "Don't be mad at me, Oliver. You have reasons to be mad, but please don't be. You were right about you and me. I'm only sorry I couldn't see it sooner." I tell him I'm just messing around like we always used to do, but that I'm happy to hear from him and that I'm not mad at him. Frankie's acting very contrite, but the call soon begins breaking up because my cellphone needs to be charged. He makes me promise to drive up to see him the first day I can during Thanksgiving break, which of course I promise to do. When we say goodbye, I think the last thing he says is, 'I love you, Oliver,' but it's hard to tell because the signal is weak. But seriously, it sorta sounded like that, and what else could it have been?

Naturally, I light up another cigarette right after saying goodbye because I'm wired now and don't know what to make of it, and lighting a cigarette is at least something to. Standing up and walking in a circle trying to figure out how I should feel about this. Was this finally the real deal like Frankie said it was? Do I still love Frankie like I thought I did a couple months ago? I know I don't love Alexander, especially the new Alexander, but sex with him is almost as hot as it gets. I kinda get off on his bossy ways, ya know. I'm definitely infatuated with the idea of sex with Randy, but I couldn't ever fall in love him with. I don't think I could anyway. And, what about my little brother, Joey, inside the dorm there?

My Joey with a hair up his ass about something. How do I feel in my heart of hearts about Joey? I've never let myself really ponder too deeply into those kinds of feelings about Joey because I've been pretty sure he's straight. Frankie definitely has gay tendencies so I let my fantasies about the two of us wander all over the place. This latest Frankie development is very exciting and I'd like to share this news with someone, maybe with Joey. But why's he mad at me? Okay, I'm going in and find out right now!

I go in quietly, finding Joey's still emailing with his high school buds. I sit on my bed staring at his back. What could be wrong? I should be the one who's pissed off at him for the way he's treating me, and after everything I've done for him too! But, ya know, I really care for him and I'm worried he's acting like this because he received some bad news or something like that, and he's just taking it out on me because he's frustrated and helpless and doesn't know what else to do. There has to be a good reason for why he's acting like this. Joey's too sweet a kid to act like a dick. I know something has gone wrong in his life and I'm going to help him with it. I'm sticking by Joey!

This Frankie thing popping up in my life again should have me jumping for joy except I'm cautious now. Frankie has issues that keep getting in the way of logic and getting in the way of the obvious too. But damn, he makes me tingle all over and I want to taste his saliva again and feel his red flat-top and rub my nose against his forehead to inhale his wonderfully sexy natural odor. Frankie makes me knees weak and my pecker hard and my balls vibrate and my stomach feel funny. He fucked me that time, although he needed my help to get started, but he finished it and I can't ever remember a stronger climax than the one he gave me with that erotic screwing. Fucking me with that perfect hard cock of his. Having Frankie's cock inside me was an indescribably delicious feeling and my whole body was alive with the kind of sensations I normally only feel just in my dick when I climax. My whole body felt that way when Frankie fucked me.

Chapter 9
Joey

I'm enjoying this trip down memory lane with Frankie when Joey turns around in his seat, asking, "Why are you staring at me, Oliver? I can feel it on the back of my neck." I tell him I'm waiting for him to finish his online business. "I want to ask you why you're treating me like shit." Joey rolls his dark blue eyes and shakes his head slightly, then slowly says, "I study with you every night so I know how bright you are, how your mind absorbs the material, analyzes it and comes up with the proper conclusion so quickly. You're so smart it amazes me. I thought I was smart in high school, but you're smarter. On the other hand, you don't know shit about real life. You're dumb when it comes to common sense." And now he has tears in his eyes as he finishes by saying, "Something must have disconnected in your brain and you simply can't read people. I'm not sure what it is, Oliver, but something is fucked-up in your head. Nobody can be this dense." I go, "What?" and Joey says, "Do you really think, in your wildest imagination, that a straight kid would do all the sexy things with you that I do? Well, do you?" I say, "Huh?" He shakes his head again, and says, "I'm gay. I've been gay. I've known I'm gay for a few years, but in the closet until I feel more comfortable with my gayness. I'm not like you running up to everyone you see announcing, "I'm gay, I'm gay!" I mutter, "I don't do that. You're gay?" Joey uses a patient voice, saying, "I know you're surprised, Oliver, that's what's so weird. Don't ya see it? I love all our physical contact as much as you do."

My head hurts as I try remembering to keep my mouth shut because when something takes me completely by surprise my mouth hangs open like I'm a toad. "So, you're saying you're gay. Right?" Joey's frustrated now, "Jesus H. Christ, Oliver, how much plainer do I need to be? Yes, I'm gay. I didn't know I was gay at age nine or whatever age you claim you knew it, but I've known it for awhile now. When I started dating at sixteen, my buddies and I would discuss our dates from the night before and I'd be thinking to myself, 'I must have the wrong girl.' My friends were all worked up talking about copping a feel and while I'm thinking how gross it was to French kiss with my date, and copping a feel never even entered my mind." Staying stupid, I say, "You did a lot of dating with girls?" and Joey begins talking to me now like he's explaining something to a four-year-old. "Yes, I tried dating girls for a year or so, but I came to understand that I enjoy looking at my best friend's mouth while he explained almost getting in his date's pants. I wanted to get on his pants much more than anything he had to say about his girlfriend's pants. I wanted to kiss his mouth, my friend's mouth. The last girl I dated really had a crush on me and she finally had to take hold of my wrist and put my hand under her blouse because I just couldn't make myself make a move on her. I pulled my hand away so fast it was like I touched a blow torch. Her nipple felt gross, with all those little bumps around it and I almost hurled. She called me a queer."

Still hardly believing my ears, I ask him how many people knows he's gay and he says that no one officially knows it except me now. He says his two best friends have to know, but they've never come out and said it to him. Joey says that they make general comments about how they don't care if someone is gay and stuff like that. I ask, "Why are you telling me all this now? Ya know, if I'm so dumb about real life. Why not stay in the closet and let me stay ignorant of the fact that you're gay? Why tell stupid old me?" Joey's eyes softened and he speaks sweetly now, "Don't be hurt, Oliver. I'm sorry if I insulted you. It's just that I was frustrated that you didn't recognize the situation and I guess I didn't know how to handle it either. Then I saw Randy with his arm across your shoulders and you gushing over him. I got pissed off, um, jealous, actually." I go, "I wasn't gushing! I was listening to him." Joey goes on to tell me that he heard one of the gay gymnasts say that Randy was taking another freshman under his wing this afternoon and it made him feel sick. He quietly says, "That's what I was sick about. But then you stayed with me here on my bed and I started to feel better because you passed up meeting with Randy. I didn't want you with him."

He has tears in his eyes again when he finishes with, "Then you left me for over half an hour and came back with a wet spot at your crotch and that big hickey on your neck. It's like Randy branded you as his boy. Oliver, I love you. I fell in love with you. I'm in love with you right now. Do ya know what I'm saying?" My mouth is open again and my brain's telling me to say, 'what?' but I don't. I managed to say, "I love you too, Joey. Honest to God, I think of you as my little brother." He makes a face at me and almost laughs. Then says, "Well, that's a start, but it's a far cry from, I'm in love with you too, Joey." I mumble, "I'm in love with you," and he grins, "You don't have a chance, Oliver, you're going to fall in love with me. I'm not usually as easy going as I've been since the accident. I'm kind of wimpy because I'm pretty much helpless. Normally I'm a competitive guy and I'm giving you full warning, I'm gonna make you love me. You got no chance, dude." He's being playful now, which is more like himself. Trying to be cool about this awesome turn of events, but a huge smile breaks out on my face anyway. I really do love, Joey, but being in love with him? Hmmmm, I don't know about that yet. It's so damn flattering though that he's in love with me. Ironically, I feel the same way about being in love with Frankie without feeling that kind of love in return.

Joey and I go into this long bull session. We talk about the frustrations we experienced being a closeted gay, like I am back home. The frustration of loving someone who doesn't love you back. I told him that the only place I'm open about my gayness is here in college, and with Frankie. Obviously the boys I had sex with knew I was gay, but it's not like we discussed it or anything. I tell Joey about Cristobal and my first gay experiences with him, but I don't mention my neighbor, Edward, or Christian. Joey tells me some of his gay fantasies. He hasn't had any real-life gay experiences to share, except me jerking him off. We get a little silly with the fantasy area. Fantasies can get out of hand, but they're fun. I get us a couple of cokes and we share some cigarettes. There's no smoking in the dorm rooms but we do it anyway. I open the window as our concession to the no smoking rule.

It's so cool to talk openly about gay stuff with another gay boy. Joey and I are back to being best buds and we kid each other about our skinny bodies and then complimented each other about our looks. Yeah, we're secretly conceited, I guess. I go a little overboard complimenting Joey on having a great penis, which gets us laughing. Then he comments on my very, common, and average-looking dick and he does it with a straight face at first, making me frown thinking he's making fun of me? Then he laughs at what a nerd I can be. "Oliver, you take everything anybody says at face value. I'm teasing you. I mutter,

"I knew that. I was teasing you back." We'd been talking and joking around for almost two hours when out of the blue Joey says, "Okay, Oliver, I've worked up the courage to ask you something. Will you have sex with me right here, right now? I've never had sex with anyone unless I count you jerking me off, which I do count by the way. Will you fuck me?" Ha! I certainly have no problem with this request, but I want it to be special for Joey so I ask if it wouldn't be better waiting until he's out of the casts? He goes, "It'd be better except I'm kinda hot for you even if you're not hot for me. I don't want to wait." I bite my lip and mumble, "I'm hot for you, Joey, seriously hot for you. I don't have a condom though and I think we should use one." He says, "You won't catch anything from me, I've never had sex of any kind," and I think of the time I said that same thing to Cris. I go, "But I've had sex a couple of times without protection," and he goes, "Please, Oliver..." I shrug, wanting to do it.

Taking a deep breath, I smile at Joey, helping him get up from his desk and steady him as he hops to his bed on his good leg. As he leans against the bed, I pull down the covers, then try doing everything slowly and deliberately the way Alexander does everything. That seemed very sexy to me. Joey's watching my every move without saying a word, his big dark blue eyes shining. I'm kinda nervous thinking maybe he'll be disappointed and I'm also shocked that we're doing this. I speculated he was gay many times but always talked myself out of it and now, like I said, I'm nervous.

I take all my clothes off. Nothing new since Joey's seen me naked many times. Then standing next to his bed, taking it slow, I get his clothes off and when he's stark naked, lightly run the palms of my hands from the back of his neck across his shoulders and down his sides to his hips, then slide my hand sideways over to his belly button and down around his hairless pubic area. Joey takes a deep inhale and holds it too long so I guess he's nervous too. When his face gets red, he begins letting his breath out slowly, then mumbles, "I'm nervous, Oliver." I cup his nuts in my hand and squeeze hard enough that he scrunches his face. I murmur, "That's the pain part, the rest is the pleasure part and it's okay to be nervous during your first time. I know I was, and I'm nerves now myself even though there's nothing to be nervous about." Climbing up on the bed, on my knees, I use the palms of both hands rubbing down the outside of his legs and up the inside. Rubbing gently up to his cock and balls and fondled them until he moans, "Ohhhh," and his shoulders shudder. Stroking his cock, then bending over to suck it into my mouth, I savor the taste, licking around and around the head while sucking on the shaft with my lips. His cock gets hard quickly and so does mine. Joey's aroma I know very well from my intimate hygiene care. It's different from Randy and Frankie's, but just as sexy.

When his cock is a ridiculously a hard boner, I ask, "Is it okay if I kiss your lips?' and he gasps, "Yes," so I slowly move my lips to his and kiss him gently. Then holding the back of his head, I kiss him wetly with my tongue splitting between his lips and he opens his mouth slightly so I can slide my tongue against his, and he moans again, "Oooh." Sucking his tongue and trying for a French kiss. At first Joey doesn't participate, but then he does and it's delicious. Breaking the kiss, I'm staring into his eyes stroking the foreskin of his cock slowly, moving it on and off the head until he grunts and a big glob of pre cum drools over my fist. Joey's shoulders shudder again and a low moan escapes his throat. His eyes are half closed and I wonder to myself if he feels a trance-like sensation like I get into so easily. Letting go of his boner, I watch it bobbing in the air. Joey's been turning me on for weeks now and how often I've fantasized about putting my cock between his hard butt cheeks. My cock's so hard the skin's shiny. Joey stares at it while I slowly unscrew the cap on the creamy Vaseline. For a first time, the use of lubricant is always a very good idea. My boner is just average. Not quite six inches long and not that big around, but it's straight as an arrow sticking out from my small pubic patch.

Joey doesn't look frightened of my boner like I am looking at his huge one. I'm a little bit scared of it and a lot intrigued by it. It's not quite as big as Pete's so I can handle it if he ever gets the urge to use it on me. Helping Joey roll on his side, facing away from me, I push a glob of Vaseline up his hole with my finger. We've done this many times, but still there's a shiver running through him raising goosebumps on his ass followed by a quiet moan, and a murmured, "That feels good, Oliver." More Vaseline goes inside him, with me moving my finger in a circle spreading it around good. After a half dozen deep finger penetrations with one finger, I do it with two fingers and there's another shoulder shudder and a quiet whimper of pleasure from Joey. Damn, I'm anxious but make myself stay methodical hoping it builds arousal in Joey like it did with me when Alexander did everything slowly. Joey's rectum has plenty of lubricant and I've loosened his anus a little, but I go back to doing deep fingering of his asshole again because it's turning me on and Joey's always telling me how good it feels. He moans a long hissing sound, then mumbles, "If I could reach my dick, I'll stroke myself off right now. You're making this very sexy for me, Oliver." Copying Alexander, I go, "Shhh," lying on my side behind him. Putting my arm over his side to steady him, I guide the head of my rock-hard boner to his asshole. The head of my cock just spreads the lips of his anus. I'm very excited myself and Joey's buttocks muscles tense as I push a bit harder. His sphincter muscle is like a fist so I quietly say, "Real relaxed, Joey, like you get when I'm putting ointment up your ass." He repeats himself from earlier, "I'm really nervous, I didn't think I'd be, but I am." Trying to get him to relax, I get up on my elbow and lean my face over to look at the side of his face, "Turn your head toward me, Joey," when he does, I stretch my neck and kiss him on the lips and this time, Joey kisses back right away with his tongue on mine. I whisper, "Slow going, Joey. I'm going to do it slowly, stop me if it begins to hurt. You taste good, like I knew you would," and I go back for another kiss that Joey gets a little carried away with, sucking my tongue, moving his head... it's awesome! I've wanted to kiss his lips for weeks now and it's everything I'd hoped it would be.

I'd had that great climax about three hours ago with Randy, but that's the only one I had all day so I'm pretty much fully loaded again and I'm very aroused by Joey. Right on cue, pre-cum drools from my cock right on Joey's anus as my boner's head disappears in his ass. I stifle a moan of pleasure, but Joey doesn't. He moans, "Mmmmm, ooooh." So far, so good. More pressure and my cock slips inside another inch and Joey's like, "Ahhhh, oh, oh, oh. That hurts, Oliver." Rubbing his shoulder, I wait a minute then very slowly, a quarter inch or so at a time, push my boner up his ass. Not surprisingly, it's very tight and feels awesome, plus it's Joey's ass! Joey's first time and I get to take his cherry, like Cristobal did for me. I don't want to hurt him though. When those muscled buttocks of his squeeze tightly on my boner, I need to concentrate not to start humping in and out right then, this really is fabulous on my boner. Each time I push in a half inch, Joey involuntarily tightened his buttocks and I bite my lip to keep myself in check with the moaning, but man this feels fantastic. I push my boner in slowly like this with no further complaints of pain from Joey, which is a very good indication things are going to go good. Finally, my pubic hairs are squished firmly up against his fantastic hard muscular buttocks. His body's as stiff as a board so I guess it hurt some, but he's a determined kid when he sets his mind to something. Then he confirms my suspicions by murmuring, "It hurt for a while, Oliver, but not much and I'm fine. I like the way I feel totally filled up back there and I like your body against mine." I quietly say, my lips right on his ear like Randy did to me, "It feels so good to me too, Joey. You have a fantastic body and an excellent ass, if ya don't mind me saying so." He says, "I wish I could hug you, Oliver. This is making me love you more. I mean the way you're being so considerate and sweet about my first time. I'm glad it's with you." Damn that's sweet and I kiss his cheek, muttering, "Thanks, Joey. I'm waiting a bit so your rectum muscles can get used to my dick and relax some more. There won't be any pain, just pleasure for both of us."

Soon there's no more mention of hurt from Joey, "Oh it feels so fucking good now, Oliver, you were right. Oh my God, it's so different, this feeling is, um, I don't know how to describe it, it just feels so damn good knowing part of you is inside my body. Jesus, my dick's so hard I can't believe it. Ohhh, it feels good." Chuckling to myself, I pull out some and he squeaks as I push back in. It's almost comical the different sounds he's making. Then I pull back about five inches and push right back in smoothly sucking air in between closed lips making a silly sound myself, but it does feel fantastic. Joey groans in pleasure. He moves his hips back towards me with the next penetrations, then I get a smooth rhythm going and Joey like, "Oh, Oh, Oh," with each thrust up his ass. This kid's got a great ass, man this is so hot! "Slap, slap, slap," sounds fill the room as my crotch slams into his ass with every thrust. "Slap, slap, slap, slap," and the sensations flying off the head of my cock have my lips moaning, "Ah, ah, ah." No more talking, just moans of sexual pleasure.

Fucking him faster now, my boner sliding tightly up and back in his rectum smoothly and every couple of thrusts, Joey tightens those incredible muscle-bound buttocks, squeezing my boner. Joey and I are now quietly moaning at the same time. We've been fucking for only two or three minutes but it's so hot fucking Joey's ass I already feel my balls tighten up and move up towards my body. My nuts are heavy with cum and I know my orgasm's close. It's much sooner than I would have liked for Joey's first time, but I'm past the point of controlling my urge to climax. It's on me strong and Joey's ass has a lot to do with that. I'm really worked-up grunting and picking up the pace even more. Very fast, hard deep humping in and out, "Slap slap slap dslap," my groin noisily smacking against his ass with every hump. Joey's grunting, "AH!' with every slam of my boner and I feel my cock swelling even more and my cock head throbs. I'm going to blow my load making desperate sounds, almost whining, but before I have my building orgasm, Joey goes, "Oh my God!" and then, a long " Eeeeee..ahhh, um, um ,um," as he's firing his cum up against the wall next to the bed. It splashes loudly followed by a second fast moving steam of cum in a tight string with Joey's moaning like he's in pain, his body bucking dangerously so I hold his back against my chest with the arm that's over his side.

I've never, in my limited experience, felt anything tighten on my boner than Joey's muscle-bound buttocks and with each of his cum shots, he tightened his buttocks beyond belief. It puts me over the top and I squeal out as if I'm in pain exploding cum into his bowels, then another shot quickly follows as Joey says, "I felt that," then he goes back to uttering sounds of pleasure as my boner slides back and forth in his rectum in the slipperiness of cum. Black dots flood my vision as another load of cum rolls up my penis and fires into Joey, joining its brothers. I tighten my grip around Joey's chest, hugging him like he's my life raft as I continue humping his hole before gasping and slowing down now as my cum drools out of his ass making wet, "Splat, splat, splat, splat,' sounds as our bodies collide. It gets kinda messy, but about as sexy a time as I've ever experienced.

After the first couple of explosive minutes, we stop flouncing around at the same time and lay there sweating and panting and moaning, me still holding Joey tightly with my cock still up his hole as far as I can get it. My crotch is dripping wet with my own cum and so are Joey's ass cheeks. I lay here savoring my orgasm. We're both breathing deeply, there's sweat between his back and my chest, my heart thumping fast against his back and his against the hand I have spread over his heart. My heartbeat is almost matching Joey's. I nuzzled my nose against the back of Joey's neck, his skin smooth and smelling real good. Putting my leg over Joey's so I can hug all of him to me. He murmurs, "I can hardly believe the way it felt on my dick when I shot off," and he does a quiet, "Ahhhhh, ohhhh, I don't know, it was indescribable how good my ass felt, Oliver. Like so many sensations I've never experienced before tonight" I mumble, "Me too, Joey, me too," thinking I'll probably remember Cristobal all my life because I had my first gay sex with him. Maybe Joey will remember me his whole life too. That's a weird thought I guess, but it makes me feel good thinking I may be in Joey's memory years from now, maybe when we don't even know each other anymore.

We lay here together comfortably with Joeys breathing back to normal and his body melding into the nooks and crannies of my body. It's very nice, but before my cock can firm up into a real boner again, Joey reluctantly says he feel he needs to use the toilet. Probably thinks he needs to take a dump, that's not uncommon especially the first time. I pull out of him slowly with him whimpering, then telling me it feels really odd back there now that my cock is out of him. I quietly assure him everything is as it should be and that he needs give it a little time and it'll close up to normal. As I say that, I stare at his ass, fascinated as my cum drools out from high up in his bowels. Grabbing some tissues, I wipe his hole for him, noticing the lips of his anus are a bit red and a little swollen. Helping him hop over to the toilet on his good leg, I ask if his hole is as sore, and he mutters, "Oh yeah, a little, but it's worth a little soreness to climax like I just did. Ya know, Oliver, I got a lot of lost time to make up for. Let's set up a schedule where you fuck me, hmmm, how about every two hours around the clock?" He's really back to his old joking self and I want to kiss him, but he's sitting on the toilet straining a stool that he may be imagining, so I just squeeze him around his shoulders.

He doesn't poop so after getting him up, I take a pee, then suggest we take a bath together. He's all in favor of that. I could have suggested anything and Joey would probably have gone along with it. Getting in the tub, Joey tells me again how he can't wait to get his cast off so he can hug me around my neck and we can make-out till he cums in his pants. Now that he's 'come out' to me, he isn't holding anything back. He says whatever's on his mind and it's usually a compliment for me in some way and that's flattering. In the tub together, we're joking around a little bit and Joey gets this idea that he should give me a hickey like Randy did. I'm not opposed to it, but I want to give him one first. Joey says, "Go for it, I've never had one," and I start sucking and licking at a spot on his neck below his ear, thinking, 'I've never given anyone a hickey before either.' It's fun discovering how sexy it can get and while enjoying the smell and taste of Joey, I almost cream in the bath water. Damn that's hot, giving a hickey I mean.

Sucking on his silky skin in the same spot, licking and tonguing and then more sucking while Joey docilely holds his head to the side. There's some quiet moaning going on by both of us. I never imagined it would be this sexy. Joey murmurs he loves me when I finish. I've wanted some cute boy to say that to me for a long time now, but I don't know how to properly handle it now that someone finally has. That's because it's Joey, who said it, and I think I'm in love with Frankie, who may or may not feel the same way about me. Being a brainiac, I know that the earth travels around the sun at sixty-seven thousand miles per hour and at the same time it's rotating on its axis at a thousand miles per hour, but I don't know what to say to Joey. For lack of a better response, I try honesty and say, "Joey, I think I'm in love with a red-headed boy named Frankie, who I worked with last summer, but I'm not sure that I know what true love is. I do know I've come to love you while taking care of you these past couple of months, but I don't think it's the same as being in love. I'm just not sure." He goes, "I guess I'm not sure either, Oliver, but we'll find out together. How 'bout that?" I kiss the hickey I made on his neck, and mutter, "Good plan, Joey." He's such a sweet kid.

It's Joey's turn so he begins giving me a hickey on the other side of my neck from Randy's, and it's a damn sexy thing to give or get one so I wonder how many other sexy things there are that I'm unaware of, and that will be fun discovering as I gain experience with gay sex. It's exciting to finally be sexually active, and so wonderful to share my body with another boy while he shares his with me. One thing leads to another and the idea of trying a bathtub fuck is enticing to both Joey and me so we try it. We both have half a boner from the hickey activity and we both appear pretty hot for each other, so mutual hand jobs raise boners on both of us, along with some sexy kisses and we attempt fucking in a bathtub full of warm water. It isn't easy as one might think, especially with Joey restricted in his movements, but after some clumsy slippery attempts, my boner plunges deep inside Joey as he's leaning over the edge of the tub, half out of the water. We're both on our knees with Joey's belly resting on the rim of the tub, his head and arms facing the bathroom floor. He grunts when I plow his ass with my boner, and I go, "Oooh!" It's tight and with only water as a lubricant, it hurts Joey early on, but the circumstances have me hot for Joey so I grunt with the pain as I fuck him hoping the hurt passes, and it does about two minutes later. "Feeling good now, Oliver," mutters Joey, and just in time too because I don't want to hurt him for long and I was just about to end this experiment. The pain in Joey's hole is soon overwhelmed by the sexual pleasure of having a cock up there and he starts humping his hips back at my thrusts and it's sexy as hell with the bath water slushing all around us. God almighty, gay roommates in college; what could possibly be better! It's an awkward rough fuck but my cock is loving the ride and after maybe ten minutes of steady fucking, Joey moaning with pleasure and me breathing hard and just about fainting from the fantastic sensations from my cock and nuts, I, all of a sudden, feel an intense urge to climax, squeal out in an embarrassing manner and shoot another orgasm, much smaller than the first one, inside Joey's awesome ass. There's a minute after climax that I'm overwhelmed with the orgasmic sensations, and I fuck him wildly, which causes Joey to squeak out breathlessly as his cum comes out in the water near the side of the tub and floats to the surface. I'm dizzy again as sensations subside and I struggle to get Joey back fully in the bath water sitting between my legs with his back against my chest and my arm around him. He nestles in nicely and I kiss his hickey briefly as we breathe deeply and lie back enjoying the feel of our bodies together.

A few minutes of silently enjoying a contented feeling of being sexually satisfied,I hug him, muttering, "Give me a kiss, Joey." He turns his head and we kiss on the side of our lips with him saying, "I don't care that my ass is sore because it's the best kind of sore and I loved my first sex, especially with you, Oliver. I love you." I give him a tight hug mumbling, "Me too," and at that moment, I do love him although it feels different than the way I love Frankie, and I'm just being honest with myself about that. I turn on the hot water because our bath is only lukewarm by now and begin to wash first Joey and then myself. We're both quiet throughout the bathing, then the tub drains and I use the hand-held shower head to rinse us both off with hot water. Getting him on his feet and out of the tub, our bodily contact seems sweeter now and maybe that's because I know for sure Joey likes it as much as I do. We're both very tired so after drying us both off, I get Joey in bed. "Let's sleep together tonight, Oliver." We cuddle together in my bed enjoying the feel and the scent of each other until falling asleep.

Waking up and being able to hold Joey in my arms is a wonderful way to wake up. I can't believe how happy I am today. Joey has a way of melding into me so comfortably and cosily, it's awesome and my dick stirs. He quietly tells me how excited he is about our sex last night. He dreamed about it, but last night he stayed awake an hour after I'd fallen asleep rehashing our sex, his first ever, over and over. I imagine his ass is still too sore for a morning fuck, so I don't mention it and we're both pretty much sexually satisfied anyway. It's Saturday so we have no classes scheduled. We lay in bed for a long time dosing off and cuddling. Finally, nature calls and we get up to use the bathroom and then get a late brunch at the dining hall. We give each other little smiles every few minutes, but we're both in quiet moods and just hang around lazily in the room and watch television. It's fun being lazy together and every so often I wonder if maybe I am in love with Joey.

We get in a routine of daily sex, although we don't do it in a routine fashion. Each time I fuck him, it's preceded with lots of affectionate foreplay followed with cuddling and kisses. It sure seems like love, and maybe it is. Whatever it is, it's wonderful. As Thanksgiving break approaches, things are just about perfect between Joey and me, but on the other hand, I can honestly say that I'm still hot for Randy and curious what he has in mind for us. We haven't made up for that one missed date and to complicate matters, Randy has the flu. One afternoon, while Joey's with the gymnastics team, I go to see Randy in his sick bed just to say hello. In a husky voice he says, "Let me feel that ass of yours, Oliver." I get close to his bedside and he massages my ass from the outside of my jeans, saying, "This is going to totally belong to men, ya know." He tells me to stand still and, leaning over from his bed, he pulls my pants and jockey shorts down past my slim hips and tells me to bend over. I don't know why I do everything he says, but I do. It's almost like we're playing a sexy game that gives me a buzzing in my balls to do what I'm told. Randy's middle finger first goes in my mouth, so I tongue and suck his middle finger as we continue looking into each other's eyes. Half a minute later, he says, "Open," so I open my mouth and he takes his finger out and rubs it up the front of my nose leaving my spit dripping from my nostrils as he casually reaches around and shove that finger up my ass. I knew that's what he was going to do. Holding me in place with his finger in my rectum, he pulls down the covers, saying quietly, almost in a whisper, "Get your face in my crotch and move it around until you can get my cock in your mouth without using your hands." Licking my lips, I can feel my cock getting hard. I lower my head smelling his three-day-old body odor, but my nose goes into the fly of his pajamas anyway. I lap at his limp damp smelly cock until I lift it enough to suck it into my mouth, my eyes to the side keeping eye contact with Randy. He has a blank expression on his face as he begins finger-fucking me and I begin sucking his cock.

When I've sucked a boner on him, he smirks at me and says, "Jerk yourself off, but watch where you shoot it," as he picks a sock off the bedside table and tosses it near my boner, "Shoot in this." My cock is throbbing and hard as wood as I begin stroking myself and sucking his cock. The triple stimulation of stroking, sucking, and Randy's finger-fucking puts me in this ridiculously hot submissive trance as I'm making pathetic mewing sounds of pleasure and submissiveness. I can't help myself, it's off the charts sexy to me. I'm slurping on his boner, pulling my pud and squeezing my buttocks tightly to increase the pleasure and it's so sexy hot I've got tears in my eyes. When Randy grunts and bucks his hips, I taste the first squirt of cum and scramble with my free hand to pick up the sock. With his first long stream of spunk hitting my mouth, I do a weak girlie squeal and shoot the cum shot of my life into Randy's sock. I can tell by the stiff feel of the sock Randy's cum in it a few times himself. And it was on the bed-side table. Duh. Oh it it's fantastic when the cum's streaming out the shaft of my boner, then the head begin throbbing with pleasure. Another squeal around his boner and another long stream of spunk and I'm weak. A few more spurts of cum into the sock, and in my mouth compliments of Randy, and now both of us have dry nuts. He lets out a long breathy exhale, pulls his finger out of my ass and forces it in my mouth next to his cock as he pinches my hair, pulling my head up off his cock. I suck on his finger, cleaning it. The acrid shit taste is unpleasant but I hear myself moan anyway. Randy's so fucking dominant and it's sexy the way he treats me. He goes, "Pull up your pants."

Someone's knocking on the door and Randy looks over, saying, "When I get a chance I'm going to spank the shit outta you and then fuck you. For now, let whoever's knocking in and you go out. Feeling foolish, I nod my head and do what I'm told. There were two gymnasts at the door, I mutter, "I'm on my way out," as they give me a look, like, "So?" I squirm by them and walk down the hall towards the stairs. Now I'm ashamed of how I behaved with Randy, but I don't seem to be able to help myself. He's a sexual magnet for me, or something. I'm like the moth to his flame, but I swear I want him to fuck me so badly. He's so fucking hot to me and I'm totally intrigued. He's my vampire and I'm under his spell. It's mysterious the way he gets me to do whatever he wants and I always have a weird, sexy feeling in my groin whenever Randy has his way with me, but no way am I in love with him. Not even close!

Outside, I light a cigarette and kill some time thinking about my situation. I'm positive I'm not love with Randy and wonder if I even like him. On the other hand, Joey sure thinks he's in love with me and he talks about it non-stop. I can't imagine ever getting tired of hearing a cute boy say he loves me. At times Joey will tell me how weird it is to be in love and how confusing it makes everything. He says when he gets the use of his arms he'll feel more in charge and maybe then I'll fall in love with him. I say, "That'll be nice, Joey. I think I love you anyway, maybe I can sort out my feelings over Thanksgiving vacation. I also told him it's not necessary to be in love to have great sex together and he said, "You'll find out it's the best sex ever when you're in love with your sex partner." Maybe I will, and then when I think how hot it is having sex with Frankie, I think Joey's probably right.

When it's time to actually get ready to leave for Thanksgiving break, Joey gets all teary telling me he's going to miss me so much it hurts his stomach to think about it. I go, "That's sweet, Joey, but you'll be getting your casts off so concentrate on that." We have a very sweet goodbye fuck in bed that morning. Boy, his cock's very big when he climaxes. We did it in the missionary position with his arms under him and me lying on his back fucking his muscled, hard buttocks for all I'm worth. This is going to have to last us awhile. I shoot off inside him and then we roll on our sides hugging and kissing and it's wonderful. We'll, obviously I did hugging for both of us but we kissed together. I really have mixed emotions. It makes me feel good that Joey cares about me so much, but at the same time I feel guilty about it because I'm longing to see Frankie. Joey's really into our spit swapping thing that Frankie introduced me to. Joey loves that! I finally get up and dress Joey and me, then pack both our satchels in time for his mother to pick him up.

Mrs. Gallo comes bustling through our door exactly at eleven o'clock, saying to me, "You've done a better job than I thought you would, Arthur." Joey goes, "His name is Oliver, mother!" Her face is looser than I remembered from our first meeting so I guess she needs another Botox shot or two. That woodpecker face of hers swivels over to give Joey a stern look, asking, "Who's Oliver?" Joey and I chuckle as I wheel him to the car and get him situated with his seatbelt buckled. Then the collapsible wheelchair goes in the trunk. Joey glances over at me, a forlorn look on his face as the car pulls away and I blow him a kiss. He gives me such a sweet smile I might have a tear in my eye too. It isn't long after that I finish getting my car loaded and I'm back on the road again, heading toward Delaware, Frankie, and Alexander. My life has really picked up and gotten complicated, but it's an awesome complication.

The End

Here is a sample from another story you may enjoy:

DICK PARKER

I DARE YOU

GAY ROMANCE

The summer between my Junior and Senior year of college, three of my buddies and I were working for a big landscaping contractor. We'd all been friends for a couple of years and like most college buddies, we did a lot of drinking and crazy shit.

Three of us were twenty-two and Alan was twenty-three. We'd lived together in an old ratty house off campus during the last school year and we managed to all get jobs with a local landscaper for the summer. There were a lot of work, both small jobs at homes, and big industrial jobs. We were all fit and loved the outdoors so it was the perfect job for us.

As I said Alan is twenty-three. He's from Georgia and kind of a redneck. He's a big guy, about six-foot four and a hundred eighty pounds. He's built like a professional wrestler and has thick curly black hair and brown eyes.

James is twenty-two like Randy and me. My name is Tim.

James is slim, with light brown hair, blue eyes and a really good build. His hair is cut in that messed up style and he always looks like he just got out of bed. His eyes are very bright blue and very pretty. He has long eyelashes that any girl would kill to have. He's a city boy, but really got into our camping and fishing trips once he tried it a few times. James is easily the best looking of all of us.

Randy is a goof. He's only about five-foot seven and around a hundred and thirty pounds. He's dark haired and has dark brown eyes and I don't think I've ever seen him without a smile on his face. He's the happiest guy I know.

Me, I'm about six-feet tall, one hundred and sixty pounds and I have light brown hair that gets what they call dirty blond in the summer. I grew up in a small town along the Wisconsin River and have been an outdoorsman all of my life. I actually worked for a nursery when I was in high school so I was the one with the experience.

Our boss was a good guy who was pretty easy to get along with. As long as we got our jobs done and did them right, he didn't mind if we had a little fun while we worked.

And we had fun.

The four of us were all practical jokers and if you let your guard down, you usually paid for it with a wet ass or something worse. We never did anything that would actually injure someone, but we came close. I think that's why we got along so well. We just loved life and loved having fun.

All of us had a girlfriend or two in the past three years of college, but this summer we were all between girlfriends. Part of the problem was our constant pranks.

Many times when one of us had a girl at our crappy apartment, someone would let a giant fart or barge in on a guy and his girl while they were having sex and squirt them with whipped cream or something. That happened quite a bit and the girls didn't see the hilarity in it and that was it.

Randy was always coming out of the shower when someone had a girl in the living room, with a towel around his waist and then conveniently dropped the towel in front of the girl.

I woke once after a girl and I had been fucking and fell asleep. I felt something strange and found my toothbrush sticking out of my ass crack.

Things like that made it hard to keep a girlfriend for very long.

"Oh well, another one bites the dust," Randy would say.

"Wa'll, we'll have to round up nother filly then," Alan drawled.

"How about we get one of those rubber pussies?" James suggested.

"Or you could grease up your butt hole and we could take turns," I said laughing.

Of course James bent over and pulled his shorts down and spread his cheeks. We all acted disgusted. But I took a second look and it didn't look so bad to me.

If you enjoyed this sample then look for **I Dare You**.

Also by this Author:

<u>**Concealed Agony**</u>

<u>**Oliver's Wildwood Vacation**</u>

From the Author

Check my page on Amazon for Updates and interesting info.

Author Central Page - http://www.amazon.com/Donny-Mumford/e/B00C8872TO/ref=ntt_athr_dp_pel_1

If you enjoyed any of my books then please share the love and click like on my books in Amazon.

If you write me a review and send me an email I will send you a free book, or many.
(Just know that these emails are filtered by my publisher.)

Good news is always welcome.

One Last Thing, For Kindle Readers...

When you turn the page, Kindle will give you the opportunity to rate this book and share your thoughts on Facebook and Twitter. If you enjoyed my writings, would you please take a few seconds to let your friends know about it? Because... when they enjoy they will be grateful to you and so will I.

Thank You!

Donny Mumford
donny_mumford@awesomeauthors.org

About the Author

Writing has always been a passion. Erotica seems to be taking up the most space in my heart or.. in my mind. Lol! I'm still young, really. But VERY legal age-wise.

I'm from Philadelphia, Pennsylvania but you can see me roaming around the streets of Boston, Massachusetts at present. Love it here!

It was during my Sophomore year that I discovered my devotion in writing. There happened to be a spark between a threesome: a paper, a pen and my imagination.

The niche I am very fond of writing is of gay erotica fiction. My first work is "Concealed Agony".

I do hope you'll enjoy reading my stories as much as I enjoyed writing them. :-)